WAR-TORN

J.E. & M. KEEP

PREAMBLE

Content Warnings:

Contains spoilers. Please skip if you have no need for content warnings.

violence, disfigurement, PTSD, war, gore, non-consent, MFM romance, and dark themes of a dystopian and war-torn world.

Word Count:

86,000

* * *

Newsletter:

Make sure to sign up for the newsletter for exclusive content, information on new releases, and free books!

http://jmkeep.com/newsletter

1

THE FRONT

The rattle of machine-gun fire along the endless trenches of the Eternal War's frontier was constant. If it wasn't happening nearby, Sergeant Levek heard it coming from further up or down the line instead. Soldiers grew used to it, along with the countless other nuisances and plagues that came with life at the front.

Ticks and fleas, the hacking cough of illness that spread so fast through the ranks, the various flesh-rot diseases which got a plethora of colourful names from the men. Just a taste of the miseries they endured day after day, until one day it ended.

And that day was always their last.

Sure, Levek knew men who had escaped. The man had served long enough at the front to have witnessed deserters running off. Most of those were shot before they ever got out of sight of the great barrier of trenches and pillbox bunkers. Most of the rest starved in the barren, cratered wastes beyond. Those who made it to the forests past that... they mostly starved too. Though a few—a lucky few —he knew...

It didn't matter. Levek was a man of commitment. He didn't believe in the war, but he valued the lives of his men. He was better than most enlisted officers; that wasn't ego speaking. The tall, swarthy man had just survived longer than most any other, and it was because he was cautious. Both with his life and the lives of those he was in charge of. He'd learned the ins and outs, not only of combat, but of trench politics, and that last part was most important of all.

As dreary as life was for him at the front, however, one day that usually brightened the moods of the men was the arrival of the new conscripts. They got little to no training, but their arrival meant forces were shored up and duties were alleviated, if only a little, for a brief amount of time. And since news from home was rare, the bright young faces of new fodder tended to perk up the men.

For Levek, though, it was a bit of a bittersweet moment. For he knew what awaited those young fools.

The horse-drawn carts arrived over what was once railroad track. The old rails long deteriorated from lack of use. They were too expensive to maintain, machine parts far too rare, and with the war being a slow slog that never shifted lines more than a couple of miles in either direction, a steady rather than fast flow of goods was important.

Watching the young faces disembark from the carts, though, Sergeant Levek couldn't help but notice one in particular.

She certainly didn't blend in with the others. Her body was too tiny, her face too youthful, her eyes far too hopeful for being in such a horrid place. With her flaxen hair held up in a bun she stretched as her feet touched solid ground.

Her clothes were ill fitted, the simple brown colour blending against her tan skin, and she looked around her with such wonderment. Her wide, hazel eyes found him staring at her, and it was the warmest, gentlest smile he had ever seen. It was innocent and pure unlike anything else he'd known as she drank him in.

Women were so rare at the front, especially ones like her. Usually when a family was forced to offer up a daughter for service because they had no or too few sons, they offered up the biggest or homeliest of daughters they had. The ones least likely to make a life for themselves behind the front. But her?

He swallowed, suddenly feeling oafish in his big brown military trench coat, having not shaved in a few days. He was over six feet tall, with a handsome, rugged look to him. Black hair and brown eyes, he would've been a handsome man back home if not for the grime of the front and the harshness it'd put to his face. He was in his thirties, though even he'd lost count of where exactly, and the beautiful young woman looked too good to be true.

His heart wept for her then and there. *She should not be here*, he thought. *It was a crime.*

He'd found himself approaching her without even realizing it. He wanted to turn away, for he knew it'd be painful to talk with her, to know what her fate was here. But it was too late.

"Ya lost, miss?" he asked in his dark voice, a bit scratchy from the smoke, fumes, and worse of the front.

That bright smile never faded and she glanced around the area once more. "Uhm, yep." She paused, her hands knitted behind her back as she looked up at him. "The medic station? That's where they told me to report."

Figures, he thought. *She was too small, too delicate for even the callous commissioned officers to assign to combat duty. Not that it'd save her. It was only a slower death sentence at best.*

He raised a hand and pointed towards a large wood-and-tarp structure. "That's the place ya lookin' for, lil' miss." He caught himself. "I mean, Private." He cracked a light, wry smile. He was her superior of course, the pips on his collar marking him as a Sergeant, but still, it wasn't appropriate from his perspective. Even if he was near alone on that mark.

The joy that bubbled forth was surreal. It simply wasn't possible for one person to radiate such feelings of warmth and tenderness just because they smiled. Just because of the way she looked at him. It was as if she'd given him something so remarkably special with simply her facial expression.

One of her hands came from behind her back, the tanned flesh looking so soft and supple despite the fact that she must have spent a lot of time in the sun. "I'm Caslian."

"Levek," he managed, though his voice nearly trembled saying it as he held her soft, delicate hand. "Here's hopin' I don't need to see you again," he said with a wry, good-natured smile, "but here's hopin' I do all the same."

So long at the front being hard and formal, yet this one woman managed to lure out the man within just like that. Got him talking like he was a real, honest-to-goodness person once more, and not the grimy trench rat he'd become.

She squeezed his hand, and for a moment it was just the two of them, smiling and bonding on death's stoop. They were both goners, sooner or later, but the moment seemed to stretch out for eternity until she finally retracted her hand. "Well, maybe a little boo-boo, then," she offered with a musical giggle. "A little scrape and I'll patch it up real good."

He found himself grinning toothily almost imme-diately. "You'll be the one I ask for." Not that they allowed such things, of course. "You'll be under Corporal Dren," he said to her, "watch out. He's not bad as they go, but he'll work you to the point of passing out if you don't fight back."

That was the least of her worries, he thought. But how could he tell her that?

"Don't worry, sir! I can look out for myself." Her voice was so teasing, that sparkle in her eyes infec-tious as she took a step back, glancing towards her little neck of the woods. "I hope to see you again, Levek."

He nodded to her sharply then gave her a crisp salute. A more precise one than he'd given a superior officer in years. "Carry on, Private. Look after your-self. Can't take care of anyone else if you don't take care of yourself first."

"You worry a lot, don't you?" she teased. "I'm as healthy as an ox!"

She took another step backwards, then another, her hands once more entwined behind her bottom. "You just make sure you come see me for something minor, that's all."

"Guaranteed," he said with a soft smile.

There was so much more he wanted to say as she walked away, but how could he? Warning her didn't change anything. It never did. She could arm herself, be on guard, but what would it do? At best it'd delay the inevitable and make the men who finally came for her more foul tempered.

2

THE SOLDIERS

The crunch of rocks and gravel beneath the wagon's wheels was monotonous and grating. The roads were so badly kept through the whole of the land that the ride had been an exceptionally bumpy one, jostling Major Hendrik Kelifron and his aide, Lieutenant Liena'sa, back and forth the entire way.

"How I long for a motorized carriage," the short, half-elven officer in black uniform said with annoyance.

"I haven't seen a motorized carriage that actually runs in years, Lieutenant." It was no exaggeration. Not that the tall, severe-looking man was prone to such things. He was all business, and did little that wasn't purposeful. If those hard, steel-blue eyes fell upon something, it was for a reason.

It wasn't considered wise to talk at length about such things. The Eternal War that had dragged on between the realms of man and elf against the monstrous hordes of the east had demanded great sacrifice from all. Machine parts were at an exceptionally high premium, and were all relegated to the remaining factories in the capital city that still churned out Gatling guns, mortars, and the few artillery pieces they could still manage.

The other two guards that were with them were non-commissioned grunts of the army who only understood that they were on some routine requisition mission to harass the local peasant farmers for new recruits and to tally the upcoming year's harvest for taxation. The two remaining tasks that the government ever managed to reach beyond the front-line or the capital for. Well, that or hunting down rebels.

Which was Major Kelifron's true mission.

In their low-grade, dusty black uniforms, the two soldiers began to talk amongst themselves as they walked behind the wagon, which gave the pair of officers an opening.

"There was something not quite right about that last house, sir," came the half-elf's voice.

"You think I don't realize that?" He shook his head and spared her only a passing glance to show his disapproval at her underestimating him. "They weren't the ones we were after, however. Simply incestuous peasant folk. He was the father of his daughter's child." He spit on the side of the road, though his aide was clearly impressed with his investigative prowess.

Her nose crinkled as she slumped back, her fair hair tied in a ponytail beneath her officer's hat. "Well, at least that's one more soldier for us in a few years."

Her ears were pointier than a human's, her jaw a bit more angular and her eyes just slightly wider, but she could pass for either race if she had to. Not that she cared to, most of the time. The bumps in the road were getting to her and she rubbed her temple for a brief second before she caught her display of weakness and fell her hands to her side once more.

"Right," he intoned in response.

The tall, slender man was usually so rigid when in uniform, but the long road was taking its tolls and he held the reins in hand, hunched over. "It's against the law, technically, but inbred or not, the front needs more bodies. They'll die before long either way."

They both knew that to be true. The Eternal War chewed up bodies so fast, and hardly any got any reasonable amount of training before being sacrificed to the grinder of the frontline. The state couldn't afford such luxuries when it barely held on in what minor capacities it still kept.

They were amongst the fortunate ones, for outside the capital city there was no order, no safety. And only the most fortunate of soldiers got a posting like theirs where they weren't guaranteed a gruesome death, just a dismal one.

Behind them one of the soldiers spoke a little too loudly. "Y'hear of the attempt on the Queen's life? They say it's what prompted her to make that alliance with the dogbreaths."

Major Kelifron arched a brow and peered back at the soldiers before looking ahead again. Lieutenant Liena'sa followed the man wherever he went as his aide, but she hadn't yet been informed of their exact purpose for this particular mission.

"Dogbreaths," she said under her breath. "Cute." She was a severe-looking woman in her sharp, black suit, though Kelifron was likely the only person alive that knew of her softer side. She certainly didn't show it often.

"Naw," she said more loudly for the grunt to hear, "I never heard that. I guess news travels low first then high." Her Major could see the smile on her lips, but the guard couldn't, and that only made it sweeter.

The Major cracked a smirk so slight that only she could make it out and appreciate it for the approval it was. The soldiers behind her didn't quite grasp the humour though. One of them spoke up and asked, "Is it true, sirs? Will the wolfkin be joinin' the war?"

The two black-uniformed officers, of course, knew the truth of the matter: those monster-bred demi-humans were long engaged in the war. The treaty was just a formal acknowledgement of what was already a reality but was too repugnant to acknowledge for the state and its shell of a leadership in front of the few civil families of the capital.

"True and then some," came his response. Though promptly he spoke in a firm, commanding tone, "Go scout to the sides. This is bandit country." Though truth be told, everything outside the capital was bandit country. They just weren't likely to be foolish enough to try anything against state soldiers. They showed up so rarely outside of battle or the capital city it was just best not to risk government involvement in their raiding of peasants and caravans.

As the two soldiers trotted off into the woodlands at either side, it left the two of them in isolation again, and Lieutenant Liena'sa knew it for what it was: a rare opportunity to speak frankly with the severe Major.

She relaxed back for the first time, though she never really lost her rigid posture. "So what do we know that they don't?" she asked, her honeyed voice so soft, as if they still might be able to hear. She was a cautious, cunning woman, but she knew not to ask questions that she didn't want to know the answer to.

This time she did.

"Where should I start?" he retorted, and she thought that was all she'd get out of him, except the glance he paid to each side told her no. "The assassination attempt exposed weakness in the monarchy. Though," he laughed derisively, "as you and I know, they're nothing but a weakness. The bureaucrats run things, truthfully."

It was one of the refreshing parts of her assignment and situation with him. He held so much over her he felt free with such statements of truth in private that no others dared. "The alliance had to be announced to show the monarchy has all that power and authority and security it doesn't really have."

She stared ahead for what felt like several minutes before she finally nodded in response. It made sense to her, and she turned to face him again.

"Well, with so many dead men and women we're going to need a lot more allies than just that. There's barely anyone of breeding age anymore." It was an exaggeration, but not by a lot.

"They plan to clamp down on the family laws. Enforce mandatory child counts and marriage deadline." He shrugged his shoulders. "They say that all the time though, but it's just another thing they can rarely ever enforce."

He went quiet, and his mind obviously drifted off elsewhere.

Hers wandered as well, and she found a small tendril of fear begin to creep into her mind before she brushed it away.

"Major, why are we actually out here?" It was the question that had been burning inside her ever since they left. She knew they weren't out here to hassle peasants, but she hadn't been able to make a lot of sense of what they were actually seeking.

There was a moment's delay, but then he said, "We're after the noble that tried to assassinate the Queen." Stated so simply, as if it were no big deal, but it was a rather earth-shattering thing to hear. A noble tried to assassinate the Queen? And they were the ones after the failed killer?

Liena'sa's throat went dry, and panic started to fill her. It was one thing to understand that everyone she knew was fodder, dead to The Eternal War. To know that the monarchy was crumbling and simply a front for the paper pushers

But to find out that the rebels had gone so far, and that distrust and contempt ran so deep that it affected the nobles was something she was unprepared to deal with.

"Major," she breathed out.

He peered sidelong at her then back to the road ahead. "Don't let it get to you, Lieutenant." His voice was so steady and firm, always in control. "The bureaucrats fear the loss of the monarchy because then everyone would know they're in charge, and they'd be accountable. But frankly, I don't think it'd make a difference. And besides, without those noble freeloaders, there'd probably be more for the front." He had a dark sense of humour, but he added on, "Our only concern right now is finding this noble on the run."

"Right." She nodded, and sanity returned to her. She trusted the man, in as much as she could or would trust anyone. "Do we know what he looks like? Any friends or relatives? Groups or associations?"

"She," he corrected her and smirked just a bit. "That's right. We're after a little princess. Enjoy this mission, Lien," he said with more familiarity than he was prone to, "not often we get a chance to chase down and put some smug noble's face into the mud." He chuckled, so very uncharacteristically.

3

THE NOBLES

The whole of the United Empire was limping along on a starvation diet, yet one could never tell judging by the opulence of the Queen's soiree. The extravagant hall — so cavernous with its marble columns stretched nearly to the heavens — was brightened with thousands of candles and lamps, lit and strung up by the palace's servants.

Throughout the ancient building were arrayed the remaining nobles of the realm, the aristocrats of an ailing empire, dressed in their finest and putting on airs while the world outside suffered. There, in their isolated halls, was the one place where true, feigned ignorance of the world beyond could be maintained absolutely.

Dressed in a trim, well-tailored black suit, which so closely mirrored the officer's uniform he once bore, was Samei Ellefor. The tall and striking Duke was known for making an understated look appear ostentatious just with sheer subtlety and his overbearing presence. He was lord of the most powerful noble family in the realm, and his high collar and trim dark hair complemented a severe face.

Duke Samei Ellefor fancied himself a cunning powerbroker, yet that evening he was slightly troubled. The approach of the Department of Finance's Chancellor, Iztira, did not improve his disposition. The stark woman was a bureaucrat, through and through; a devotee of the state yet someone he would rather not have present at all. Though affairs of the nation were what they were, and she herself held a not insignificant influence on events despite her austerity.

Dressed in a slinky black dress that hugged her pregnant form, with long, glossy black hair, she gave a muted smile.

"Duke Ellefor," she said with courtly respect. "Congratulations on the marriage of your daughter to the Duke of Rensford. That marks quite the achievement. The union of two of the realms most powerful houses, ending countless generations of rivalry."

With drink in hand, Samei shifted in his knee-high military fashion boots.

"And congratulations to you on yet again providing for the state," he said, paying not a glance to her pregnant belly. "My, I swear I never see you in any other state but gravid," he managed to slight even as he complimented.

She laughed, the sound a bit grating.

"Well, hopefully your daughter will be in the same position before long. She's at her peak, after all." Iztira's hair fell in waves over her shoulder and she lifted her glass. "In fact, I haven't seen the young lady at all tonight. Perhaps that is what she's working on now?"

Most fathers in his position did not prize their children highly, not beyond the material gain they could get for them. After all, Duke Samei Ellefor had gotten a Queen's ransom for his daughter, Caprice.

Yet the Chancellor of the Exchequer knew exactly how to dig a knife into him with her words. His daughter was a prized possession. And he gave up no possessions lightly.

"She is just in the powder room, doubtlessly," he replied and took a sip of his drink as he peered about.

"Ah, I see. She still needs to look her best, I suppose. It does no one any good to let themselves go." Iztira smiled placidly and sipped her sparkling drink. She opened her mouth to speak once more before her blue eyes spotted something in the crowd. "Well, speaking of..."

Iztira's gaze lingered long on the proud young woman with her brown hair pulled into a painful looking updo, careful curls tumbling down along her temples and the nape of her neck. She was dressed in an elaborate red gown, her black necklace snaking between her pushed-up cleavage.

"Daddy." She smiled as she joined the two of them, Caprice curtseying towards the bureaucrat. "And you, Chancellor."

Samei took her arm in his.

"Ah, there you are, my sweet child. The Chancellor here was just enquiring about your new marriage," he said with as little sound of interest as possible. "Reading about it in the broadsheets just isn't enough for her. She has to enquire personally about our family's affairs."

"Well, I can hardly blame her," Caprice said with a tight-lipped smile. "After all, there's certainly nothing else of interest happening around here. Oh, and look, you're pregnant again. Or still." Iztira returned the look of barely hidden disdain.

"It's one of the many duties I fulfill to keep this country strong and stable. I do hope you'll soon be following in my path." The woman glanced around, her brows knitting. "Yet I haven't seen your husband anywhere. He paid so much for you yet leaves you to your father for such auspicious occasions?"

"Well, he's quite busy." Caprice's eyes narrowed. "And my father has many friends here he'd like to see." "Oh, of course, dear. It's just so nice to see a father stand by his daughter after receiving payment," Iztira bit back.

Duke Ellefor's hand tightened on his glass. "Leave it to an accountant to speak of marriage in such crass terms." The bitterness edged into his voice just slightly. "I do wonder, are these children of yours you keep popping out all part of your tally sheet? Do you have a number value printed on each one, Chancellor?" He squeezed his daughter's arm inconspicuously.

She smiled, the first warm smile of the evening. "I don't think there's anything wrong with using tally sheets to plan for inevitabilities. Surely you knew your daughter's worth the moment you saw those sweet little eyes."

Caprice's gaze narrowed, but she quickly looked up at her father.

"She has to focus on such things, father. When you're a glorified whore, surely that's where your focus needs to be, and is why she's so skilled at her job." She looked back at the Chancellor. "Who's the father for this one, anyways?"

The barbs had gone well beyond subtle, and reining his daughter into his side, he said, "You'll have to excuse us, Chancellor. My daughter's mind is on her new family. Another time." He began to lead Caprice away.

It wasn't, however, until they were out of earshot and had rounded a column that he turned his dark gaze upon his daughter. "My my," he tutted in such a blasé manner. "Your tongue could cut diamonds tonight, my child."

Though, of course, he knew exactly why she was so on edge.

"I still don't understand why I have to be here, talking to that overstuffed woman," she huffed, her eyes like daggers. "We've better things to be doing this evening, and drinking," she gazed at his glass, "will not help."

"Watch your tongue," he insisted with her more harshly, that reprimand for her having the nerve to boss him around the first chance he'd given her, even after the harsh public display with the Chancellor. The glare faded rather abruptly, however, and he spoke to her in muted tones. "You know very well we have no choice. We couldn't very well turn down an invitation from the Queen herself. Not after what had happened with the assassination attempt."

Though between them both they knew it was more about what had happened in the privacy of their own affairs.

She pouted for a brief moment before sighing dramatically.

"We're going to be here all night. Who knows what could happen in our absence." Her eyes went back to the party, scanning over the crowd as she fixed her ruby dress and pushed up her large breasts further. "I do like this, though," she admitted, watching the necklace fall deeper into the dark crevice. "I'd like another one in gold and black."

Those piercing, dark eyes of his followed her hand movement, and he watched her fondle the fabulously expensive necklace.

"Gods dammit, girl," he muttered and took another sip of drink, tearing his eyes from his daughter's chest. "You're a maddening child," he half-heartedly reprimanded, for his daughter had always been his one weakness. "We have to put on a show of normality. I assume you realize what rides on that, hmm?"

"You're the one being indecent. I'm just fixing myself up to go face the crowds. Besides, you're my father, you're the one who has to be normal and responsible." Caprice's full lips pulled into a dark smile, her brown eyes staring at him beneath her heavy lashes. "I'm just capricious. Isn't that what you always said when I was a child?"

Almost without realizing it, he'd reached up and took hold of one of her curls, fondling it between his thumb and fingers.

"Never was a more appropriate name given to a child," he mused. Though as he met her gaze he let the silky strands drop. "Be on your best behaviour, child." He glanced around then leaned in, his voice a husky murmur for her ears only. "After tonight, you'll be a widow. A very rich and powerful one at that."

As he pulled back, his gaze on hers, she felt his hand trail down, the backs of his fingers stroking her arm and grazing her breast.

She swatted him away as she squared her shoulders.

"Then I suppose we're off to apologize to that wicked wench," she said in her rich, honeyed voice. "Besides, maybe we can use her later. If she only cares for money, and we have a lot of money, she might be useful one day."

He sized her up again and brushed down her shoulders and arms, this time nothing but official and serious as he made sure she was ready to mingle once more.

"I wouldn't waste your energy, child. That woman is a bureaucrat. And nothing more." He extended his arm to her again in a fatherly manner, looking as formal as his stiff military attire warranted.

"We have higher aims anyhow," he said with a self-assured half smile.

4
____

THE REBELS

The blonde noble was clad in leather. It clung to her large breasts, her big hips, but it was so different than the regal wear she was used to. Even dressed as a peasant, she couldn't chance going to a town, or even a farmhouse. She was still too close to the capital, and she knew she simply had to keep walking.

The leather's shade of brown helped the curvaceous young woman blend into the forest and the brush a bit better. Her skin was fair, almost white, and she kept her hair long and back in a band. Her bangs skirted her dark eyebrows as she stumbled through the woods.

The assassin wasn't trained in such rugged conditions, and she cursed herself as she snapped a twig.

She was exhausted from being on the run, and there was no reprieve in sight.

And she hadn't even succeeded in her mission.

For that reason she doubted her contact would be waiting for her at the meet-up spot. After all, the plan was for her to succeed and give the rebels a chance at overturning the crumbling state leadership. Without that success she was likely just another spoiled young noblewoman who lashed out ineffectually.

When night fell and she was forced to set up camp in the woods again, she deflated. Her supplies were enough — she hoped — to take her to the meet-up spot, but beyond that? She had no idea what she'd do. The leather kept out most of the chill of night as she bundled up in the sleeping bag she toted with her, but worries were inescapable. She'd make the meet-up site sometime before lunch tomorrow, a little later than she should've due to her unfamiliarity with the wilds. After that...

Sleep had overtaken her worries at some point, exhaustion of having trekked through the woods for two days straight beating all else. Though awaking to the crackle of fire and the night still in full swing was not what she expected.

"Morning, m'lady," came the smooth, charming words, though she knew there was some derision there for the title. Immediately her eyes darted open to the sight of a tan man before her, a long machete-like blade near her throat.

Her mouth opened as if to scream, the sound beginning to rise before she swallowed it back. It was all a dream. It had to be. She blinked her eyes free of the groggy sleep, but still the darkened vision of the man remained, her body pumped full of adrenaline. Her blade was near, but not near enough, and she didn't dare move.

"I don't have anything!" she said, her tiredness making her think it was a simple bandit attack until she realized he had said her title, and she deflated back into the hard ground. Her entire body felt stiff, and her clear blue eyes glistened in the fire light.

"That much is obvious," he responded, and as her eyes adjusted she watched the enshrouded man come slowly into focus. He was strikingly hand-some, and too much so for a normal human, though the thick mane of golden-blonde hair kept his elven ears partially hidden. He was dressed much as she was. Dark leathers, though his were more ragged and worn, patched up. The suit fit snugly to his body, showing off a lean but fit physique.

He was no lordling, and the scar that crossed one of his eyes and another on his chin — the only blem-ishes on his otherwise flawless features — attested that he hadn't known a soft life like her aristocratic associates.

"I did my best," she pleaded, but she knew she had choked. That one, little miscalculation, that one second of hesitation; it was all she had to do to fail.

"Please! They're going to kill me if they find me. I need to escape!"

His own golden bangs dipped a bit over half his face, partially hiding the scar over his eye, but not quite. His emerald eyes were such a strong shade of shimmering green they stood out even in the dark, faced away from the fire, and she knew then he had to have elven blood in him.

For all his masculine beauty though, he studied her in silence a while, scrutinizing her.

"With your failure went a lot of planning. A lot of wasted sacrifice by people who could spare no more. Lives were lost in your failure," he chastised her in such a calm, cool demeanor, though she could tell emotions smoldered beneath thanks to a life of political maneuverings in the capital. He cared for the lives he spoke of.

Tears burned her eyes, but she refused to shed them.

"I have blood on my hands, but if you kill me, then it's all for naught. I can still be of use to you now!"

The noblewoman was not used to begging, or pleading, with anyone. For anything. She was proud, but with a blade so close to her throat, her pride had dripped away to be replaced only with a desire to live.

It didn't seem to upset him though, or throw him off. He kept his position so tight, so rigid. Never budged.

"The Bucketheads are following you, aren't they?" he said, referring to the special forces guards — the Landed Knights — that carried out the will of the state. They were so named because they were always fashioned with steel helms, regardless of the fact that they rarely saw the front line and real soldiers there often went without helmets at all due to shortages. "Did they catch you after the botched assassination and offer you some deal? Or were you always playing us?"

"If they caught me, I'd be dead!" she pleaded, her body so stiff beneath the blanket. She wanted to jump up, to flee from the calculating elf, but that blade was so near to her throat. "I haven't sold you out. I just fucked up. I made a mistake."

Those piercing emerald eyes of his seemed to bore through her. There was no softness to them as he stared across at her, bent down upon one knee, the knife extended and motionless. It seemed as if he'd never take her word until finally he moved that blade an inch away from her neck.

"You were slow getting here," he stated plainly. "Word got here of the failure over a day ago, and I sent the rest of the group on. No need to sacrifice their lives on a fruitless attempt at revolution now that you've failed. So if the bucketheads are following you — knowingly or not — they'll only get one new head to mount at most."

"Terrific," she said bitterly, her eyes narrowed. "And it took me longer to get here because I'm a pampered fucking noble, remember? Even if I am trying — and failing — to help, that doesn't mean I'm suddenly used to fleeing through the forest in these rags."

At her words his eyes dipped lower to her outfit — and the curvaceous form it hid — though instead of feeling titillated he just curled a corner of his lips in distaste. She realized then that his leather outfit was in far worse shape than hers, the contrast so stark as to make the quality of her wear seem lavish by comparison.

"Sorry, hun," he said with mock compassion as he lowered the blade towards his side. "Shame you failed. With the Queen gone we would've had a good shot at upturning the tables and making people's lives a little better."

He did well at hiding the bitterness in his voice, but she knew when he said "people" he didn't mean nobles like her.

"Yeah, well. If you'll remember, succeed or fail, I risked a whole hell of a lot. Including my house, and my family, and my friends. Succeed or fail, I'm left with nothing, and it was a price I paid knowing that."

Her clear blue eyes were hard and stern, though she still didn't move from her pinned-down spot.

Slipping the large knife into its sheath along his thigh, he shrugged his shoulders.

"Now you're like the rest of us then," he said dryly. "Welcome to the real world, princess. Shit sucks." He rose up from his crouched position and she saw that standing he was just shy of six feet tall. He circled about the fire he'd set while she slept and warmed his hands.

"Fantastic," she hissed as she rolled onto her side, her bicep acting as her pillow. "Except now I don't even have a gang of rebels to protect me, so I'd say I'm a bit worse off."

With a deep intake of breath he said, "Spare me the sob story, princess. Some good people gave their lives to help set us up for this plan, and all of us sacrificed a little something to make it happen. And that's all gone up in smoke. And considering none of us had anything to spare to begin with, excuse me if I'm not too sympathetic to your plight." He added wryly, "You've got misery to make up for."

Even in her bitterness she saw the truth of it, but her face hardened to try to hide that fact from him. She pushed herself up from the cold, hard ground and moved to the fire, across from him.

"Yeah, well. There's no turning back now."

He studied her a moment before turning his gaze back to the fire and his hands that he twisted about it. The flames did a good job of keeping the cold chill at bay.

"That's one thing you've got right at least," he remarked. "And despite anything they might've told you, there's no negotiating with them. A traitor noble counts for nothing. Any deal you might offer them they'd only break once they got what they wanted. So even if you offered them the whole Resistance on a platter, they'd take it and shoot you for thanks."

"I lived around these people for twenty years, I know how they are. You don't ever wonder what it was that even made me want to help you? Those people in there, they could give two shits about you, and I could have lived the same way. Been the same type as them. But I'm not. Maybe remember that when you try to tell me how shitty they are."

"So what?" he retorted. "I should be grateful for

you deciding to turn on the state and live like us plebs?" He shook his head and laughed with amusement, and though it was laced with derision she couldn't help but notice how beautifully smooth the sound was, masculine yet pleasant. "You tried, and that's good. But what matters in this life is results, hun. There's no ribbon for effort out here," he said with a shrug of his shoulders, as if the reality were beyond his control.

"I don't need your gratitude, but I want you to remember. I could have had a nice, cushy life and never given a second thought to the dregs and fodder out here. I did. And now I'm here, on your side. Don't act like I'm the first one in the Resistance to have fucked up and blown a shot," she said, her voice groggy as she stared at him with her blue eyes.

He spared her a moment's glance then undid the top button on his leather jacket, loosening the high collar just a bit as he stood before the fire. The getup he wore was riddled with straps and patches, keeping the suit in place about his leanly muscled physique.

"When we blow a shot we don't typically get a second chance," he said. However, after a brief pause he conceded, "Sometimes we're fortunate like that. Though you..." He looked her over again, this time slower. This time she detected just a hint of male interest as he lingered on her figure. "You got off lucky. Don't see a scratch on you."

"Apparently I'm better at hiding than killing," she hissed, her voice filled with self-loathing and regret as she drew her legs up a bit higher, feeling the heat warm her shins. "There's not many friends in the city. Doubt there's any I can call on to help us out."

"There's none," he stated firmly. "And get that stupid train of thought out of your head right now." He spoke like someone used to leading, though there was a special urgency to that insistence. "Anyone you used to know is a liability now. They will turn you in, because to do anything else is putting their and their loved ones' lives and privilege at risk. You understand?" He stared at her hard. "That's a dead avenue. We face that reality all the time. So get it through your head right the fuck now."

She glared at him, even as she nodded and pushed herself up off the ground. Her curvaceous body glowed in the soft firelight as she began to pace.

"Well, fine, but what now, huh? I have people coming to torture and kill me, who wouldn't think twice of taking you and tearing you into two, and you might be used to that, but I'm not. Besides, you must think I'm of some use or you would have killed me already to hide your tracks."

"You're the would-be assassin here, not me," he

replied immediately. Though after a moment he looked her over. "I value life, unlike most of the aristos you're used to. Even the life of a noble... to an extent." He flexed his fingers over the fire. "I sent the others on without me so I could see the truth of what happened. To find out whether you were on our side or not."

To find out whether she was worth saving, was the unspoken part.

"Of course I am," she hissed. "If not, you'd have been caught before I even woke up to you brandishing a knife at my throat."

He shrugged his shoulders again, confirming to her that matter was done and over with. What was before him now was determining if he thought she was worth the effort and risk to save from her new exile.

"This is no small matter," he stated simply.

"Obviously." She paced again, her arms beneath her breasts. "Look, there's still going to be ways to fuck them up, to make them pay," she told herself more than him.

"There are always going to be ways to make them pay," he said matter-of-factly, and he only seemed partially interested in her as a tool. Perhaps the handsome young rebel was interested in her human side. It was hard to say. She didn't have experience with men — people — like him, who knew this life outside the city. Even her contacts back home had been people more akin to her, who grew up in the relative safety and order of the capital.

"Then tell me what to do," she said, stopping and staring at him. She was the picture of royalty but for her crass tongue and her leathers. Her soft body, her slightly rounded face, those wide eyes, and sparkling blonde hair all screamed of her noble birth, but there was a glint, something not quite right behind her gaze.

He studied her for a while, those sharp, emerald eyes, almond-shaped and narrowed. It was almost like he was piercing her skin and peering into her soul.

"There's more to this than just me. Every step of the way I take you, I put more danger on a lot of good, innocent people and other brave rebels alike. If you were in my position, what would you do, huh?"

She went silent, for she knew what she'd do, and she turned her back on him for a moment to try to hide it from that strange gaze of his. She still felt it on her back, her skin prickling, even though she knew it was all in her head.

"Look, if I need to do this on my own, I will."

How he must've snuck up on her in the night and done all the things he'd accomplished remained a mystery, because without her realizing it he'd slunk up just behind her.

"You won't last a week out here on your own. If you don't know that yet, then I'll have to readjust that down to two days, tops." The words were not full of recriminations as before. Simple, sad fact.

"I've already made it two days," she protested even as she jumped forward, away from the stealthy man, and felt her heart begin to race. She didn't like someone being sneakier than her.

"Two days on a full pack using our guidance," he corrected her. "Now the bucketheads and worse are after you, your supplies are run low, nearly out, and you have no idea where to go from here. Don't kid yourself or me about your chances," he chided, a hand on his hip with the elbow cocked to the side. He brushed back some of his golden hair and it was hard not to appreciate the male beauty of the rebel despite the situation. Even those scars only seemed to enhance his looks, adding a bit of ruggedness to his smooth features.

She hated when others were right, and she could feel that pride and annoyance mix within her, but she stamped it out.

"So what, you'll keep me around then?" She bit back her tongue as she stared at him. "Why? What do you need from me?"

"Nothing," he said definitively, "I need nothing from you," and the serious look on his face said he wasn't fucking around. "If I decide to rescue you, it's out of the kindness of my heart. Because at this point you're not worth a damn. You don't have any useful connections for us, you're penniless now, and if you failed the first time you sure as hell couldn't have a shot with taking a second attempt at taking out the Queen. Not without your pass as a noble." He crouched down to the fire, faced away from her so that his firm rear tightly clad in leather showed. "You're deadweight out here. And you'll need training just to learn how to survive."

Something about how he'd said that suggested he'd perhaps already made up his mind to help her. Though under the circumstances...

She was glad his back was turned so that she could brush away the angry tears that threatened to fall, but her voice still held that telltale quiver.

"I can still steal. Kill. Whatever. I still have value."

"There's no stealing from our own," he said, crouched down, legs splayed before the fire. "You trade fairly, and you go out and get things to bring back to help everyone. Or else you make yourself *very* useful around the camp. There's only one way I could think of you making yourself that useful, and you need time to learn the skills to raid or steal from the military. Otherwise you're just throwing your life away."

Her pale cheeks began to glow hot, and her skin prickled in anger and annoyance beneath her skin-tight leather outfit.

"Then I'll do that," she responded, her voice more terse than she had intended.

The mysterious rebel turned his head to the side and gazed back at her.

"That simple, huh? You were a pampered noble two days ago, and now you'd be willing to sell your-self to get by to some filthy rebel plebs?" It wasn't the mockery she might've expected. It sounded like a genuine test question.

"What? Sell myself?" Her eyes widened. That was not what she'd understood him to be saying. She felt a cold chill run down her spine and her breathing picked up as she took a slow step back from him.

"I'm not some... some... whore for your friends."

The corner of his lips screwed up and he looked at her with something akin to disappointment.

"What? You think that's something special or odd?" He gave her an obvious once — over, sizing up her rather full figure in an attempt to goad her. "The body of a princess would probably fetch you enough to get by pretty well. As far as us plebs reckon such things, that is."

"Oh, fantastic! A few copper for something that'd be worth a golden throne to some people." She threw up her hands in frustration. "I can do other things rather than lie on my back and let your unwashed brethren move on me, you know."

He rolled his eyes.

"We all can," he said dryly. "But circumstances don't always allow for it."

She didn't catch it in her rage, but he seemed to be testing her more than anything. He wanted to see how far she was willing to go to survive. And she was doing badly.

"Look." She moved towards him, facing him directly. "I might have fucked up. I have blood on my hands, and I have nothing to go back to. I'm at your mercy, but what fucking good am I as a whore, huh? What's this anyways? Your idea of punishing me for failing?"

The man couldn't help but roll his eyes again at her and brush some of his golden hair back.

"What? You think you're special?" He snorted in amusement, which seemed so uncharacteristic of the handsome man, perhaps done just to show his derision at her outrage. "I've done it before. Why? Because I had to. That's all there is to it. I want to survive. You only seem to want to survive if it's done the way you like it. Well, let me clue you in, princess," — his voice had risen and grown harder — "out here we don't get that luxury. Nobody lays out the velvet rug for our survival. You fucking do what you have to, and you don't regret it, because there's no damn time for regrets."

It was quite likely she'd never been spoken to so roughly before, because her face tightened and her jaw clenched, her face going red. Regret and anguish were behind her eyes as they narrowed and twitched.

"I want to survive," she hissed. "I'm just saying, I have more to offer than a simple whore. I'm not going to spend my life just having sex with strangers."

He rose up and said simply, "Idiot." He pulled some piece of fabric out of his pocket. "You just don't fucking get it. You've been pampered all your life, and you just don't understand how the world works for the bulk of us, do you?" He shook his head, a slight sneer on his face. "You'd never survive with that kind of attitude out here. And I thought you'd be worth saving."

"Why, because I think I can actually do something to help you? Because I think I can do something worthwhile?" Her eyes burned with anger and panic, her hand reaching out to grab his bicep. "Look! I was to be married off in a month's time, right? Do you get that?"

He gave a stern look to her as she grasped him, displeased with her touching him. As if she were the filthy peasant laying a hand on a noble.

"And what? So you've run off to get out of some arranged marriage? Please, give me a break." He yanked his arm from her grasp. "Out here it's not always a matter of what you're best at. It often comes down to any act of desperation you can do to keep going another day longer. Y'hear me there, princess?"

She quaked in anger, her eyes staring at him so hard it felt like she could burn him with that alone.

"I'm going to survive," she hissed, her voice trembling with her attempt to hold herself back from doing something she'd regret.

"Well, you could've fooled me," he said plainly and pulled the dark flap of material over his head, showing it to be some mask to cover up his golden features and long hair. He began to walk off into the woods. "I don't waste my time training brats who'll turn up their nose every time they have to roll in the mud to get the job done."

"Oh, when are you going to get the time training me to fucking raid when you're too busy teaching me how to spread my legs, huh?" She chased after him for a few steps. "Who's to say you won't just figure I'm better suited to that? Then leave me to waste away?" She couldn't help it, and the proud noblewoman began to sob. It was all too much for her, and her entire body was trembling. "Don't leave me!"

He was out of her sight, but she heard his voice come back through as if not far away. "If you need training on how to spread those thighs of yours, you're more hopeless than I feared."

He was gone, it seemed. Though she noticed, even in her anguish, that his voice hadn't receded as he talked.

"Yeah, well, I know a lot more about stealing than about how to do that!" She twirled around at the nothingness, her ponytailed hair smacking her in the cheek as she stopped, trying to catch her balance.

There came no answer. Nothing. The forest returned to its normal quiet, and the fire, she noticed, had already died down low, nearly gone out. Sunrise wasn't far off, she realized, some birds beginning to chirp, but she no longer heard or sensed his presence near her.

She toppled, exhaustion and fear making her land hard into the dirt. Sharp pain traveled up through her knees, and she sobbed into her hands. For the first time, the direness of her situation truly struck her, and terror gripped her heart.

She was alone.

5

THE MATRON

War raged all across the continent, from the deserts of the south to the cold arctic chill of the north. Though both sides struggled to maintain a defensive line along that entire frontier, at the ends it frayed. The near so-called "Endless Trench" became a broken line in the southern deserts, and in the north became little more than scattered outposts.

After centuries of war neither side could afford to maintain a strong presence in either area. The occasional attempt to bypass enemy lines by going through the poorly defended climates was usually self-defeating, leaving at best a scraggly, diminished force that was driven out immediately.

Not that such lessons ever lasted long as new

generals and marshals on either side took over with the naive vigor of a new generation pushing them.

Spring was on its way, but on the cold plateau above, one could hardly imagine that. The permafrost there kept it a white dome year-round. Though from the edge of it a green-grey Kron stood in white furs, peering out over the edge into the brown-and-green lands below.

The Kron men ranged from squat sub-five-foot grunts to towering goliaths, and at nearly six and a half feet tall he was at the extreme end. Despite the chill, the furs covered only the Kron's shoulders, and draped about his legs in a kilt, leaving much of his bulky muscular form on display to the blowing snow.

Satisfied with his search, Saghar turned, a steel staff in hand fashioned from human piping with an ornate assemblage of bones and fetishes at the top. Kron were known by humans as primitive, superstitious monsters that believed in mysticism, and dressed in his scant furs with a witch doctor's staff, he looked the role.

The snow crunched beneath his feet as he approached a pair — one of which was even bigger than him — of huddled figures in heavy, covering clothes. He didn't say anything to them, just jerked his wide jaw northwest along the plateau then began to lead them. He wore his black hair in a single braid down his neck and spine which swayed with the wind as he guided them to a cave, which descended into the plateau itself and out of the harsh winds above.

Ramtok shed off his thick overcoat, revealing a broad physique — more muscled and bulky than the first — clad in metal, strapped to his form with leather strips.

"About damn time," he said in his guttural tone, so heavy and harsh as he shook off the snow, only the drip of melting ice and the distant howl of the winds above to challenge that earth-shaking voice.

The third of their party was by far the smallest.. Aleena was easily a foot shorter than the pair, yet her motions were anything but meek. She was the colour of snow, her hair an unreal white, her skin holding just the faint trace of pink beneath her cheeks from the cold. She was clad in white fur, and though it was for practical, camouflage purposes against the permafrost, she rarely traded it in for more neutral colours.

Aleena's daggers were strapped to her hips and those piercing green eyes were keen as she moved. She was sandwiched between the two brutes, but her movements were confident and smooth.

"You know I hate being idle just as well as you," she reprimanded lightly.

The two Kron were quite similar beneath their garbs, though their skin colour differed — one was grey green, the other brown grey — and there was the obvious difference in bulk. Ramtok bore a great spear and rifle upon his back, with a scimitar at his side, while Saghar merely toted his walking staff.

"My brother only worries for you," came the guttural, grunting words of Saghar as he stood beside her. "The snow-lands are harsh, Matriarch." It was an odd term of respect and affection applied to an elf of all beings; an unheard-of twist for their kind, whom had been at war with one another for longer than mortal memory could recall.

She stayed so near to both of them, and there was no questioning that she was in charge. It was a quiet understanding between the three of them, and they all accepted it for what it was. She had plans to help them and their people, and in return they offered her submission and so much more.

"Once we're out of here, I will feel a lot safer, that much is certain," she agreed, their bulky frames offsetting her own toned body. She had wide hips, thick thighs, but her limbs were strong and agile. "Hopefully we'll make a good pace."

Saghar nodded to her and led the way. Though

lesser armed, he had keen senses beyond Ramtok's, and always managed to guide them through any situation.

The caves down into the plateau split off into a myriad of little offshoots that spider webbed out. One could get lost in them for weeks without proper guidance, so the trio relied on the witch doctor to take them through.

The monotonous drip of water from the cracks above was the only accompaniment to their footsteps, though the temperature grew more hospitable the further down they went. They came at last to a great cavern, the ceiling of which stretched upwards so high. It appeared empty, though their sight was limited to what the shimmering crystalline objects embedded into the stonework revealed. They made for faint lighting at best, but before they set out Saghar had warned them that to shed more light would be a reckless danger.

Saghar paused, stood motionless at the entrance to that mighty cavern, and his brother shifted a bit anxiously, hand gripping the hilt of his weapon. Though that was nothing special, he always seemed agitated and protective of the other two.

Aleena's elven eyes worked over their surroundings, as cautious as any as her hands gripped her weapons. Beasts and animals were always a potential threat, though more sentient things were always the greatest danger. People were desperate everywhere she went, and she knew the depths of insanity that desperation led people to.

It was not something she wished to have to succumb to, which was why the deal was so important.

The silence dragged on long, but at last Saghar jerked his head off to one direction and the trio moved on. They were newly joined together, but already the pair of Kron brothers seemed absolutely dedicated to Aleena. Despite the tales of her own people, they'd shown themselves to be faithful to their deal, and more civilized than most humans and elves she'd known.

Not that it was the case for most of their kind, as she'd met plenty of ravenous Kron that fit the picture of the legends too.

As they made their way across the open cavern Saghar finally spoke. "Ramtok. Up."

Immediately after, they heard the shriek of some terrifying creature as it descended towards them.

Upon the warning, Ramtok pulled out his scim-itar and in a smooth arc sliced through the skull of the ice- blue coloured creature. It was like a wingless bat, with large ears and a snout, though it cleaved in twain from the large Kron's strike.

"Kreelengs." He practically spat the word out as more shrieks sounded from above, and Aleena heard their claws skittering over the stones.

Her blades were in her hands before anyone could blink an eye and she crouched down before springing herself in the air just in time to stab one through the belly. She deftly leapt aside as the thing careened to the ground, propelled by its prior momentum.

She was fast, almost blindingly so, but every step she took was precise and planned.

The three of them fended off the skittering assault of spiderlike bat-creatures. The shrieks of their assault and wails of their cries filled the air as the group fell back towards their destination tunnel, leaving the cavernous floors splattered in their blood.

Saghar wielded his brass stave with uncanny grace for so large a Kron, and though it did not look like an effective melee weapon, he swung it about in such lavish arcs as to smack away and injure the crea-tures en masse.

"Our way is through the tunnel, Matriarch," he called in his gruff voice, that new title she'd earned for herself still so odd sounding.

Ramtok let loose a bellowing war cry while slicing and chopping at the creatures as they advanced. He had not the finesse or grace of his two companions, but his reach and strength were impressive. In his spare hand he grabbed one of the attacking limbs of the kreelengs and snapped off a talon with the crunch of bone.

She led them, the three fighting in tandem. Their styles were so varied, yet she was quickly learning how well they complemented one another. Anything the bigger two missed, she easily struck down, diving between the two hulking bodies with such agility and grace.

The brothers were seasoned warriors, which was a rare thing. Few reached such a point where they could claim to be seasoned anything, especially not a warrior. And as they left the screeching kreelengs back at the entrance to the cavern — the things seeming frightened and wary after their great losses — the two men gave her an appreciative look.

The humans and elves may have had their legends of the savagery of Kron, but they had their own tales of the weakness and machine-cruelty of the fairer races.

"This way, Matriarch," led Saghar, taking them down the twisting cavern, the stone worn smooth by countless years of runoff from the glacier above.

Ramtok added as his heavy metal footfalls came down on the rock hard, "They aren't followin'."

"They know that only death will find them,"

Aleena said confidently. Her blades were bloodied, yet somehow she'd managed not to stain the white of her hair or the fur covering her body but for a brief speckling across her cheek and shoulder.

The trio carried on, the two Kron having no issue carting the great load of goods with their personal belongings down the stone slope. After a while Aleena felt the stirring of air ahead, and so knew they were reaching an end before Saghar even announced it.

Getting to the end of the tunnel, all they saw was a field of brown and green, rising and falling, as the forest carried over hills and valleys.

"Careful," cautioned Saghar, "we'll need to climb down a rope."

She could see it for herself as she neared the ledge. The tunnel's opening came to an abrupt stop, yet there was still such an immense distance to go before they reached the ground below. She sighted another ledge further down that they could reach using her climbing gear.

Aleena nodded and shrugged off her own back-pack. Their bulk was intimidating, and for a moment she worried about the strength of the rope but quickly brushed the thought aside. Strangely enough, she trusted them and their capabilities, even as she went to help set it up.

"I guess you'll go first, Saghar." She motioned with her head. "Then me. Then Ramtok."

The two Kron looked about to protest, but instead they sealed their lips shut tight and obeyed. In the weeks since she'd met with their people and negotiated their servitude, they'd come to address her with the same fealty they would a Kron matron.

Ramtok secured the rope as Saghar tied it about his waist, and then in concert the pair got to lowering the witch doctor down. With the staff strapped to his back, Saghar moved down across the rock face with surprising agility. It was as if he were made for such a task, as he swung from one hold to the next with the grace of a mountain lion.

When at last he reached the lower ledge, he took a look around then secured the rope tight before calling out, "We'll have you from both ends, Matriarch." His thick muscles went taut as he held the rope in a firm grasp.

She held her smirk as she began her own way down. Following her own path, her slender elven form made a graceful and speedy plunge down the rock face. Whereas Saghar may have moved with the surprising grace of a mountain lion, she spun and rappelled as if she were flying upon gossamer wings until she was on her feet once more, the leather soles of her boots firmly on the rocks.

Saghar stared at her with his dark eyes wide, and mouth hung open just a bit. The bulky Kron was more impressed than she'd seen him even in the cavern above. He bowed his head to her in reverence and helped her — needlessly — to the comfort of the ledge.

As Ramtok then made his way down, the large warrior sending stones and pebbles spilling down the cliffside, she couldn't help but notice they were at another cave entrance. It curved around but did not go in too far, and she saw at the back were a high concentration of the glowing crystals. So many of them it lit the area rather well, and even radiated a soft warmth in the cool of the waning spring day.

"I hate to say it," she admitted, "but we might want to settle in for the night." Her head motioned towards the mouth of the other cave. "We will clear it out and set up watch. Hopefully it'll be easy to protect."

Ramtok was noisily making his way to the ledge with them as they heard her order. Saghar helped his larger brother to safety then unwound the rope from around him, coiled it back up then handed it to Aleena.

"Yes, Matriarch," chimed the more sagely brother.

The larger merely took out his scimitar and carried out her orders, inspecting the cave top to bottom. When at last they were done and satisfied with the security of the place, they laid out their supplies and set about getting ready.

Saghar was fast at work on a fire, using some tinder kit he brought with him when Ramtok pulled out some wrapped meat to cook from a parcel in his backpack. They knew their roles to serve her well already.

She, meanwhile, was looking over a small map, not for the first time. Despite the fact that she had the two Kron as guides, she didn't use that to be lazy and ignorant about the route they were planning on taking. They'd outlined it well and she'd committed it to memory, but it was like a security blanket as they prepared her bed and food.

They'd already spent so much time waiting, but the trek made her feel that comfortable exhaustion, to the point that she knew she'd have a good rest that evening.

"Ramtok, you'll take first watch, then Saghar. I'll take final."

"Yes Matriarch," they intoned together, sounding so obedient, though she had been warned back in their village that they were troublesome. They were the best of their clan and they had let it go to their heads, it was said.

With the meat fried — though she knew not what

kind it was exactly — they brought to her on the flat metal pan the full of the meal.

"First offerings for you," spoke Saghar, and Ramtok grunted his agreement. Despite her race they looked to her, a pale white elf, as their leader now, and both remained on their knees as they offered her the prepared food.

She didn't rebuke them, instead plucking some of the meat from the pan and chewing it thoughtfully. She gave a brief smile of acceptance and her eyes went to the mouth of the cave.

"You two share up the rest," she said as she stood up. Though she was a hippy woman, she'd never eaten much in their presence and seemed no worse for it.

They divvied up the rest between them with no apparent hierarchy there, the two brothers just working in concert as they devoured the rest of the fried meat. When they were done and they cleaned up, Ramtok gave her a deep bow then went to the mouth of the cave. With the curve of the shelter it put the larger Kron out of sight as Saghar looked to her.

His broad frame, though muscular, was not the extreme bulk of his brother, and so to look at the green-grey man, he appeared more like a large, powerful human than the caricature of Krons. Only the broad jaw, the upturned tusks, skin colour, and fashion marked him for what he was.

The white furs he wore about his shoulders and in a kilt were his usual wear, even before she set out with them.

"You move with the grace of legends," he stated to her as he arranged that long ebon ponytail of his around his shoulder and over one of his pecs.

She shrugged off the fur cloak, revealing the leather-clad figure beneath, and spread the cloak over the ground as she settled down. Aleena didn't really know what to say, but her green eyes found his and a smile turned her lips upwards.

"You don't live to be my age by being clumsy."

Saghar was appealing, and not just for a Kron. It was only that wild, barbaric-looking garb that really hid it. Though as his gaze looked over her hippy form, the obvious appreciation for her was hidden beneath wonder.

"How old are you anyhow, Matriarch? You look like but a young matron, barely ready for her first harem of males." His fingers curled on his legs, the sharp dark nails digging into the fur there. She'd learned some of their culture in her journeys with them, and the fact that women ruled their society infected everything they believed.

She laughed, and it was the earnest music of elven joy.

"Well, let's just say I'm older than you imagine, then, Saghar." She stretched out on the fur, her hands planted behind her as she watched him, curiously. "They warned me of you. Do you know that? They've warned of both of you."

He nodded to her diligently. He had but a short triangular tuft of black hair at the center of his chin, and he stroked the little beard thoughtfully as he eyed her.

"Aye, Matriarch. I assumed they would." There was a certain little light in his dark eyes then. A glimmer of mischievousness. "The Matron of our clan found me very disagreeable. She was eager to be rid of me." He licked along his lips from tusk to tusk.

"How'd you manage to piss her off, hm?" she asked, leaning in. She, too, shared a history of being thought of as a troublemaker despite her stern persona. All of them, she supposed, were more than what they appeared to be.

He shrugged his broad shoulders, though that look of wishing to elude her question faded. He might've been a troublemaker, but he seemed reluctant to refuse his new Matriarch's questions. Or perhaps it was growing respect that urged him on.

"I questioned too much," he said simply. "I

always asked for more during lessons. I always sought to do things a better way." He grinned across at Aleena wryly. "The Matron of our clan did not care for such things. It tried her patience more than anything else, for her inability to answer questions weakened her authority in her eyes."

"You haven't questioned me much," she replied simply, and pleasure sparkled in her emerald eyes. "Perhaps she had weak authority to begin with and you just reminded her of it."

He gave a gruff chuckle to that and nodded to her slightly.

"It's true, she was a weak Matron. She did not earn her position through cunning or effort. She inherited it." He shrugged his shoulders. "As for you? I am still appraising you," and he added on in his gruff voice, an air of husky desire to it, "Matriarch."

Her light-peach lips parted, brightening that pale, icy look she usually had. She was so fair, so delicate seeming, but that deviance in her eyes was anything but innocent. She leaned towards him, her fingers running through the thick fur beneath her bottom.

"And what do you think so far?"

Saghar strummed his fingers upon his chin as he watched her, studying her in his quiet manner.

"I think you are likely more cunning than you

seem. Definitely more cunning than the Matron thought you," he added with a smirk. "You have angles you are working that we do not yet understand. But—" He paused, reluctant to say more. All she had to do was look at him to get him to continue. "But you are an able leader and a stunning fighter. Thus far," he added in his gravelly voice.

"Subject to change," she teased as she moved closer, prowling like a shadowy cat. Her hair fell down along her shoulders, framing her face in that pure white down, but her smile was dark and secretive.

Interracial relations between humans and elves were tolerated because of the need for more bodies at the front.

With members of the other side, however? It was considered abhorrent. Vile.

They were at war for a reason, despite few knowing what that reason was, if any.

Yet still, the pair looked to each other in the glow of the cavern, desire obvious in their gazes.

"You do have the fire of a true Matron in you," he remarked as the elven woman stalked closer to him. His tongue lingered at the corner of his lips as his chest rose and fell with his rising breathing.

She was almost upon him, knelt on her hands and knees. She looked angelic with her pale features, but that dark, sinful look in her eyes was anything but. She didn't care for social convention, and she'd been gone too long from the rest of civilization to care anyways.

"I do," she agreed as her hands went to his knee, propping her up and squeezing her small breasts together. "Will that be a problem?"

A low growl emanated from the large Kron before her. His muscular physique radiated heat and her breasts drew his gaze in.

"I knew what would come when I was traded off," he said lowly. He smelled of pure, masculine musk. Not unpleasant, not malodorous, just virile and strong. "Even the lowliest Matriarch needs to breed a kinship of her very own. Even if it is mongrel half-breed."

The way he said that almost made it sound to her ears as if he liked that filthy idea.

She laughed again, but the sound was deeper, tinged with lust. Longing. She had always been a curious girl growing up and that had done nothing to dissipate as she aged. She'd never been with one of his kind before, and a heat started in her belly, flowing outwards and making her sex throb.

"I thought you two always shared. Isn't that how it goes?"

With a light shrug he said, "In a manner of speaking." With a glance towards the cave entrance he said, "But you gave Ramtok a duty. So he'll do it until you tell him otherwise." He gave a wry smile, and one of his hands came up and reached out to cup her pale cheek, brushed the coarse, alien skin against it. "It makes no difference, Matriarch. Now or later, he and I will work in you to provide you a powerful brood." The corner of his upper lip curled as he looked ready to bite at her with arousal.

Decades of prejudice and hatred had been taught to her, and even she was surprised by how quickly it melted away to curiosity and desire. She licked her peach lips, taunted him with her closeness, her feminine scent so near to him. She was so delicate, her skin so tender against the coarseness of his palm, her face so beautiful compared to the monster she gazed at with such lust.

"Do you get jealous over one another?" she asked, leaning in to whisper it into the shaman's ear, her voice tinged with something so dark and primal. The Kron believed that it took many males to create a child, and the elves had no notion of that.

The large man was rather timid for a male from her experiences, but then she'd never dealt with a Kron man before. His fingers felt out her cheek and went back to her ear and neck as he leaned in to the other side of her face, his breath hot on her ear as he hovered close to her flesh.

"Jealous? Only if you wish it by showing favouritism do such things tend to happen," he said with a shrug. "He is my brother. And our seed shall mingle in you, Matriarch, to breed a strong child for you."

His full lips moved in then, and wrapped about her ear, the sharp tusks pricking her skin as he suckled there.

Never for a moment did she feel like she wasn't in control of him, of the situation. Her grip on his knee faltered for just a moment as her hand began to snake up, feeling out the strength of his thigh as he toyed with her pointed, elven ear.

She was so small compared to him, but she felt no fear until her palm rested atop his package, and even through his fur covering, she could feel the heated loins. They pulsed under her touch, and exhilaration ran through her.

Saghar wore little, but that impressive shaft of his remained covered in the white fur of his kilt as his chiseled pecs rose and fell with his growing breathing. As he released her ear he moved down to her neck, nipped it accidentally amidst his kisses as his other hand came up to one of her hips.

"You've a strong breeding frame," he husked in her ear, "for an elf."

Her hand stroked him, feeling that obscene masculinity throb beneath her hand, and her eyes fluttered shut. She enjoyed the warmth, the heat between them, and her breathing picked up in pace as her thighs pressed against his leg. Her free hand came up to the string that kept her leather top together, deftly untying it down the center of her chest.

She was loathe to remove her hand, but she sat up straight on her knees, tugging off the tight leather and revealing her perky breasts, the dusty pink nipples already tightened atop them.

Aleena did not cut the figure of an ideal Kron woman, yet Saghar's eyes dipped and went wide at the sight of her bare breasts. She had stayed amongst his people for a while as she bartered, and she knew the hippy, busty proportions of those towering amazons. She was not it. Yet still, something about her figure, her pale skin, those perky teats drew his attention.

He shrugged off his white pelt and reached his hands to her chest. Palming both breasts, he squeezed gently, the contrast of his dark skin so pronounced against her white.

"You are very different, Matriarch," he said in a

low, gravelly voice, his exquisitely carved male physique on display as he fondled her chest appreciatively.

She sat in such a way that he could feel her out, those large hands dwarfed her small breasts, but there was no self-consciousness or hesitation as he touched her. She was confident in her form, and her head dipped down so she could appreciate the sight of him groping her. Her heart pounded beneath her ribs, and her lips quirked as one of her hands went out, her finger sliding along his tusk so curiously.

"It must be quite a task to be careful of those things," she purred.

The remark surprised him, or at least confused him. For him the things were a part of his being, so he never thought about it, of course.

"I am careful," he intoned simply, his voice rich with arousal to match that large swell of cock flesh in his fur kilt.

He reached one hand from her breasts and tugged at the leather that held his kilt in place. It loosened the garment, and it gave way enough that she saw the tuft of sleek black hair emerge, then the throbbing, veiny mass of flesh beneath. A cock so large it dwarfed any other she'd experienced in her life amongst the fairer races of the world.

The strange colour of his skin, the bulky

physique, his height, it all had tried to prepare her for the baser differences between them, but it hadn't. Nothing could have prepared her for the sight of that large girth, and her thighs pressed together tighter to try to ease the painful throbbing between them.

A soft sigh passed her lips as her hand moved to free him, entirely, of that covering. The fur peeled back, revealing the hefty sac beneath, almost more impressive than the shaft above. Heat radiated off it, and the lining of veins were so still and full, more prominent than on any man or elf's.

Saghar leaned in and licked at her neck, his two hands squeezing her breasts again harder in his eagerness for her flesh. Despite the Kron male's inferior position in their own society and the taboo of this tryst, he seemed eager for her to take him.

And she was only too happy to oblige. Adrenaline ran through her, egging her on, and she reluctantly stood, stealing her breasts away from him. Her fingers worked to loosen her belt and lower her pants, kicking off her boots all in one easy motion. She was an ethereal beauty with those full hips and that soft, white down trying to hide that bright red sex, but it couldn't hope to succeed.

Her arousal was too obvious on her body, and as she quickly moved to straddle him, her legs were just a tad too short to do so comfortably. She pulled herself up close to his body and wrapped her thighs around his hips as she felt that throbbing member pulse against her sex.

It was how most Kron matings went, and he wrapped his arms around her as his thickness rested to her. It caused the foreskin to roll back, revealing the bulbous crown, a dark shade different than that of what she was used to, though so alike. Only bigger. Much bigger.

It glistened between their bodies, hers so pale and fair, his so dark and hard, those abs ribbed and obvious. One of his palms cupped her rear, and he supported her body as she moved to get in position to take him. A husky growl rumbled from his lips, and she could practically smell the excitement off the virile male.

His arousal only pushed her past that fear, that brief wonderment if she could actually do such a vile thing, though really, there wasn't any question. She'd always known she was a deviant, and that there was no way she could possibly travel with the two Kron without trying it out. Seeing how it felt. She leaned forward on her knees, and her slender hand grabbed his hard cock in her soft palm. Tugging down the flesh, she placed it against her sex and already felt the pleasant heat prickle her.

Lowering herself upon him, her breath held, but

she was already so slick. Her scent was obvious in the air, and terror gripped her when she realized just how large he was, but she wouldn't turn back. She'd not risk his respect like that, and so she let herself drop, inch by agonizing inch, as the beast spread her open.

He was vocal as his cock slid into her, a guttural growl of satisfaction — she could only imagine — ripping the air of the cave as he slid up into her. The further he got, though, the more she realized just how different he was. Those thick veins were more than just prominent, they ribbed his length and rubbed her canal, producing such a stimulating effect on her honeyed folds. It was as if the Kron male's very loins were made for serving their matrons.

She heard him hiss a "yess" in his native tongue, and his powerful hands clutched her ass cheeks so tight as their chests mashed together.

It was so wrong, but her arms slid about his back, her breathing growing hot against his ear. She rested her chin against his shoulder as if to steady herself as she stayed still atop his cock, feeling it work to please her in such a new way. Her eyes rolled back in her head as she moaned a quiet, feminine curse.

It contrasted with his harsh tongue, his hard body, and her nipples prodded his pecs as she clung to him so eagerly.

"Good boy," she murred to her new pet. She'd claimed him, and now he was hers in her mind as well.

The pale, petite elf astride the large Kron could hardly have looked more wrong, yet he accepted her claim. He clutched her in his arms, those bulging biceps prodding her sides. He bent his head down and kissed and nipped her pale flesh. That thick girth throbbed inside her so pleasantly, those sleek black pubic hairs so nice against the red vulva and clit as their loins mashed together.

His breathing was heavy already, and she realized just how aroused he was. He was primed for her, the whole of his body waiting for her to claim it.

"Matriarch," he growled out in his deep tremor of a voice.

She pressed herself down to his hilt and grinded there, momentarily surprised that she was able to take him all. It was lucky that her fleshy rear helped to pad her a bit from injury as her mouth went to his neck, biting him far harder than he had dared to bite her. She licked it, then repeated the sharp sensation contrasting with the soft, her hips beginning to undulate atop him.

It was something familiar to him, and he groaned in her ear as she did so. It wasn't the wild up-and-down riding a human or elf male might expect, but he ate it up, only giving the most satisfying and carefully angled of little thrusts into her. The large brute was quite skillful at adding to her pleasure.

That warmth in her cunny spread north, and her entire body flushed a beautiful light pink as she crested that point of ecstasy. She gasped in shock as it gripped her so powerfully, so quickly, her eyes flying open. His body was made to please her, and no amount of shame or disgust could hide that fact from her.

"Cumming," she hissed into his ear before biting down on his shoulder, muffling her moan.

Her pussy contracted against that pulsing, throbbing organ with those ribbed veins, and warmth flooded them. Her wriggling grew more erratic, more hurried and passionate. She knew what her carelessness would reap, what he expected from her, and she didn't care. He and his brother would breed her, stuff her full of powerful, mongrel children, and her fingers gripped into his back in desire.

Saghar gasped, and she felt that hard, muscular body of his stiffen as his cock reacted to her release. Again, as if nature had designed him so, he quaked in response. The warm honey of her climax caused his sac to tighten against him, and that bulging shaft convulsed as it spewed out the virile ropes of seed.

It was more than any man or elf could've given

her, more than she would've anticipated his relative size to provide. Instead it was a seemingly endless stream of eager cum that shot into her depths, raced for her fertile womb.

The Kron believed no one male made a child. A woman gave birth to life through the combined efforts of her males and their continued ruttings throughout her pregnancy. For him it was but the first step in a process, but what a step it was. He cried out his satisfaction as that dark shaft twitched with the thick spurts of his release, the end finally nigh.

She felt so strange, as if her body was full, and she could feel it begin to ooze out of her, soaking them both with his wet release. She licked his shoulder where she had bit and marvelled at the intensity, at the beauty of a male Kron's body.

It was so taboo and forbidden, considered to be so degrading, but she knew at that moment that it was all just wives' tales, passed around to keep her from leaving elven men behind for all time.

As the big brute cradled her pale form and stroked over her delicate skin with a sort of doting and energy no human or elf ever had after his finish, she couldn't help but think of the business ahead. She was a focussed woman, and her goal lay south, in the underground hideaways of the rebels.

6

THE SOLDIERS

*M*orning hadn't yet broken when Major Hendrik Kelifron arose. He had always been an early riser, and even on the road as they were, he kept his uniform in good condition. Lieutenant Liena'sa knew better than to linger in rest when on duty with him, because though he may have let protocol slip in his cold appraisal of events with her in private, he did not brook sloppy work on the job.

It was what made him so admirable. He was harsh, but not arbitrarily so like other officers, and she knew he followed it up with competence and an attention to details that kept himself — and therefore her — alive.

They had commandeered the ground floor of one

of the farmhouses they'd come across, the family huddled together in the loft above, having suddenly found themselves short on room with four soldiers in their midst.

Moving to the sleeping bags of the two grunts, Kelifron kicked them in the side enough to startle them awake.

"You two," he commanded the pair of soldiers with a point, "scout along the roads for any sign of passage during the night."

One of them grumbled, "What about food, Major?"

"You'll get it when your morning duty is done." He called out to the family, "Have it waiting for us when we return." Then he stressed authoritatively, "Nobody eats until I'm sat back down, however. Nobody."

Liena'sa was quickly up and alert at the commotion, almost as if she could sense her Superior's wakefulness. Her hair was up in a bun and she quickly went to untie it, letting the silken gold strands fall down around her shoulders, her pale skin looking refreshed. She'd slept well, truthfully, despite the disturbing thoughts that kept threatening her mind.

With the others ordered about — including the

poor peasant family — he turned his dark gaze back upon Liena'sa.

"With me, Lieutenant." He strode outside into the pitch dark of the predawn morning.

She followed after him, though she felt a little more cautious with him alone. Still she kept pace. "Where are we going, Major?" She was short for an elf, though fairly tall for a human, standing at about his shoulders.

"To the top of the hill," he instructed, indicating needlessly the tall, craggy hill covered in trees that they would be climbing that morning. It was not that impressive, truthfully, but for the mostly flat farm-land and forest area, it was the only piece of elevated land for some distance, so it appeared more daunting that it really was.

His tall, shiny black jackboots carried him over the increasingly harsh surface as he went from one rock to the next in the dark, armed only with a dim lantern for light that did little to illuminate their way. Though, she noted, it didn't seem to impede the tall, slender Major's movements.

She followed after him, though her brows furrowed.

"You think we're going to spot her from up here?" Liena'sa's voice was a bit lower, as if even speaking the words might frighten their prey off.

The climb was pretty arduous for those unaccustomed to such harsh terrain travel. And since the pair spent most of their time either in the city or at one of the outposts near the front, she was surprised to find him pushing onwards at an impressive rate and showing no signs of exhaustion.

"I don't know what we'll find," he stated in his stern voice, "not until we get there. But I want a look at the land as sunrise comes. At the very least get a picture of possible directions she might've travelled."

She was falling behind, though her elven grace kept her from suffering too much embarrassment, only a couple feet behind him.

"Right." She could feel her heart begin to pound at the exertion, and her jackboot hooked into a loose root, giving her a secure footing until she pushed herself up another bit.

She knew when it came to work that she couldn't expect him to ease up on her. So together they went, with her pushing to keep up.

When at last they crested the hill, the Major put out the lantern entirely and stood stiffly. It didn't take her eyes long to adjust to the moonlight, and she watched as the black-uniformed officer scanned the landscape with such intense scrutiny.

She joined him in her own serious manner, her back facing his as she scanned over the flat of the land, over the road and through the forest. Liena'sa was used to following such orders and took pride in her duties, and the fact that she had a relatively safe position.

A position made safer by the man at her back.

It was some time before he satisfied himself with the search enough to speak again.

"Lieutenant?" he said, his voice having lost none of its authority as he pivoted on his heel and came to face towards her, though his gaze was slow to meet hers.

"I don't see anything, Major," she said, her head tilted to the side. Her hair was long, and she'd left it down beneath her hat as protection from the early-morning breeze. "Any sight of her?"

"We'll hold out until sunrise," he stated, and then she saw his harsh gaze turn towards her, a reflection of the moon in those steel-grey ovals. "Tits out, Lieutenant," came the abrupt and crass command from the severe Major, as if it belonged in the conversation as much as anything else he'd said.

Her breath stopped and her eyes moved away from his, even as her deft fingers unbuttoned her collar. Her pale flesh grew a brighter pink and she swallowed, but she knew they were safe. At the top of a steep hill in a remote area of the country. No one would find them. No one would hurt her.

The second button popped open, then the third. She didn't dally or protest, and when finally that last brass piece was pushed through the hole, she shrugged off her blouse, revealing the slim, toned figure beneath. She was so brilliantly pale, her nipples a lovely shade of pink atop her small breasts, and her held breath pushed them out to him.

His attention was so cool, emotionless. She watched as he slowly plucked the gloves from his fingers one at a time before pulling one off his hand, then moved to the next. His hard grey gaze swept over her slowly, soaked in those pale features in the moonlight.

Few women served in the military, and most that did took positions away from the front lines. Hers was something in between, though no less dangerous. The only thing that kept her from the untempered lusts of the soldiers was him. A commanding officer who kept them at bay. For as much as morale and order had broken down, the men still knew not to cross an investigator of the Royal Ministry.

He turned and walked a few paces to a side of the hill where the trees grew and blocked sight of them better.

"On your knees, Lieutenant," he ordered, and gestured to a flat stone before him.

She moved, though it wasn't too stiff. She didn't

fear him, or what he would do to her. She understood him at times, and felt that cold, hard stone beneath her knees. It sent a brief shiver up her spine, and her head tilted back. Her lips had dropped open, showing the white teeth within, the warm muscle of her tongue prodding her lower lip as a puff of breath clouded the air.

She watched as he stuffed his gloves in a pocket and looked down at her, ogling her exposed chest with a cool detachment and twisted enjoyment. It was with the same meticulous gestures he did his work that he unbuttoned his black jacket then the trousers beneath.

"Time to earn your keep," he said crassly as he reached in and plucked out that long, sizable member. Pale as the man, it throbbed full of veins that crisscrossed its length to the sheathed tip.

"Yes, Sir," she said on an exhale, her hands going to his thighs to hold herself steady as she leaned forward. Her entire body felt so warm, the pink buds on her chest stiffening in the cool morning air. She was conflicted about him, but her respect for him overshadowed her doubts, though it certainly didn't make them disappear.

As her mouth parted around the swollen, purple tip, her warm breath enveloped him. Her eyes closed, the lovely half-elf devoting herself fully to her new task. Her tongue laved along the underside of his cock, playing with him just the way he'd taught her.

All the while he watched, enjoyed the sensation of her peeling back his foreskin to suckle at his bulbous purple crown. He only intervened to reach down and take hold of her jaw, twist her head to the side so he could appreciate the sight of her fair-skinned face stuffed full of his length. It swelled out her cheeks as she fellated him, and he licked his own lips in his first outward sign of enjoyment.

"Drop your pants and get on your hands and knees," he instructed as his hand pulled her face back, leaving the shaft glistening with her saliva as it popped free of her lips to bob in the cool morning air.

Her mouth still hung open as she quickly stood. It was so formal, so quick the way she dropped her black pants over her pristine, slender thighs, her firm ass, those strong legs. She was a fit woman, a bit on the skinny side, and as her legs spread and that fair prize glistened betwixt them, it was a lovely sight to start the morning. Her hands dug into the earth, the chill making her nipples poke out further as her breasts succumbed to gravity pulling on those small tits.

It was bizarrely formal the way they interacted, even in their illicit trysts. He bent one knee and came down behind her. He took hold of her slender waist brought his cock to her lovely, waiting slit, where he wasted no time in filling her moist depths.

She didn't fail him at any of her tasks, and she knew how annoyed he'd be at finding her dry. Instead he was able to waste no time. With his hands on her he began to pump that large shaft hard and fast. This was her price, and he exacted it to his full satisfaction, his balls slapping against her clit noisily atop the dark hill as he grunted.

She didn't loathe him for it, or resent him. In fact, she figured herself rather lucky, considering her options, and she moaned her enjoyment. Her eyes fluttered behind her lashes and her head tilted back as she helped him ram into her.

She was lucky, she told herself. It was better him than the countless others who'd lusted after her, who'd cornered her and threatened her, only to be batted away by her Major.

Those hands of his, so deceptively strong despite his lean stature, moved up and grasped her petite breasts. Her nipples were pinched between his long, slender digits and he rutted into her harder.

It was one of the few moments he ever seemed truly vulnerable, when the sex got going and he truly started enjoying it. He seemed nearly human, then, and not simply a military commander. She heard him groan, gasp, and moan as he plowed into her. The

slap of his sac peppered between his sounds of satisfaction.

He was so much stronger than her, and her moan
was part groan as he pinched her aroused nipples a
little too hard. Her pussy quaked around him, and
her body slammed back into his. They made a pretty
pair, rutting in the forest. Their slim, pale bodies slapping against one another, the way her back arched
into his pinch and made the stiff bud tug against his
strong grip. Her breast stretched and she cried out at
the exquisite mix of intense pain and pleasure, her
body flushing deep pink.

She felt him begin to tense then, and knew his
release was at hand.

The thrusts had grown erratic, and he bent nearly
over her as a shudder passed through him. With such
a powerful moan of satisfaction he hilted himself into
her and shuddered. His cock spasmed inside her as
he flooded her depths with his virile seed atop the
hill, those cruelly strong fingers gripping her tight
until the last of his cum had spurt into her and he
was left drained at last.

She was left on the peak of ecstasy, so close and
yet so far away, and she felt her eyes burn with agitation. She would never show it, though. Not to him.
Even though her lip trembled as her head hung
down, looking over his hands containing her breasts,

seeing his balls slap against her cunny one final time. She sucked in a breath of cool air and shuddered.

The stillness of the morning as the very edge of the horizon began to turn orange with the rising sun was only broken by the heavy breathing of her commanding officer.

After a delay, he reached into a pocket and pulled out a kerchief. With careful precision he reached down, slipped his shaft from her, and wiped himself clean before leaving the cloth pressed to her messy cunt.

He rarely said much after such sessions with her, but he showed consideration beyond most men with his care for the mess. Then after he stood and buttoned his uniform again she saw him take out the familiar metal case that contained those precious, illegal pills that would prevent pregnancy.

"Ready, Lieutenant?" he asked, a bit of the edge taken off his voice.

She held the cloth to her, wiping her sex partially free of his cum as she nodded, still on her knees. She looked so small, like a dog begging.

"Yes, Sir," she said in her sex-laden voice.

He lowered himself to one knee, and she saw that tiny little betrayal on his lips. It wasn't a smile, but it was near one. He enjoyed this part, for whatever reason.

Cracking open the metal case, he took out one of the tiny pills. They were banned, in conjunction with breeding and family obligation laws. Contraceptives were something only the richest of nobles typically had access to. Yet she knew her commanding officer could get or accomplish anything he put his mind to, and he held out the little morsel to her and placed it on her tongue like a treat to reward her.

She held it there, her gaze intent upon his before she slowly pushed it back to her throat, swallowing it down. She never looked away from him through the entire process, and a true smile laced her lips when it was safely down.

"Thank you, Major," she said with gratitude.

There was a brief moment of something special there. Or almost. It was hard to tell with the stoic Major. He stroked a hand over her beautiful elven hair then stood up.

He trotted upwards to the crest of the hill again and looked out over the countryside.

"Come here, Lieutenant," he ordered.

She moved quickly, dressing herself back up as she went so that she managed to still look impeccable, just as a woman of her station should. She tucked in her blouse as her gaze followed his. "What is it?"

"See that?" He pointed off into the trees, a small pinprick of orange light amidst the dark of the forest further northeast. "That wasn't there before." He turned and began to head down the hill at an impressive rate, though never lost his cool composure.

Liena'sa followed after him, and wondered if perhaps he was just seeing things with a clearer head. The thought made her smile as she deftly moved behind him.

7

THE REBELS

*R*osa cried out as her foot struck a branch, toppling forward before catching herself. She cursed herself under her breath. The noblewoman had been wandering for days and was already out of supplies. She only had her backpack with a sleeping roll and two pieces of hard tack left to get her through, and she didn't even know where she was going.

The road would be instant torture and death, so she stayed in the forest, knowing that she had no allies left, no friends. She'd tried to assassinate the Queen, and all she had to show for it was a starvation march. She'd given up her friends, her cushy home, her lovely marriage proposal, all to help the lower class. To stick it to the rich monarchy that thought they could buy and sell people's lives so cheaply.

She'd sacrificed it all and then botched it at the last moment. It was sheer luck that she was able to escape the city, but when she'd pissed off the only man that could help her, she was left stranded. Deserted.

Even the self-pity had begun to bore her, though, and she was trying to come up with a plan. There had to be some farmers around that she could hide with. It would be a risk to their lives as well as her own, and even though the thought made her stomach knot, she was starving.

Her legs ached, and she already felt those large curves begin to give way to muscle, protesting with every step. The brown leather outfit she wore fit a bit looser, and her once pristine golden hair was just tied back in a bow, keeping it out of her face.

She hadn't seen a soul since the mysterious contact had disappeared, but she knew there were others out there. People who would make use of her skills and abilities without making crass propositions such as he had done. There had to be.

Rosa came at last to some sign of humanity. The scent of roasting meat carried on the air to her, and as she followed it along she found it didn't come from a farm house as she had expected. Instead, it was a small clearing in the trees where a fire burned. It was the first time she'd come across other human life since she'd angered the golden — haired rebel before, and it was satisfying just to hear the faint sound of whistling. Loneliness and desperation had a way of wearing on the psyche, after all.

She realized she was clasping her fists so tight that little half-moon indents were left on her palms, and she tried to relax. One hand found her knife as she slowly began to scout around the area. She wanted to leap out, to beg for help, but she was smarter than that.

There was just the one man at the fire. Dressed in an old, tattered trench coat with ragged furs about him for extra heat, he huddled at the fire with the hare he roasted suspended over it. In the middle of the woods, as they were, he whistled, carefree, as he watched the meat slowly roast against the will of the cold air.

She felt her mouth water, and stared at the spit with such longing that she'd never felt before. Her stomach rumbled and her free hand went to still it as she moved closer, her dagger still clutched in hand. He looked like a peasant, that much was certain, but she didn't know who she could trust.

The answer was "nobody," but she didn't know that yet.

Abruptly she felt her shoulder and arm grabbed from behind, a powerful hold keeping her knife hand from moving.

"Go to take a piss and come back wit' a girly," came a harsh, growling voice behind her.

The brute that held her locked in place looked worse than the one at the fire. He had missing teeth, and he grinned so broadly down at her.

She gasped and jerked her arm, feeling that tension as she struggled fruitlessly. Her face went red with anger more than fright.

"Let me go!" Rosa's voice felt so pinched, but it sounded strong and commanding regardless.

"What's all this?" came another gruff voice behind her, the man from the fire approaching.

"Found a lil' birdie on me way back from a piss," came the response from the filthy brigand who held her. She could smell the sweat and grime off him she was so close. "And ain't she a pretty one," he remarked, a glint in his eyes.

Her disgust outweighed her panic, and she tried to swirl, only causing herself more pain. She had fought mock battles with two foes, but never had she been at such a disadvantage, and she let herself go limp. It was the hardest thing for her to do to let her body go soft, for that rage to fall from her face.

"Please, let me go," she said, her voice filled with

as much pleading as she could manage, "I'm lost and scared!"

"Awww, don't worry, lil' one," came the voice of the other man behind her as he petted his grimy hand over her blonde hair. "We'll take real good care o' ya. Won't we, Grit?"

"Oh ya bet we will," came the retort, as she was pushed between the two filthy brigands. "Ya ain't lost no more. Sam an' I know these woods real well. Been out here long enough," he said, and she could see the scars upon his pockmarked face. His nose crooked from having been bashed in a few too many times.

"Let me go." Rosa narrowed her eyes, the resolve to remain calm dissolving almost instantly as that dirty man touched her. Her arm was strained, but she didn't care. She wasn't going to let them touch her like that.

"'Ey, whassa matter, lil' girly?" said Sam behind her, his arm going around her waist to keep her pinned to him.

"She don't seem ta like us, Grit," said the other one. His fingers dug into her shoulder and arm tighter. "She prob'ly just needs a bit of time ta get used ta us," he said with such a malicious grin.

"Some breakin' in," came Sam's addendum.

Her free arm instantly went back, her elbow

aimed for Sam's rib just as her knee jerked up towards Grit's groin. There was no way she was going down to these two dirty bums without a fight. She'd rather die than have them touch her, and she grunted as she tried to beat them away.

Sam took the elbow strike and his hold on her loosened, but Grit blocked her leg and in a blinding flash head butted her. All the world was black.

She awoke mere moments later to the cold dirt in her face as she felt one of their knees press into the center of her spine. "Rotten bitch!" said one of them, Sam, she thought. Her hands were tied in some corded rope as he bound her up.

"Fuck you!" she cursed right back as she squirmed, feeling lightning-hot strikes go up her spine. She didn't care, though, and her legs flailed, her arms tried to get free, regardless of how fruitless it all was. Even just making it slightly harder for them would be worth the pain.

Her head was pushed into the dirt at the side and one of their fists impacted the other. The world was ringing, she couldn't hear a thing, and all around her reality spun.

She didn't hear the first thud. Nor the second. Nor did she even notice when the pressure upon her back suddenly vanished. It was only when she was being pulled up onto her knees by the handsome elf in his dark leathers that things began to make sense again.

She was so dizzy, her head still spinning, and for a moment she thought it was all a lovely fantasy. A dream brought on to see her through the terror, but when her hand tightened around the elf's wrist, he didn't disappear.

Her mouth dropped open as she stared at him dumbly, then over at the bodies of the dirty scumbags. "You... took care of that easy enough."

As her vision cleared she saw the scowl upon her rescuer's face. "Yeah, they were distracted," he responded dryly, and she saw the severed pieces of rope dangling from her wrists as he helped her to her feet then led her towards the fire.

"See, I make a great distraction, too. Think of how useful I'd be. I could just stumble into the people you want to kill and distract them as they punch my face," she said sarcastically, but she stayed so close to him. Her voice lowered, and she looked up at him with sincere eyes, "Look... thanks. Really," she sighed. Her pride was bruised, her ego was almost nonexistent, and her face felt swollen, but he'd saved her.

He took a deep breath as he sat her down where Sam had previously been, the rabbit stuck near to the fire to keep it warm. "Couldn't very well let what was about to happen occur," he said plainly. With a sigh he added, "And I didn't kill them. I told you, I'm not a killer." Looking to their tied, unconscious bodies, she realized more time must've passed since that last hit to her head than she realized.

She blinked the thought away as she sat on the ground, still feeling woozy from the blows. "You've been following me? Or am I just exceptionally lucky? Well... either way I'm lucky."

"Luckier than you deserve," he said, and she watched as he freed his own long, lusciously golden hair from the hood that he still wore. Despite his dislike of her, he remained a strikingly handsome man. That near-flawless face of his marred only by those two scars, which made him look rugged and tough despite his elven heritage.

He bent down and retrieved some grungy cloth from the two men's supplies then held it out to her. "Here, you've got mud all over your face," he stated, though the dingy cloth looked barely any more appealing to her refined gaze.

Her finger reached up to touch her face, sneering as she took the cloth, trying to clean herself up as she glanced back to the two men. "You're not going to kill him?" she asked with disdain.

"No," he stated firmly. "They're bandits, but they're still people." He left that as is, as if it somehow justified sparing the lives of two mongrels like them.

"They're still people that are just going to do that to the next person they come across, and they're not going to be so lucky as me," she hissed, her eyes narrowing. "They're a menace. What if it was someone else they caught, huh? Someone you loved?"

He narrowed his eyes right back at her, that smooth, golden skin of contorted into displeasure. "I don't deal out death and judgement lightly. These men are desperate. Fleeing slavery, murder, and certain death. If life has made them vile criminals in the process, I mourn for them. But I won't rush to end their lives." He gave her a once-over. "If I valued life that cheaply, I'd have left you to die the other day."

He closed the gap between them in such a surprising speed. "How many died for your pleasure over the years, huh? How many of my kin and friends had to give up everything so you could grow up in a lavish manor in the comfort of the capital?"

"Too fucking many," she hissed back, her clear blue eyes hard beneath the dirt and grime that sullied her pale face. "Too fucking many have been dying for no reason, but that doesn't excuse what they did to me. The Crown isn't protecting your people from the beasts it creates." She motioned her head to the two passed-out bodies. "So how can we protect them?"

"They'll have their chance at redemption," he stated firmly, eyes narrowed at her. "But if you think I'm going to slaughter off the hard-luck cases of the world on your behalf, think again, princess." He grabbed the rabbit on the spit and offered it to her. "Go on. Eat. They owe you that much, at least. And you've not eaten decently in days. You'll waste away before long if you're not more responsible."

"Already am," she muttered as she took the meat in her hands, suddenly unconcerned about the messy, ugly picture she made. She was just grateful for food, for company, once more. It wasn't until she'd practically finished the small beast that she gasped for air, blinking up at the canopy of the forest. "So you think I'm worth a second shot or something?"

"No," he stated firmly. He'd spent her time eating arranging the two unconscious men against a nearby tree. "You're clearly not. I just don't treat life so cheaply as you do." He shot her a momentary glare.

"You're not responsible for me or my life," she said as she stood on weak legs, though the food made her feel stronger than she had in a day. "But if you've come back all this way for me, I'm not going to argue."

He gave each of the men a slap across the face, waking them both.

"Listen here," he said to them harshly, that smooth, masculine voice of his taking on an air of command she'd not heard in him before. "You're alive, but I saw what you did. And don't think for one moment I'll let you both go lightly."

They stared at him in surprise and the cowardly nature of both seemed to be brought to the fore. It was something drilled into every peasant and plebe in the land after all, and to be put back in their place the old nature took hold.

"Put your energies to the fight for freedom. And don't dare let me hear about you out here harming travellers or innocents again, you hear me?" he scolded, the fiery rebel full of his righteousness. "Our kind are slaughtered wholesale each day, and those who linger behind are enslaved. You can fight for them or against them. Your days of preying on them are over."

Rosa was rather impressed, but she grabbed for the knife she'd lost, placing it quickly back in her scabbard, "Yeah!" she said emphatically. She was still dirty, looking every bit the peasant, but for the first time, she didn't care. "You never know who has friends that'll help'em out. Or be able to help you out," she added on.

The anonymous rebel that'd saved her gave a curious look in her direction. He seemed surprised by her words and didn't have anything to reprimand her for.

"Here," he said as he rose up and tossed a knife towards them into the ground just within reach of her feet. "You'll get your way out of those ropes before nightfall if you keep a clear head. Remember our words," he said and moved off towards Rosa, taking hold of her arm and scooping up her bag as he took her off towards the north.

She still wobbled on her feet a bit, but that was hardly any different from how she was walking when she first went into the forest. She'd been getting better, but that blow to her head had made her balance a bit off. "Where are we going?" she asked quietly when she figured they were far enough away from the bandits.

"Heading in the wrong direction for a while," he said plainly. He let go of her arm when she seemed to regain her balance, though he kept her backpack in hand. "You don't have time to linger around anymore. You've dawdled too long as is," he stated firmly, leading her quickly through the forest at a hard-to-follow pace.

Desperation somehow helped her keep up with him, though she felt her pulse begin to quicken. "I don't know these forests," she reminded him. "I was lost. Were you following me the whole time?"

"Not the whole time," he said. "But you're not hard to find. You leave an easy trail to follow." And the way he said it made that sound so terribly ominous. Though his smooth, strikingly handsome face showed only the clear determination it always held.

"I'm a lot better in the city," she said sternly. "I'm just not used to being out here, but I catch on fast." At least, that's what her teachers had always told her growing up. "Is someone after me? I mean... I know they are but..."

He furrowed his brows and looked at her as if she were insane. "Of course they're after you. Always assume they're after you from now on. Don't be daft," he reprimanded and shook his head, that flowing mane of golden hair shifting just slightly as he led her on.

"I mean, are they on my trail?" she asked as she moved over a gnarled root, feeling more pleased at herself than she should that she didn't trip up.

He shrugged his shoulders but said, "With how obvious a trail you leave, I'd be surprised if they weren't. Though the incompetence of poorly trained soldiers motivated solely by fear often surprises me."

"Where are we going?" She frowned.

With a look to her he said, "Good question." He appeared troubled, though he added, "Anywhere you go, you'll be inviting trouble. But it's either let you die out here or take a shot at holding you up somewhere." He sighed, "I'm taking you to one of the outcast hideaways."

Even she knew the significance of that. The fabled underground cities of those who spurned the war and civilization were the stuff of popular legend, and had been for ages. Even the nobles wrote stories of such places and the aggrandized tales of what went on there.

She was shocked, but she tried to keep her face neutral as she moved in tandem with him. Her thoughts were dark, but she had no interest, for the first time, in sharing them. She didn't want him to leave her again, and that reliance upon another person made her heart feel heavier.

"You haven't even told me your name," Rosa said, her words softer, sounding more kind than usual.

"Marin," he answered simply.

8

THE NOBLES

The nobles of the Union all held residences in the capital. Their wealth and power all sprung from the strips of countryside they owned or were technically responsible for, but there was only one safe and civilized place for them to live anymore: the big city.

The private armies of the noble families were abolished long ago, and they relied — like everyone else — upon the state forces to protect them. The Landsreck, special forces of the state, patrolled its streets and saw to the safety of capital residents, especially the wealthy and powerful.

For once, though, that played to Duke Samei's detriment. Following the Queen's latest soiree he was not headed to his own manor, but that of his daughter. The rival city manor of the Rensford family was large and opulent, and, like his own, it had a handful of personal guards. They were the last lingering remnant of the armies nobles once commanded.

It would've been an impossible feat for the well-dressed Duke to sneak in normally, but now he had something special on his side. More aptly put, someone special.

She'd barely been married for a month, but she'd learned enough about the large, old-style manor to tell him of a secret back entrance. Duke Samei accessed it through a dark doorway beneath a bridge at a nearby royal park. The place looked like a tool-shed, but the hidden doorway behind a shelf was its true purpose.

Slipping through it, he moved on through the dark brick tunnel. The pathway was crafted centuries before, as a means for the nobles to escape should the people of the city rise up and come for their rulers. His own manor had something similar though better hidden, he thought. However, his mind was on other things.

As he came to the end of the tunnel, his daughter opened the door to him, showing a rich study behind her. Books, maps, and extravagant furniture filled what must have been his rival Duke's private sanctu-ary. "The servants are still away?" he asked out of anxiousness, but he knew they must be. She would've warned him right away if they had returned early.

"Of course," she hissed as she ushered him in, offended that he'd question her capabilities so. Her long, dark hair was more casually curled around her shoulders, though the gems that sparkled through her tresses were extravagant. Her smile was as dark and devious as she stepped aside and revealed her slinky, gold-and-teal dress that ended at the floor.

He gave her a look-over. "You changed fast," he remarked. They'd barely had time to spare since the soiree ended, but she'd managed to find time to change her dress for him.

"I could barely breathe in the other one, and I already told you, I wanted to wear something gold-en." She smiled, lacing her arm into his.

With a final look about the chamber he locked his gaze back on her.

"Is he still in the room?" he asked, unable to keep himself from appreciating his daughter's youthful beauty. That vibrancy she exuded, so starkly contrasted to his own stern, well-aged exterior. He was healthy for his age, but the silver at his temples betrayed the fact that the years had set their hooks in.

"He is, just as we left him. I almost like him like

this," she said softly, but a trail of malicious hatred ran in the undercurrents of her tone.

Samei couldn't help but soften that stern exterior of his, and he reached up, cupped her pristine, youthful cheek, stroked the flawless skin there back towards her ear. "My sweet child," he said affectionately. "You'll never be slave to another husband for as long as you live," he promised, then bent his head down and to the side. He was such a tall, statuesque man, and it took some doing — even with her in her heels — to reach her, but he gave her a sweet kiss upon her sumptuous lips.

Her nose crinkled and her hands went to his chest, but even as she pushed him away, her eyes sparkled with mischievous delight. "Father, you must behave," she chided lightly. "We have a guest in my home that we need to take care of."

The Duke couldn't help but crack a wry smirk at her playful nature. Despite his own reprimanding of her, he enjoyed her impish nature. Missed it in his own manor.

He licked around his lips, tasting what he could of her there before he led her onwards through the halls. It was a distinct style, different from his manor's architecture. The woodwork was lighter, taken from some exotic southern forest, no doubt. He loathed the place. It had housed generations of his rivals, yet now...

"This shall all be yours," he murmured to his daughter beside him as they walked. "A small consolation for having put up with that old fool for so long," he nearly spat bitterly as they made their way through the sprawling building.

Months had felt like decades to the young woman, and she patted his hand soothingly. "And I will dress in black to mourn the dead," she agreed, that smile parting her lips once more as heat flushed her pale face.

As they came nearer to the chamber he nodded. "That, I'm afraid, is required." He took a deep breath and sighed. "The old fool doesn't deserve your tears, real or fake, but he must have them."

With that, he pushed open the door and revealed the sprawling bed chambers. The massive canopy bed, the two tall windows with thick drapes on either side. The focus, however, was on the old, hawkish man tied to one of the exquisite chairs off to the side. He struggled to lift his head and look at them, his beady eyes filled with hate and anger.

"I'm home, husband." Caprice smiled. "I do hope you missed me. It was the most wondrous dinner, and had you not made me miss the last three with your wicked hands, you could have been at my side." She sighed wistfully as she walked into the room.

"Well, my sweet," said the boisterous Duke to his daughter. "That bruise I gave him seems to have cleared up nicely thanks to the ointment." A broad, feral grin contorted his devilishly handsome face.

She inspected the flesh that her father had struck with keen eyes, staying far enough from him that she was protected from his anger. "Ah, and yes, you've healed so quickly for a man of your age!"

Her father unfurled his arm from hers and stepped between them. The old Duke Rensford couldn't talk, tied up as he was in his underthings, and a gag was placed firmly in his mouth to keep him quiet.

"Leave this all to me, sweet girl," he said in a rich, soothing voice. He cupped her two cheeks in his hands and bent down, kissing her forehead tenderly. He lingered there awhile before pulling back up. "You needn't sully your hands any further on this vile thing." He smiled adoringly at his daughter, stroking back her curls from her face.

She sighed as she nodded, brushing past her father and sitting atop the bed. "I'm not going to leave the room, so don't even try." Her legs crossed and her hands pressed into her lap primly.

With a wry smile he watched her a moment.

"Very well. You've earned the right to do as you like on that matter, my darling." Samei looked to the tied-up old Rensford. "A man simply cannot stand up to the insistence of his daughter, can he, old boy?" He walked over and gave the old man a heavy pat — which was more like a slap — on the cheek, in mockery of some sign of familiarity between an older male and youth.

The Duke began to undo his jacket. "This shan't be a pleasant undertaking," he told the beady-eyed Rensford, who struggled against his silken bonds. "I imagine it could take a while for you to succumb, but..." He shrugged his shoulders as he tossed his jacket beside his daughter, his white shirt beneath on display as he went to the bathroom nearby. "Once we're done, we'll have everything you possess," his voice echoed from the washroom, "and nary a thing to say in contest."

The tied-up and gagged Rensford struggled and glared daggers at his "wife," the scrawny old man trying to break free in futility.

"Don't worry, husband," she chided. "It shall be faster and more pleasant than what you'd done to me, and perhaps you'll find you can take the same amount of pleasure in it. Perhaps this will make you hard, even," she teased as she glared at the older man.

She was the vision of youth, of a fresh woman just recently wed to a man that was almost ready to die when she married him. Her loving, doting father was just quickening things as far as she was concerned.

When her father returned from the washroom, his sleeves were rolled up like some common worker. "Time for the show to begin, old fellow." He dragged Rensford's chair towards the washtub. The water was running and she could feel it was cold from the increased chill in the room as she followed after to watch.

Her father simply lifted her husband up, chair and all, then tipped him back so that he faced down towards the flowing water upside-down. Samei gripped the leg of the chair, balancing the older man there as if it were some mechanism for dunking him.

Caprice looked on, curiously, her head tilting to the side. "What are you doing?" she asked, watching with rapt attention. Her nose crinkled. "If he drowns, won't he be all bloated?"

With a malicious chuckle, Samei shook his head and peered back at his daughter over his shoulder. "Only if we left him in the water afterwards. But no. I'm not going to drown him. That'd leave water in his lungs and they'd find it on autopsy."

As the pair spoke so casually, the old man fought

harder, and his wriggling nearly caused Samei to lose his grip on the chair.

"Hold on, old boy, your time is coming soon," chastised the younger Duke.

"I guess he doesn't like being afraid," his daughter cooed, and she tut-tutted gently. "It's so sad when someone can be so cruel, and so cowardly."

"Don't worry, love," comforted her father. "It shall all be over soon." And taking hold with both hands on the old man and his chair, he levered him down into the water so that it poured over his face, upside down.

The resulting show was not what Caprice had expected. She thought the old Duke had struggled hard before, but now she watched as the chill water poured over him and he convulsed wildly. She could hear his struggled attempts at crying out through his gag and the futility of his situation as her father held him in position.

After some time he released the man from the flow of the ice-cold water. "How was that, old boy?" he asked darkly.

Caprice took a step back, but she was fascinated by the tepid and terrifying torture. It looked so harmless, water just careening down someone's face, yet he'd thrashed so.

"Daddy?" she asked quietly as she stared.

Her father gave the old man another moment then dunked him back under again. As the disturbing struggle replayed itself out, he looked back to her and said, "It's a form of interrogation we used in the officer corps, darling." He gave a smile. "Simulates death in the individual." And he acted oblivious to the noisome struggle before him. "It's been known to induce heart attacks at times. And in this old fellow?" He laughed cruelly and turned back to his work. "We'll get there, won't we, old boy?" he said in a raised voice.

Her breathing held, but she wouldn't look away. Couldn't. It was the most horrific thing she'd seen, but it made her feel so alive. So in control. Just to see how delicate another person's life was, how easily they could disappear in a flash.

"Yes, father. We'll get there," she agreed, and felt a wave of heat flood her body beneath her fine golden-and-teal gown despite the chill in the room.

The struggle came to an abrupt and erratic change. Duke Rensford bucked and struggled against his bindings more than she could've dreamt possible for such an old man, and her father remarked, "Got there sooner than expected. Sooner than you deserve to be sure."

9

THE FRONT

No new recruits got it easy. The simple fact of the matter was that forces couldn't spare anyone from being thrown into work immediately, and the second part to that was the exhaustion and weariness of the veterans already at the front meant the "new meat" tended to get it worse than anyone.

So it was that when Sergeant Levek managed to find the opportunity to make his way outside the medical tent, he found Caslian working hard at scrubbing the bloody medical sheets. She was up to her elbows in the scrub basin and working all by herself, as no doubt the other medics took a moment to rest their weary selves or tend to some more urgent problem.

"Lookin' good, Private," he chimed in, face shaved, hair combed back in a sleek look. As much as anyone could while at the front, he'd managed to turn his appearance around and looked nearly presentable. "Them fingers worn to the nub yet?"

She wiggled her wet, pruny fingers at him before she went right back to work with a smile. "Don't think so, sir!" Even though exhaustion tensed her shoulders and made her face look a bit red, she still seemed in such good spirits. "You scrape your knee already?"

The woman was so sweet, and the smile she gave him lit up the darkening sky. Her flaxen hair was still tied back, though her bangs had come loose and threatened her eyes as she scrubbed.

Seeing her like that he could almost imagine her back behind the front at some farmhouse, living a life that approached decent. Somewhere she belonged. It warmed his heart to think of it, even as the sound of some mortal exploding in the distance took him back to reality.

"Where ya grow up, Caslian? You don't seem like you're averse ta gettin' yer hands dirty with some hard work, that's for sure," he added with a big, toothy grin. He wanted so bad to forget the rest of their bleak reality.

"Same place as anyone, I guess. Just south, one of

the fishin' villages." She grinned broadly. "I can fillet a fish faster than you can even blink, I bet. And everywhere you go there's always sheets needing cleaned." It went unspoken, though, even in her expression: Usually they didn't have to clean blood off them.

She stood, taking the sheet with her and draining out the cool, soapy water. Some of it splashed on the front of her simple brown suit, but she didn't pay it any mind. "What about you, Levek? Sir, I mean," she added on cheekily.

"Levek's fine," he said with a smile, though he refrained from pointing out she'd not see a single fish here, nor likely ever again. The ocean was far, far off, and any bodies of water here were drained of all life thanks to the pollutants of the front. "And I'm from a small ranch down southwest," he said, "on the cusp of the desert. We raised goats mainly."

He leaned against the wood post, watching her with no small amount of satisfaction. She reminded him of a place less hellish than where he was, even as he stood in that well-worn uniform of his.

"I like goats," she said as she squeezed the water from the material before hanging it up and grabbing for the next. "I mean, I only saw one once and he screamed at me, but he had the cutest goatee." She paused. "Oh, that's where that came from?"

He broke into a chuckle at that then rolled up his sleeves. He carried over the next load for her without asking. "Must be," he said with a toothy smile, that smooth, sandy complexion of his alight with joy for the first time in ages. "But goats can be nasty creatures. Eat anything, bite the crotch off you if you give 'em half a chance, kick it in if you don't."

The sun was setting, leaving the horizon a blood red that matched the horror of the trenches. Though they thankfully resided on one of the rearmost fallback lines.

"Fish can be nasty too. Some have barbs you gotta be careful of," she said as she took another bloody sheet, dumping it into the water and pressing down on the brush to get it under. "Though mostly they wouldn't kick you."

With a smirk he settled down near her and dipped his forearms into the tub beside her, helping out. "I don't imagine, no. I've heard tell fish legs are pretty stubby. Well, unless ya mean those weird scaly ones from the deeps. The, uh, what'cha call 'em? Kape'lar." Scourge of fisherman everywhere, the nasty things were allies of no side, and made the seas a treacherous place for all.

"Got a lot of family back home?" he asked, genuinely interested.

"Yeah." She nodded, her hazel eyes staring at him

over the basin, and he could see the light sprinkling of freckles beneath her tanned skin. "Bunch of us out home. Dad always joked that mom's as bad as a kitten, always poppin' out litters." She laughed. "Three sets of twins, one set of triplets, then me."

He laughed at that too; it was a pleasant thought. Though bittersweet, which was as good as it got, he told himself.

"Sounds like my old ma," he said with a faint smile. "Last I heard I had a good six brothers and five sisters." It'd been a long time since he'd heard from his mother, however. Many years. Mail didn't make it to the front often, and families usually ended up letting go after so many failed attempts. After all, it was not like their sons and daughters ever returned. Even on the off chance that they did, they were not the same. It was best to let go.

He rose up with another mass of sheets, moving to hang them up. It was then he caught sight, in the fading light of day, of some soldiers with their collars undone, looking off duty, making their way through the medical section. They didn't belong here. No soldiers came here like that, not unless it was to see a dying comrade off, and they were too cheerful for that.

"Thanks," she said jovially, scrubbing one stubborn stain with a pursed face before she sighed in satisfaction. Even though she'd seemed pleasant when he first came along, it seemed he'd rejuvenated her spirits and helped relieve her exhaustion. "I hope my ma has a few more. No boys," she sighed. "Always wanted some boys, they both did."

He'd barely heard her last words, but they registered a moment late and he smiled and nodded to her. "Yeah."

That was what he figured. Families didn't give up daughters to the war unless there were no more sons to sacrifice. Though that was far from his mind then. As he saw that group of soldiers approaching he knew what was afoot. They were headed down the row of medical tents, peeping in each one. They weren't here to see anyone injured. They were after the new female medic they'd heard about or seen.

Levek turned towards her. "Say, I gotta show ya somethin'." It wasn't the graceful or gentlemanly way to do it, but he didn't have time, he took hold of her arm firmly and tugged her from the basin, leading her back away from the tent.

"But the sheets!" she said with a gasp, turning to look at the abandoned basin, her fingers still pruned from the water and rubbed nearly raw. Already her hands were toughening and there were small sores developing from her hard work, though she'd never let on about them. "I don't wanna get in trouble." She didn't tug away though, looking up at him with wide eyes.

She had been too loud. Her girlish voice would carry, he realized. He led her on around behind the racks and through the alleyways between tents and wooden supply caches. "Don't worry," he told her, looking behind them again and again, for all the world looking nervously anxious as he took her forcibly by the arm through the sprawling maze of makeshift structures. "I'm an officer, remember?" he told her with a smile, though it was forced and obvious.

"Right." She was practically being dragged, but her legs worked to try to keep pace with him at the reminder. "Where are we going? I've not been 'round here before, I don't think," she said as she gazed, wide eyed, at her drab and dreary surroundings. It almost seemed like she lit up the area before it dissipated back into the glum drudgery of war barracks.

Levek heard footsteps from behind. They'd heard, of course, just as he'd feared. He tried to tell himself as a Sergeant he could usher them off, but he knew how frail a hope that was. They weren't his men, and the command structure only went so far out here. Even if he managed to frighten them off with threats of his authority, they'd just ambush them both separately later.

Besides, only a new recruit would be fooled by his threats. Whatever punishment he could mete out would be miniscule, nothing that would deter a group of desperate soldiers. And no commissioned officer over him would severely reprimand some soldiers for so "minor" an offense as this. Not when the grinder always needed new bodies.

He was leading her through blindly, down alleys, up others. He had no clue where they were. "Me either, I don't think," he said, and the cries of the men calling out to one another behind them carried forward. "How about we keep a bit quiet, huh?" he said to her with hope in his dark eyes, picking up his pace as his heart thudded in his chest. Damn it, he had to get her somewhere safe!

Her nose crinkled in distaste and confusion, but much to his relief, she didn't speak. She stuck a bit nearer to him, as if sensing the worry and urgency in his voice, finally. Her legs were much shorter than his, but she kept pace with him on those toned limbs.

The sound of a man shouting out "here!" did it. He nearly had a heart attack, but he grabbed her, swept her up into his arms, and carried her.

Levek dashed ahead with his trench coat fluttering in the dim of early night as he ran as fast as he could down the labyrinthine corridors of old crates, makeshift buildings, and endless coffins.

She clung to him, though she had no idea of the menace behind her, of what he was trying to protect her from. Still, her clammy hands held tight to his trench coat, her weight so easily lifted by him. She couldn't have even been a hundred pounds with her slender, waifish figure.

He had no idea how close they were, but he knew he couldn't outrun them all forever. Rounding a corner, he saw it. What might've been her only hope.

He slid down into the latrine ditch and clutched her to him. The stink of excrement was nearly over-powering, but he did all he could to hold her to him and keep a low profile.

The sound of those booted feet moving above them was clear as day, the men within a few paces as they looked about. It occurred to him only too late that if they gave up but went to take a piss they'd be caught, and it'd all be for nothing.

"Where'd they go?" He heard one of their voices, the men making guesses, arguing. Arguing so near.

She held her breath, and he could only imagine part of it was the stench. Her eyes were clenched shut as her small body pressed against his larger form, like a small child clinging to a loving, protective parent. The darkness of war didn't befit the angelic woman, and she trembled against him.

He could detect defeat in some of their tones, but

at least two others went off in further search. Levek cradled her form against him, buried his face to her beautiful hair, and tried to imagine they were anywhere but in that ditch. He swore he could detect her feminine scent even through the awful reek, and he shut his eyes, tried to imagine they were elsewhere.

It worked. For just a brief moment he was holding that delicate young woman by the pond near where he grew up. It was a rare spot so close to the desert, but he caught fish there at times. She was in a beautiful yellow sundress that complemented her, and she was ready to teach him how to fish, for he'd never been any good at it. They always got away from him. And the only time he met any success was when he fell in and grabbed one. Which had only worked because the damn thing bit him in turn, allowing him to yank it out.

She'd have laughed, that beautiful, musical laugh that was ethereally perfect. No malice in the tone as she saw him flail.

It all vanished immediately, though, as the sound of one of the grunts relieving himself in the ditch but a couple feet away broke his reverie.

She tightened her grip, her trembling nearly uncontrollable yet she didn't even make a peep. She was perfectly silent as he held her in the lowest point of their hellhole. She was fresh to the gritty realities of war and couldn't possibly be expected to understand why they were being chased, why they were hiding. She was pristine.

"Damn bitch," came the other man's voice as he relieved himself. "Wanted to wet my dick," he remarked crassly.

As he finished up and trundled off, Levek didn't dare budge or say a thing for some time. It wasn't until all had been silent for a good quarter of an hour that he breathed a quiet sigh of relief. "I'm sorry," he said softly.

He couldn't tell with her silence, but it was only then he could notice that she'd been sobbing, the front of his trench coat stained as she refused to let him go. Her fingers were white and her face looked green under her tan, but still she nodded. "It's fine."

It had been dark, and that was all that saved her. The hiding spot wouldn't have passed muster even minutes before when there was still some glimmer of daylight remaining.

He rose up, carried her out of that stinking pit, and spoke softly. "I'll take you back now, safe and sound," he promised. And though the whole ordeal had endangered him nearly so much as her, and was far from done with, his smile was at least somewhat genuine. He was happy to have spared her something worse. If only for now. "Swear it, Miss Caslian."

"Hope the sheets won't be cold," she replied, but her voice lacked that spark, that glimmer that had been so pronounced in everything else she'd said and done. It was if a little part of her had been snuffed out, darkened by the cruelties of war, and she hadn't even seen combat.

When he rested her back upon her feet, he reached out with his hand. "Cold sheets never hurt no one," he said, taking hold of her hand with a warm, comforting grip. Trying not to let the reality sink through his own stubborn skull.

10

THE MATRON

The glacial plateau was to her back, but still the chill winds blew from on high down the cliffs and into the sparsely forested area below. Aleena travelled on the edge of the permafrost, and the scraggly trees did little to mask the bleak nature of the landscape. With the two large Kron at her sides, however, the trip wasn't all that bad.

They all kept their cloaks bundled tight to them as they braved the arctic winds from the north, Ramtok and Saghar's massive forms doing more than she would've thought to block it from her as they trailed behind obediently as was the way of their people. The "savage" giants bowed to the authority of their matrons at all times.

Since leaving the plateau, Saghar had even taken to covering himself more. He'd braved the cold of the arctic in little more than his fur kilt, but now that he was beyond there he donned a thick cloak like the other two. "You trust these people then," he said, not daring to phrase it like a question, though she knew it was.

The frontiersmen of the area were different. They were given special dispensation from the state, requiring fewer recruits to meet their quota in exchange for them using their skills and knowledge of the area to patrol and keep the Union's enemies at bay. That was to say: the Kron. Though like any group, Aleena knew they were eminently bribable.

"I don't throw around that word, no," she said as she shivered beneath the heavy fur cloak. Her white, porcelain flesh was reddened from the wind, and her hair flowed from behind her. "But I believe we can come to a mutually advantageous agreement, and that's even better than trust."

Ramtok chuckled at that, seeming to enjoy her take. Saghar, however, grunted and nodded in appreciation of her pragmatism. "Caution shall serve us well indeed," he intoned, though she got the impression he was immensely uncomfortable now that they had ventured beyond territory familiar to him.

The barren wastes had only a spattering of snow

left, and as they trudged on further the flatly uneven land became increasingly littered with the scraggly northern trees. She'd traversed the area many times, and knew the terrain.

It wouldn't be long before they ran across one of the kaliak patrols. Despite their inevitable corruption, they did keep to their side of the bargain and patrol regularly. Though it was more for their own benefit than the Union's. After all, bandits operated even this far north.

And they were the hardest type, to even be living in such a place, but it didn't bother Aleena much. She tugged her white fur around her tighter, her fingers freeing her eyes from her white tresses. "Keep your eyes open for bandits," she said as she tied her hair back, leaving her long, elven ears exposed. She couldn't risk not being able to see, and the wind whistled past her.

For the first time since they'd set out, it was Ramtok rather than his brother who sighted the danger first. "There, matron," he said, his dark eyes glued off towards a patch of brown shrubbery near a thicker tree line. It took her gaze a moment to adjust, but she saw it then. It was at least two of the kaliak camouflaged in the tundra, and most definitely aware of their encroachment.

The negotiation of this would be tricky, even for

her. Her two Kron mates would definitely stand out under any close scrutiny. Yet she needed to conclude her deal and secure a place to rest from the elements. And on the flat tundra, it wouldn't do to just camp anywhere.

Aleena's footsteps stayed the same pace, her body still holding the same poise as she watched them, watching her. She began to move towards them, her hands unseen beneath the fur coat. The metal of her dagger touched her left hand, the cool wood of her pistol's handle clasped in the other.

"Stay back," she said as she made her way forward, her hands squeezing around her weapons before she relinquished them. "I've come to negotiate. The large brothers obeyed, as she knew they would, but she felt their unease. They hadn't left her alone since they'd acknowledged her as their new matron and set out together, and being in a strange land of their enemies heightened their sense of agitation.

As a show of faith I've left my guards behind," she called out loudly over the wailing of the wind, moving her arms from under her cloak and spreading them in the air.

Ahead, however, she saw as the silhouettes of the scouts crouched in the shrubs rose, rifles at the ready, aimed for her. More came out of the trees with bows and arrows, but as one of the men studied her then waved the others to lower their weapons, she knew it was fine.

"We know this one," came the voice, and when he pulled back his hood she saw it was the familiar face of the short-haired militia captain she'd dealt with before. That made initiation easier, but the rest... undoubtedly harder. This one was a slippery negotiator. Too cunning to rise to any higher a position amongst his people, as he was safe and in control right where he was. "Long time no see, elf witch," he remarked loudly and wryly as he folded his arms and let her approach.

"Aleena, actually." She smiled amiably as she moved forward, letting her arms rest back at her sides. "And I've missed you too." Her white hair whipped across her face, freed from the hair tie, but she ignored it.

"So what brings you here this time, huh?" he queried, seeming only half interested. "Smugglin' some drugs on through again? Or is it 'medicine' this time?" He smirked just a bit, but she had to watch as his keen, blue-eyed gaze slid over to her two conspicuously large Kron brothers and saw the danger there.

"Why, are you wanting for something? I do get around, if you have any special requests." Aleena was cold and anxious to get back to her Kron, but her posture was artificially relaxed. She seemed at ease, yet every muscle was at the ready, danger still prickling her scalp. "If you don't want to say it in front of them, we could discuss in private."

"I've no secrets from them," he said, though all the same he looked back to her then waved them off and they retreated, giving them space to speak. "What'll it be this time, elf? Whatever it is you're after, it won't come cheap. The state's breathin' down our necks, lookin' for excuses to conscript more of my men on any flimsy pretext they can come up with." It was hard to miss the slight dip his ice-cold eyes took down over her though, sizing her up in a less-than-professional manner.

"Well, perhaps I could help with that. I'm here to give you a break." Her nose crinkled slightly. "I'm sure you can use it. The weather is beautiful this time of year, after all. However, I'd like a private lodge. In return, well, I think me and my guards can let you and yours take some time off from patrolling."

The look on the tall, dark-haired northerner's face was sceptical, to say the least. But businesslike at its core. "I'm sure," he responded in a gruff voice. He paid her new Kron mates but a sparing glance more then leaned in. "Like I said," he began in a lower tone. "This isn't a good time for us to be cuttin' deals that could endanger us." With a shrug of his shoulders he glanced to the brothers once more, raising her anxiety. "There's somethin' more you could do for us though. Earn the 'privilege' of helping us out at one of the lodges." His lips crooked up in the corner.

Her expression softened, even as she inwardly cursed him. "Please don't say cook you a good meal. I'm a lousy chef," she said lightly, her green eyes narrowing as another gust brought hard debris to her cheek. She swatted it away and blinked back at him.

"You have quite the small army amassed," she added.

The man gave a dry laugh at her remark then shrugged. "We got somethin' to get to tomorrow. A trade," he stated. "Gotta meet some folk and trade 'em some of our specialty crafts for southern goods. Y'know, the usual." He smiled cooly. "And don't worry, rather not be eatin' any elf brew anyhow."

"Oh, my delicate sensibilities," she exaggerated with a playful roll of her eyes. "I'm assuming you're expecting the trade to go... sour?"

He shrugged his shoulders. "Not particularly. But y'know, anythin' could happen." She detected it wasn't quite the truth, but then, nothing said ever was in her experience. "What's really important is that we not be caught tradin' directly with these... sorts, with the state breathin' down our necks. So an intermediary like you would serve the function just right," he said with a toothy grin, the fur-clad north-erner so smugly full of himself.

"Ah, because I'm so objectionable in the first place. I'm your fall girl." She gave a saccharine smile. "Aren't you sweet. Well. You have me by the toe, don't you? Tell me what and when and where, and I'll tell you what types of sheets I'd like for my lodge."

She saw that hint of a sneer on his face then as he looked at her, not much appreciation for her tone. Though it faded fast as he was more of a busi-nessman than anything else. Which worked for and against her. "There's a lodge just a couple miles to my rear," he said with a thumb towards the tree line behind him. "You'll find the goods there for trade. You make the switch, we pick up the supplies two days from now, and other than that... the lodge is yours. How long you need it for anyhow?" he asked with only professional interest.

"A month or so, and I'll leave it in better shape than I left it." She offered her freezing cold hand out to him. She didn't trust him, or his deal, but one thing she did manage to trust in was herself. It'd kept her alive so far.

She could see the look on his face as he seemed about to debate her on the length, but instead, reluc-tantly, he reached out and took her hand. He gave it a firm shake and nodded. "All yours for that time then. We'll give you a wide berth after we pick up our supplies. Don't care to know exactly what you're up to anyhow," he added truthfully enough. "So with that, I'll see ya again in two days' time."

She knew then the deal had to be worse than he let on, for certain.

Her hand squeezed his, and her piercing green eyes locked on him. "And there's absolutely nothing else I need to know about who you're trading with?"

The captain gave a dry laugh at that as he took his hand back. "Really? You need me to say any more?" He turned and began to walk off instead. "You got enough of a warning." And it was true. Anyone trading without sanction of the state was someone to be wary of, for they were either bandits or crooked black-marketeers like her who knew how to protect themselves either way.

She rolled her eyes at his back before trudging back to her Kron. She pushed her hair back from her face, though the red in her cheeks was no longer just from the cold, but anger at the obnoxious, insulting man.

The large, armoured Ramtok took a long look at her then stared at the back of the captain as he receded into the distance. "It's not too late for me to gut him for you, matron," he said, solely inferred upon her angered reaction he seemed ready to do just that on her behalf, his hand gripping his scimitar hilt.

"It's fine. He's a peon. Besides, I could use a little adventure in my life." As if what she was doing wasn't already adventurous enough. "We'll be doing a trade. Then you might have to actually kill some people." She smiled. "In return, we'll have a cozy little lodge all to ourselves."

The broad Ramtok gave her a toothy, almost lecherous smile. "Very well, matron. By your command," he stated respectfully, and together they set off towards the lodge in the woods.

11

THE SOLDIERS

"They're up here, sir," said the black-uniformed Landsreck — the Landed Knight, special forces of the state — as he led the pair of officers through the woods. "We found them while searchin' where you told us."

Major Hendrik Kelifron moved along at a brisk pace, forcing the man to pick up speed to keep astride him. "And they were tied up when you found them?" he asked brusquely, the stern man's voice so firm and resolute. All business.

"Yes, sir, that's correct. We didn't ask them anything, as you instructed. We waited for you and your adjutant."

He was surprised they managed that amount of adherence, but he gave just a firm nod in approval. It was hard to say what went on beyond those steely eyes of his as the tall, slender man strode through the woods so speedily.

Liena'sa was close at his heel, her walk just as formal and purposeful as his. Her blonde hair was tied up and away from her sharp features, half hidden beneath her officer's cap.

She was a stern-looking half-elf with a purposeful stride and her shoulders were squared. She understood what it all meant, finally.

They were hot on the would-be killer's trail.

As they reached the small clearing with the dead fire pit, the two bound bandits were hard to miss. They were knelt down at the center, with the second Landsreck's rifle at the back of their heads. "Step aside, Sergeant," came the Major's firm voice, and the two guards took up position to the side.

The two scraggly-looking ruffians peered up at the stern captain with wide, terrified eyes. "We didn't do nothin', sir! I swear! We was on our way ta sign up when we was waylaid by bandits and—"

The Major pulled out his pistol and struck the quiet, shorter one with the hilt of the gun. He spoke with an eerie calm as if he hadn't nearly just bashed in the jaw of the other man "Don't waste my time with bullshit. Just tell me the truth."

With those steely eyes upon him, the first swallowed then spoke again sheepishly. "I swear, sir, what I said about bein' tied up was true—"

"Obviously," butt in the Major coldly.

The man flinched at that. "Was two of 'em. A man dressed in dark-brown leathers with blonde hair, spoke a bunch about fightin' the power and stuff."

Major Hendrik Kelifron's brows furrowed in a rare display of open thought at that. "And the other," he urged.

"She... she was a pretty lass. Real fine lookin'. Too good ta be true," he said with a nervous swallow.

The Major studied the man intensely, satisfied himself that this was the truth based on what he knew already. "Keep going. I like honesty."

Liena'sa didn't flinch at the violence but spent almost as much time studying the Major's expression as she did the two bandits'. She was a clever woman, but he was cleverer, and she watched as the gears turned in his head.

The ruffian jerked his head up to the north. "They went thataway sir," he blurt out immediately. Nodding to his own words, he was insistent, eager to appease the Major. "After the feller got a drop on us, tied us up, and took our stuff for the missy, they went off in a rush. Even though she was lookin' ragged!"

The Major never let his eyes slip from the man, that unrelenting gaze boring through him to the truth. "So you were waylaid and hog-tied by two rebels in the woods, who then robbed you and preached about their cause," he said in accusation.

Flinching a bit, the man nodded. "Well... we was... we — " He glanced to his companion, whose jaw was already a mess. "We took ahold of the lady and... while we was busy with her the feller got us."

Liena'sa's eyes were as cold as the Major's. "Poor dears."

The Major looked at her for a split second, giving the bandit his first reprieve from that harsh gaze. "So were they working together or did he just happen to drop in on you three while you were 'busy'?" he asked with his eerie calmness, barely slipping with the derision on that last word.

"He... he" — the man swallowed again — "they seemed ta be separate. But... but after he tied us up they talked like they was real familiar. They definitely knew each other, sir. I swear, that's all I know!"

Taking his time, the Major nodded to that then walked around the man. "Alright then. Moving on to other business," he stated, much to the barbarian's relief. Hendrik grabbed the filthy man's arms, going down to the ropes that bound him. "You're going to tell me the location of the nearest outcast hideaways."

The man flustered for a moment. "What?" He

jerked his head about but couldn't see the Major. "We don't know nothin' like that, sir, I swear!"

Liena'sa saw as Hendrik took hold of one of the man's fingers and bent it back at such an obscene angle as the sound of cracking bone filled the chill spring air. "Not good enough," he stated firmly over the sound of the man's screams.

"Try again," came the Major's insistence, and even amidst the man's cry of "I don't know

The next bone broke.

"We swear we don't!" cried the other man with the near broken jaw. "If we did we wouldn't be out here!"

He earned another blow for that one. "Parasites like you two doubtlessly were kicked out. Now tell me what I want to know and I can send you on your merry way."

The Lieutenant saw him take out a tool from his pocket, and she knew what it was even before he had it ready. If the bandit didn't start talking soon, he was going to have much fewer fingers.

12

THE NOBLES

Through all her years, Caprice had never had the opportunity to witness her father get his hands dirty with work. Yet she'd just watched him torture and kill a man.

She knew, of course, that he had been an officer. A Marshal of the Union Military. He'd commanded men at the front in combat, and spent years organizing the Landsreck behind the lines before he took over as head of their family. She suspected the skills she'd witnessed him display were earned during the latter.

As he came out of the bedroom, his sleeves still rolled up and his normally brushed-back hair a bit tousled, she could see him in a different light. The silver that brushed his temples did not diminish his vigor there before her with his jacket over one shoulder. "He's in place now," he said to her smoothly. "Tidied up and waiting to be found in the morning," he explained to her calmly, as if he hadn't just murdered a man — her husband by law— — on her behalf.

Duke Samei was such a tall and imposing man, but he gave her an uneven smile as he reached up and cupped her cheek in his palm. "It'll all be done and over with soon, sweet child of mine." His voice was so rich, his tone so fatherly despite the topic.

Relief flooded her and she let go of the breath she'd been holding for so long. Her entire body seemed to yield to exhaustion after the ferocious and trying evening, and her bared shoulders slumped.

The gold-and-teal dress still covered her arms but left her cleavage and shoulders scandalously exposed, but it was expected of youth to rebel a bit. To let others enjoy their bodies as everyone pretended to be offended.

"Thank you," she sighed, her pale flesh seeming a bit flushed.

He bent down and kissed her forehead tenderly. "You'll have to check in the morning to be sure before you send for help, but otherwise that's it." He stroked his strong thumb over her smooth, fair skin.

The same hand that had just been responsible for murder touching her pristine, virginal flesh. "Make sure the Landsreck or a doctor get here before you send for me."

Her lower lip trembled and she glanced past him for a moment. "You expect me to spend the night alone with a dead body?"

Samei slid his hand back, stroked her beautiful dark hair and its carefully coiffed curls. "Not in the room with him, but yes. I can't stay the whole night, it'd be too risky," he explained to her with a calm patience. The sort of control she was used to her father exhibiting with her. "My poor girl," he said with deep fondness, "your trials are nearly over. I swear."

"What if he wakes? And I'm all alone and can't protect myself?" she asked, her tone an annoyed hiss. "Father, you can't leave me all night like this."

His gaze hardened, but only for a moment. "Come along," he said and took her by the arm. He guided her to the bedroom down the hall, led her into the lavish residence, and slung his jacket to the side. He took hold of her hand and lifted it up, squeezed her palm then kissed the backs of her fingers in the dark room. She could make out the reflection of light on his eyes though, the silhouette of his form against the window behind him.

She blinked as her eyes slowly adjusted to the dim light, her body aching with exhaustion. "Tucking me in won't calm the monsters when the monsters are us, Father," she protested but squeezed his hand at the same time.

"None of that," he reprimanded in his velvety husk. There was no harshness in those words, just tenderness and care. "Come here," he said and led her by her hand to the bed. He sat upon the edge and guided her along with him. "I'll stay a while," he promised.

The gown gathered beneath her as she sat beside him, the lush duvet so soft against her weary muscles. Caprice leaned her head against his shoulder as her eyes fluttered down. "It could have been so much better, couldn't it have?"

He put his big, reassuring arm about her, held her close, and kissed her luscious hair. "Don't worry about such things, my sweet," he urged. "Could-have-beens are a thing for peasants, not lords and ladies." His hand stroked down her arm then came to rest on her hip as he tugged her close. "You're a free woman now. Once word is out, you'll be a widow officially. And never need worry about the whims of another ever again." His dusky voice had such a soothing way of reassuring her in between the kisses of her hair and forehead.

She stayed so near to him, letting her breathing return to normal as her fingers stroked up along his thigh gently. "You enjoyed that. Taunting him."

He gave a soft but abrupt and curt laugh. "That vile thing?" he asked, then squeezed her tighter, his strong fingers digging into her flesh at her side and over her stomach. "Absolutely," he stated. "I enjoyed every minute of it, he deserved it all, and it set my daughter free."

Her breath came quicker and that strange flush swept over her pale flesh, the dim light of the stars and the moon all that lit up the room. It cast everything in a soft wash of colour, and her fingers circled his thigh. "He only wanted me to get back at our family," she lamented as she felt her father's warmth against her side.

"He didn't even want me. What if they don't let me keep the manor, daddy? What if they take it all away from me?"

He kissed down her face to her cheek, the touch of her hand so tantalizing to him. So wrong. "It'll be yours," he urged. "His family will challenge it, but we'll take measures to secure it for you." He squeezed her hip and stroked his strong hand up her side as the other came over to rest on her neck, to feel her smooth, pale skin. "As long as they can't prove the marriage wasn't consummated, they'll never make a convincing case."

Caprice's pulse raced and her fingers dug into his thigh. No longer was it the soft caress. Instead it was fear and apprehension. "How could they prove it? How could they tell?"

It wasn't right, especially not under the circumstances, but with her hand so close to him, the exhilaration of events... her fingers grazed the bulge in his black pants. It had swelled out so far, the accidental brush of his daughter's digits was unavoidable.

"There's only one way they could attempt it, darling. But it'll prove nothing, which is why they so rarely approve such tests of noble ladies." He kissed her cheek, admired her fragile beauty in the dark of the room. "With any luck, my agent will be able to trick the rebels and hand us the Queen's would-be assassin, and nothing would be denied me any longer by the Crown."

She nodded eagerly, her head brushing past his lips, and she swallowed. His daughter was normally so composed, so in control, but the moment she'd come to him for help, everything had changed. She'd been relying on him more than when she was a child even, and the way her hand didn't stray and escape the press of his masculinity was either an oversight on her part or terribly wanton.

Slowly her hand returned to her own lap, bundled there like a flower, and she exhaled deeply. "I'd do anything for you, daddy."

It was like time froze then. He stared into her gaze, held her, but remained unmoving. It was as if a battle raged within him, silent and hidden. A storm within a box. At long last he spoke, his voice sounding hoarse. "You are too perfect a daughter, sweet Caprice." It was almost as if he lamented that fact. "I am so sorry for marrying you to that vile, old vulture." He looked like he wanted to say more, do more, but his hand trembled at her cheek as he gazed at her longingly.

"A few months of misery for a future of ease. It was a worthwhile trade." She smiled, her full lips pulled taut as she stared at him. A cloud passed by the moon, blotting out the silvery light for a few moments, and her hand brushed his side as it went behind her. "You don't have to regret it, daddy. Any of it," she reassured him.

It was torture. She was such a vision of beauty, so curvaceous and lovely. He swallowed down his doubts and anxieties. Forced them to the back of his mind. But failed. "I should've kept you to myself as I longed to do," he said softly. "Locked you away in our manor where we could chat and trade tales till the end of my days." He shook his head slowly. "I very nearly did, darling. I very nearly did..."

"But instead you did the right thing, and you got me anyways. Brought us closer together," she said softly. She seemed so calm and put together, even as her body felt so heavy with world-weariness. "You protected me from him."

He leaned after her, let her descend towards the bed just a bit. "I'd do anything to protect you, my child," he said with such sincerity. His lips found the corner of hers again and smacked lightly in the large room. "And when you rule over a noble House of your very own, you shall still have your doting father. Always and forever."

She smiled as she lay back, feeling that full duvet beneath her as the cloud pulled away from the moon and illuminated her refined features, her sharp eyes and the halo of brown curls around her head. She kicked off her heels, her bare feet swinging slightly. "Thank you for coming to the party with me tonight. I don't know what I would have done if you weren't by my side, father. Keeping me safe."

Gazing down over her angelic form, he leaned in and kissed her forehead. "You'll never be alone, for you'll always have your father's love, sweet Caprice."

She shimmied out from beneath him, moving her

body in such a slinky manner to raise herself onto her elbows. "I should bathe, daddy. With everything that's going to happen, tomorrow... it'll seem suspicious any other way." Her eyes were drifting down already, but she twisted her spine about to face away from him. "Will you get the clasps in back?"

Such a different style than she'd worn for the party, the gown was rich and smooth. It was lighter and let her fresh, peachy skin show through at the shoulders and back, and she pulled her hair away from the golden clasps.

He'd resisted her already, but she hadn't relented with her teasing, even in such a moment. He took hold of her bicep and leaned in, kissing her shoulder near her neck. "Very well, my child," he said in his husky voice, the restraint audible as his other hand came up and took hold of the top clasp, undoing it, then moving down to the next golden binding.

Her lashes descended as his fingers brushed her creamy flesh, and she felt the gown begin to give way, falling from her chest, and she took in a deep inhalation. The dress was not so restrictive as her ball gown, but it still made free breathing a luxury.

With the last of the clasps undone, he saw the gown slip away from her, exposing the smooth skin of her back. He knew then how dangerously close he was to doing something wrong. He couldn't help, though, but touch that milky flesh of hers, trail his digits down over it. Though he stopped and rose smoothly. "I'll run the bath for you, my sweet," he said and made his way to the attached bath chamber.

As he began to run the water from the pipes — a luxury few knew anymore — he couldn't help but let out a ragged sigh. *How she tests my resolve*, he thought.

It was only moments after that she came in, stripped down to nothingness and leaving her creamy, voluptuous body exposed. She kept herself half hidden by the doorframe, her hand running up along the wood. "Use the golden oil" — she paused — "and just a drop of the pink."

She'd always been one for her fine oils and creams, so it was no surprise that she was so specific.

Looking back to her he said in a husky, almost anguished voice, "You are a merciless tease, Caprice." Though he did as she asked. His sleeves still rolled up, he bent down and added the oils, exactly as she specified. He tested the water, found it pleasing, and choked off the flow before setting a towel along the edge so that she needn't touch the cool surface of the tub as she climbed in.

She was silent for a while as she shifted into position, her creamy flesh slowly disappearing beneath the water. She had curves that most women lay awake at night dreaming of, and her pink nipples were tight atop her breasts. "I didn't realize you had such delicate sensibilities now, father. You always used to bathe me."

He licked around his lips as he watched her sumptuous flesh through the scented water with such fascination. "You are more woman now than most men can handle, Caprice," he responded, and without being asked he lifted the wash sponge and dipped it into the water. He soaped it lightly and brought it to her flesh, started at her shoulder and began to make little circular motions as he moved over her.

Her eyes fluttered shut and she sighed, inhaling the rich, floral scent of the oils. She trusted him, completely, and her body shifted to always follow the sponge. The water rippled, but it could do nothing to hide her flesh from him. Her thighs, however, were kept together, and he could see that promising tuft of downy hair pointing down.

"Am I the only one you bathed, father?"

As the swirls of the soapy sponge made their way down, leaving her arm and shoulder coated in its light foam. "Absolutely," he said honestly, moving about the sumptuous curve of that hefty breast. "You were the only one of my 'brood' that I ever cared to spend any time with beyond what was necessary,

Caprice." The pale foam coated her stiff nipple. "I have my sons in the service to be proud of, your sisters, but they could hold no candle to you."

She smiled, the expression almost devious as her back arched and she tilted her body towards the sponge, forcing him to wash over her tit. "It's the only way I really feel I can relax. The handmaidens couldn't do anything the way you could. They couldn't give me the same experience." Her eyes fluttered open. "Daddy knows best, after all."

His hand trembled for just a moment at her breast before he steadied it. "You'll cling to that term forever, won't you?" he said, though they both knew he enjoyed her calling him "daddy." Despite his attempts to deny it.

He didn't skirt it then. He cleaned her breast, soaped and rubbed it. His fingers grazed her flesh in the process before he moved across her chest to the other, repeating his slow, meticulous movements. Lathering her teats with such careful attention, and enjoying every moment he had to appreciate her nubile flesh.

"You don't stop being my father just because I grow up and get married," she said, her eyes opening slightly and watching as he moved the sponge across her body. She shifted and her legs parted, revealing more of that untouched place. "You'll always be my daddy, for the rest of my days."

She watched as his dark, piercing eyes moved down over her to that sweet, forbidden nexus. "Forever and always, sweet Caprice," he said, and his hand rubbed upon her flesh, brought the sponge down across her lower stomach in its circular fashion. He skirted the tuft of pubic hair before brushing through that.

He leaned in, unable to tear his eyes away from her as he spoke. "I have seen and bedded many women," he said in a low voice. "Many more than just your mother" — the confession was not exactly unexpected — "but you, my child?" He managed then to tear his eyes from her body to meet her gaze. "You are the loveliest by far. Not a single tart in all the Union holds a candle to your luscious form. But yet you sprang from my own loins." And his hand moved between her thighs, and he rubbed over that still virginal slit and cleaned with such dutiful attention.

Her devious smile didn't fade, and the shrug of her shoulders sent the water cascading over her breasts, lapping at his wrist. Her legs parted further and her pelvis tilted up slightly, a moan filling the air between them. It was so sweet, a reward for his gentle care. "Perhaps that's why, then, daddy," she offered. "I inherited my looks from you."

Samei lifted his free hand and caressed her cheek with the backs of his digits. "Yet your mother, as fair as she is, couldn't hold a candle to you. You are too precious and lovely for this world, my girl. By far."

She struggled to keep her eyes open, to look at her father through the partial lids and thick lashes as her knees touched either side of the tub. Her skin grew warmer, turning pink under his ministrations, and she inhaled sharply. "Daddy," she whimpered on her exhale, leaning in against his hand.

He watched her writhe beneath the water, murmur for him, and drank it in like it was the finest of liquors. He tentatively rubbed her needful quim, the lap of the water at the side of the tub accompanying his skillful ministrations.

Through it he leaned in towards those succulent, pouty lips of hers. He kissed them sweetly, then again like no father should. "Always and forever my favourite, sweet Caprice. Daddy's girl till the day I die." And he admired her so completely as his fingers brushed along her cheek and her sensitive labia below.

She pushed her lips back against him, her tongue darting out for a brief, daring second before she leaned back, her breath increasing and sending the water rippling about her breasts. Her nipples were so hard, still partially covered in soapy suds as she lamented, "He wouldn't touch me. Said I disgusted him."

His hand increasingly moved at a more vigorous rate, the soft yet coarse feel of the sponge rubbing over her delicate cunny. "He lied," he nearly hissed, his bare arm shaking with the movements below the water. "He was a sick fool who got off on torture, and would deny you your rightful credit, sweet girl." He kissed her again, firm and wantonly, tasted those luscious lips. "Cum for daddy," he urged. "Cum for your father like a good girl, pet." His voice was so harsh with his own denied desire.

If she was shocked by his words, it was only in the best way possible, for it wasn't soon after she gasped and bit down on her lower lip. She drew it between her teeth to stifle her moan as she thrashed in the water, losing control of her body as he rubbed over her throbbing sex. Her eyes squeezed shut and she couldn't hold back any longer, that familiar refrain of, "Daddy," cried out in the throes of orgasm.

Duke Samei Ellefor watched his daughter squirm before him in the water, drank in the sight of her climaxing to his hand. He stroked her affectionately, upon her cheek and sex, brought her down from her high with attentive care, stoking her pleasured clit delicately until she could handle it no longer. "Good girl," he husked approvingly. "Your father's pride and joy." He laid the sponge aside and kissed her sweet lips.

The exhaustion clutched for her once more and her eyes dropped even as her arms reached out for him. "I know what I said about the monsters, about you not being able to tuck me in and protect me from them. But I'd like you to try," she said hazily.

The stern duke put his arms about her, held her water-slick form against him, heedless of the mess. "Of course, my child. Of course." He kissed her dark curls and reached out with one arm.

He plucked a towel from nearby and wrapped it about her before he pulled her out of the water. She was so light in his hold, and he lifted her with ease, swathed in the rich fabric of the towel. "I was always going to anyhow," he said with a smile as he carried her out to the bed and laid her down.

With meticulous care he peeled back the blankets, picked her up again then put her in them before pulling them around her snugly.

"I wish you could stay the night," she lamented once more, arms wrapped about his neck. "I don't like being alone anymore."

Samei kissed her forehead tenderly, gave her a final squeeze in his arms. "Hush, don't fret, my girl.

Once things are settled, your loving father can visit you more often," he said with a warm smile. He tucked her in tightly, in such a fatherly manner that contrasted what he'd just done in the bath. "We shall probably have more time to ourselves than ever."

"I'll call for you as soon as it's safe," she murmured, but already she was beginning to drift, secure in the knowledge that he could see her through. That he would take care of her. That he'd always be there.

13

THE MATRON

The kaliak hunting lodges were made to serve as host to the scout parties they sent out to watch the tundra and forests of their territory. They were moderately sized, enough space to fit a raiding party in fairly close quarters with their supplies.

As Aleena and crew approached the appointed long stone-and-wood building, Ramtok and Saghar split up to check out the area. The witch doctor took the outside, inspecting the area surrounding, while Ramtok went to the building itself and cautiously probed before opening the door. He caught the trap there, which the kaliak scouts left to protect their lodge then nodded to her. "It's safe now, matron."

Safe and cozy, she thought. As she peered inside,

she saw the spacious room with its generous fire pit at the center would make for a very welcome respite for her after the long journey to and from the Kron lands on the other side of the border.

The moment she stepped inside she felt sweet relief that she couldn't remember feeling in months. It was comfort that she'd almost forgotten, and she shook off the fur cloak and tossed it on a dresser. "Finally."She moved to the fire pit and began stoking it.

There were no supplies waiting for them in the lodge, other than a generous supply of firewood, which she used to great effect. Ramtok went about unpacking some of their things, and when Saghar returned and shed his overcloak to stand in the long lodge in only his white fur kilt and harness, he shut the door and reported. "The area is safe, matron. Or" — he hesitated — "as safe as I can judge it at least."

Ramtok gave a brief glance to his brother then rested his scimitar on the table near the fire pit. "He is never wrong, matron," he stated with absolute certainty as he removed his belt and sheath.

"Still, I like his caution." She grinned as she rested back, her fingers stroking the heat of the fire in the air. Slowly the red drained from her face, and her pure white skin returned to its normal hue. "We'll just have to make sure to keep the curtains drawn now."

The two Kron men were towering figures, like larger-than-life sculptures of men carved from stones of various shades. Their muscles so outlined and prominent, as if etched by a sculptor. The windows of the lodge were already shuttered by wood hatches, but Saghar checked them all the same as Ramtok shed his outer layer of armour, down to just his leathers beneath. It left his pecs and biceps exposed, and his thick thigh and calf muscles bulged through as he crouched beside her. "It is not quite time to eat yet," he spoke to her in his deep, gravelly voice. "But shall I start some food for you anyhow, matron?" The brazen brute gave her a wry smile as he reached out, and touched her hand with his, his heat so prominent since they'd only recently come in from the cold.

"I'm not hungry," she said, her lips contorting into a wry grin. She always ate light, if at all, though her ample thighs and behind still remained. "I think I'd just like to focus on getting warm, truthfully."

They were so close, the pale, elven woman seeming so small in the shadow of that giant Kron. Her green eyes danced over his dark, strange flesh before resting on his lap. "I could use some relaxation."

The brothers were never shy of sexuality. They

were used to being treated as objects of sexual use or desire back amongst their own kin, and at her words the large male very obviously twitched beneath his leathers, his groin swelling.

"Whatever you say, matron," he husked with some amusement, rubbing her fingers in his hand as he brought the other to her knee and rubbed up over her, across her thigh to her hip. He very obviously licked his lips in a suggestive manner to her as he reached for her belt.

Her palms pressed into the floor as she leaned back, her body arching her small breasts up and giving him access to the white belt beneath. Her outfit was just as pale as she, the leathers bleached and treated until they were a snowy white. "Saghar" — she glanced behind her — "I have a kink in my shoulder."

She didn't even need to ask, for the other brother was already coming up behind her. "Of course," he said to her in a light rasp, those large hands of his finding her slender shoulders and rubbing them tentatively.

"Here," he said, reaching around her from behind to undo her top and pull the white leather from her chest. Her hips were so ample and rounded, yet her breasts were so perky and small. The tight, pink nipples pressed against him as he felt her bare flesh.

His strong hands rubbed over it raw then, and he grunted in approval at his own handiwork, or the feel of her smooth skin.

Ramtok, despite his great size and muscular bulk, undid her belt deftly, and curled his fingers into the tight leggings, tugging them down and off so he could touch and rub at her lower body as well. Though his dark gaze was obviously glued to her exposed chest, and his breathing had risen.

Aleena hadn't felt so relaxed in a long time as she pushed the tight leathers off her arms and ankles, her body so lovely. It wasn't the form of a Kron woman, certainly, but she held her own unique appeal. She leaned against them both, desperate for the feel of their warm bodies and strong hands.

Her green eyes fluttered closed as the two brothers worked over her, and a sigh passed her lips. "Ramtok, my thighs feel tight."

The large warrior put his hands to her thighs, and despite his immense strength he managed to massage her firmly but with care. His powerful thumbs kneading her inner flesh and parting her thighs with their pressure. "You have had to go a long time roughing it, for a matron," he said in his deep, dark voice.

His brother Saghar agreed with a grunt, his finer touch working such sensational feelings through her slender shoulders and neck. "It is hard to provide real comfort on a journey such as this."

She could smell the scent of their masculine arousal on the air. The two men such a powerful force to be around. To be between.

It was the exact thing she needed, and her head rested against Saghar's chest as her legs parted for Ramtok, that thin slip of fabric all that separated him from her sex. The soft material delved between her slit, outlining it so sensually as her thick thighs were massaged by his powerful hands.

She moaned and her eyes fluttered closed. "Just like that," she murmured.

As the brothers' two pairs of hands worked at her fair skin with their dark digits, she could detect the increase in their breathing with her sensitive ears. They were diligent mates, much more so than what she was normally accustomed to. They tended to her needs and wants first and foremost, and she never felt Saghar's hands stray to her breasts again while her knotted muscles needed the soothing rubs.

Ramtok was a little more daring, however, and she felt his thumbs graze her clothed slit as he kneaded her inner thigh flesh. The larger brother looked over her elven form with such lust, despite the inherent perversion of their interbreeding.

"You are not like the tales, matron," came his

gravelly voice as the Kron knelt before her in his leather vest, muscles bulging out from beneath.

"Ah, the tales," she practically moaned, her body writhing subtly beneath their attentive fingers. She was teasing them, surely, but with how heated her sex was, it was torture for her. Exquisite torture. "What did you figure I would be like? A witch, like that uncouth Captain?"

Saghar chuckled at that, though his hands never ceased their attentive rubbing, the firm but soothing touch working her body as she was propped up against his hard chest. His fingers reached far, and skirted her breasts as he moved.

Below, the larger brother worked in closer to her sex, leaving her thighs less tended as his thumbs began to work at her slit more and more. "No, matron," he said with a husk and a lick of his lips. He had skill with his digits, and the way he strummed her quim was so delightful. "They just said your kind were all..." He hesitated a moment. "Unappealing. Stick thin. And weak." Though the little swirling rub about her clit said he didn't think that of her.

Her pulse quickened and she felt so warm, yet it didn't matter. Her body cried out for them as the two sets of hands caressed her and she grabbed for Saghar. She drew his grasp down from her shoulders until he palmed her small breast, pressing him into it almost violently.

"Well, you two lucked out," she managed, but her throat was dry.

The witch doctor bent to her neck, nudged her pale hair out of the way, and put his mouth to it. He had to be careful of those large, Kron fangs of his, but he suckled at her pale stem, kissed and licked her neck as those large palms squeezed and manhandled her breast flesh. He went to his new task with a dedicated fervor to please and enjoy.

Below, Ramtok leaned in and she could feel his breath on her inner thighs. "We crave adventure," he said in a low growl, and she felt his tongue lap over the thin strip of fabric that covered her slit. "We crave excitement," he went on with another lap of his broad tongue, feeling it move across her folds, tugging her panties up into her tighter. "We crave the exotic." And to them, she certainly was that. Ramtok gripped her thighs and pressed his mouth to her cunt, tonguing it over her panties in a show of his desire.

Her legs were so lewdly spread, the alabaster thighs parted around Ramtok's large skull. She felt his fangs graze along her outer sex, and that dangerous sensation made her clit throb harder. She was already so wet from their exquisite touching and she felt that she was the lucky one.

For the first time in decades she felt like she'd finally caught a break as the brothers pleased her so eagerly, their bodies moving against hers so readily. Her hands grasped Saghar's and forced them to squeeze, to tug at her so wantonly, and she gasped with need.

On the journey she'd never had an opportunity to enjoy them simultaneously. It was never safe to do so, one always had to be watching. But now with the two brothers gripping and pleasing her in tandem, she got an idea of what she'd been missing out on.

Saghar obeyed her urging hands, and he squeezed and groped her pert breasts with intense enthusiasm. She felt her stiff nipples dig into his palms as he worked his tongue up across her neck until he was nibbling her ear.

Betwixt her legs the larger brother bit her panties and tugged them from out of the cleft of her pussy, baring her slit entirely before he returned his hungry tongue to taste her honey directly. The mighty groan of lust he gave was a delightful tremor through her loins as he lapped eagerly.

The white down tickled his nose, and her pelvis lifted slightly, urging his tongue deep into her sex.

She arched her back against Saghar as he tweaked her nipple hard and shuddered as the intense sensation traveled through her. "Yes," she hissed, her green eyes shielded as she ground herself into Ramtok's face.

As that large tongue worked over her slit and sensitive clit, Saghar teased and tweaked her nipples. He tugged those stiff peaks and brought such a tingling fire of sensation to them as the brothers worked in concert to bring her satisfaction.

They were so well behaved as lovers, so well intentioned. Ramtok delved into her cunt but never ceased to give her needful clit the satisfaction it craved, his hands rubbing her thighs and keeping them pinned back as he lavished her quim. He groaned against her almost as if he was getting as much pleasure from the act of cunnilingus as she was, his large, muscular body bent to her needs.

She'd learned something so strange about them, that uncanny ability for them to cum only after her, and had delighted in it every single time. Yet she knew, in the safety of their lodgings, that she finally needed her fill of them. To enjoy them for hours, without fear of being caught.

Or, at least, without as much fear.

She moaned as Ramtok pushed her thighs back so far, folding her back as she felt that intense pleasure begin to flood her. "Yes," she hissed as Saghar pinched her light-pink nipples, feeling her cunny pulse harder against his brother's diligent tongue.

"Right there," she moaned to the both of them and her head knocked back against Saghar's hard chest. "Cumming," she gasped as her eyes flew open and her body struggled to contort. The two brothers held her in place, but she bucked and writhed as warm juice flooded Ramtok's mouth.

They held her throughout it. Saghar's grip upon her breasts, those arms around her chest. Ramtok's tight hold on her thighs as he tongue-fucked her to orgasm. He never ceased throughout, just continued to lash at her sensitive twat to continually prod her to new heights of pleasure as her climax went on.

Together they dragged out the sensations, made it the longest and most satisfying orgasm of her life. Their hands and mouths working separately but cooperatively upon her. As she neared the end of her tolerance for it, Saghar moved his mouth to hers and kissed her deep and hard there, probing her with his tongue.

Her moan reverberated through them as her hand mashed his larger head to hers. His mouth was so big, his lips so full as she traced her tongue around his. She could barely stand it, the exquisite talent of the two brothers making her body buck and spasm, and as another orgasm crashed through her, she broke off the kiss. "Stop!" She gulped for air, her entire body on fire with sensations.

Despite her order they did not cease abruptly. They were too attentive and skilled for that, and they eased off in a soothing manner, gradually winding down so that they were rubbing and kissing her in less sensitive, but still sensual manners.

Ramtok moved down her thigh, kissing and nipping her pale flesh there with a fascination and interest for her elven body while Saghar nuzzled her neck and kissed along her jawline. "Was it too much, matron?" rasped the striking witch doctor behind her, his hands gently massaging the less sensitive underswell of her breasts.

She moaned and hated having given the order, but her body still trembled with the doting caresses. She was nearly stupid after having lost count of her orgasms, but she shook her head. "To the bed," she managed through her dry throat.

There was no hesitation. Saghar put his arms in underneath her and lifted her body with ease. As the slender brother carried her to the hide-covered bed, Ramtok stripped out of his leather vest and pants, so that when Saghar laid her out upon the large but tough bed, she looked up and saw that hulking warrior completely bare. His bulky form, jutting with muscles, and peppered with dark hairs across his chest then pointing down in a trail towards his impressive loins.

The two brothers looked so stunning side by side. As tall as giants, both so exquisitely muscular, but in different manners. Ramtok's exposed cock twitched to life, throbbing with its thick, ridged veins in the air.

She'd been vaguely worried about jealousy, about how it might affect their ability to work together, but she understood their relationship a bit better after spending so much time with them. She knew she was safe, for she appreciated both of them. Two parts of a greater whole, and she beckoned them both to join her.

The two brothers worked together well without much outward indication of it. As if, she presumed, to compensate for the time Saghar had spent with her already, Ramtok went to her first as the other brother disrobed.

The heavy warrior climbed atop the mattress where they carried her and loomed over her, leaned down and kissed her on the lips as he palmed one of her pert breasts. He gave a husky groan as he tasted those lips his brother had so recently supped upon, and when he finally smacked their lips together as he broke away, she saw Saghar climb to her side, nude and with a raging stiff cock that rivalled his brother's.

It was exquisite, both of them, yet she tried to hide her awe and appreciation. It still registered on her pale, elven face, however. She leaned back, her white hair framing her face as she looked between the two Kron brothers.

Elves found them repulsive and vile. Hideous.

She knew how wrong it was, how easily her people would cast her aside if they knew what she'd done with them, what she wanted to do with them, but she didn't care. The other elves would soon learn her prowess, and her eyes narrowed in determination as she reached for Saghar's cock.

The thick, ridged organ fit into her hand, but just barely. The brothers were well endowed, even for their sizes, and that heated girth swelled so large against her fingers and palm, a lewd groan escaping those thick lips of his. She could see a clear bead of precum form on the dark tip, and knew these Kron brothers were not so different from the men she knew after all.

Above her, Ramtok kissed along her cheek, down to her neck, and massaged her teat as his own cock dangled down, brushed against her thigh, and grazed her slit. He was hungry for her, she realized. He'd not had the personal time with her his smaller brother had, and perhaps it wasn't jealousy that motivated him after all, just desire and need that had built up over the trip.

Or perhaps some of each.

She could feel her slickness all down her thighs, his saliva and her cum making her so sticky as her free hand went down her firm stomach. She hooked her finger into the panties and pulled them aside once more, making the reddened sex puff out towards his needy member.

Aleena tugged the foreskin back from Saghar's dark crown and her eyes partially lidded in excitement to be pinned between the two beasts.

They were huge, and powerful, and they pleased her in a way no elf had ever even cared to, and her pink tongue darted between her lips to whorl about his head.

The guttural groan of satisfaction that Saghar gave was followed by his larger brother taking the offered opportunity to nudge his broad crown to her puffy slit. With her legs pushed back far, he began to force that gargantuan shaft into her. It was no less daunting than his brother's, which she'd had an opportunity to enjoy, yet they were both so large it felt like being a virgin all over again.

Ramtok managed to cram that thick, ridged tip into her though, forcing her canal wide as he began to sink down into her, and his brother watched as she tended to them both at once. He reached out and stroked her white hair as she suckled him, the two brothers grunting in unison.

"*Lha*," she cursed to her Goddess, her body going lax as she almost lost a grip on Saghar's rigid shaft. His cock fell against her thick lower lip, but she wouldn't let herself stop so easily. Her tongue pushed out again, licking off that smear of precum as her red pussy contracted tightly around Ramtok. He was so huge and her body was protesting, but she was too wet for it to make a difference.

The mighty warrior grasped her by her breast and hip, and whenhe'd gotten a few inches of his girth into her, he began to tug back a bit then force himself in just a bit further. He repeated this motion again and again, pushing more and more of himself into her with each new thrust of his dick. All the while he grunted his pleasure and never ceased to squeeze and tend to her flesh.

Saghar, meanwhile, kept his place, and only his pecs and abs moved, twitching as her mouth moved along his rigid cock. The sensations prompted such uncontrollable reactions in him as he watched her lips move against him, and his brother rut her with increasing intensity.

They were subtle, but she watched through lidded eyes while moaning lewdly. She felt so full, her entire body still buzzing with energy, and her legs pressed back further towards her chest.

Her tongue whorled around Saghar before she dove down, her mouth spreading open nearly so wide as her cunny, feeling both of the Kron throb in her body.

Ramtok was so much larger and physically stronger than his brother, and he couldn't help but begin to ram that thick dick of his into her a little harder than the more slender Saghar ever had. Those thick, ridge like veins on his cock providing such stimulation to her stuffed quim as he plowed into her again and again with an increasing speed and force.

All the while, she supped at the other brother's cock with her mouth, those dark eyes of his, so strange and different — so keenly aware, as if they held more cunning secrets than his brother ever could — locked on her. She could almost read it in his gaze then. How strange it was for him to have a matron suckle at his dick like that. And how much he liked it. If she doubted her eyes, the little spurt of creamy seed affirmed it for her as her body was jostled by Ramtok's thrusts.

Her body flushed with the awareness, with that strange pleasure that their cocks contained, but she never stopped. Even as she was fucked so hard, her body screaming with such delight, she didn't stop licking Saghar's dick, massaging it with such interest. Every time her tongue swept over those bulging veins she had to quiet a moan, the hum traveling through his flesh.

Her hand grasped his thigh, held him to her tighter as her cunny massaged Ramtok's pounding flesh, her slickened sex beginning to drip down onto the bed.

The loud slap of those heavy balls striking her pale, honey-wet ass filled the longhouse. Ramtok's grunts and groans as he did his best to angle that thick girth into her pleasurably, it all added to the sound to produce a musical number unlike any she'd heard.

All the while Saghar's eyes held to hers, and they glimmered with something unseen. As if dark secrets were hidden there as she worked his cock with her mouth and hand. That thick cock twitched in her hand, and his brother's throbbed wider in her cunt, one then the other in quick succession as the glistening muscles of Ramtok heaved over her.

She surrendered herself to them, to the ecstasy they promised, and she sucked Saghar harder, more purposefully as she felt herself topple over the peak.

Already her body was exhausted from the intensity, but it didn't matter. Aleena still wanted more, to experience more, and her hand pumped his cock as her tongue begged for his release, for the three of them to share in something so special.

Yet all the while Ramtok hammered into her, and as her tight quim responded with a flood of honey at his satisfying thrusts, he toppled over that precipice. He bucked erratically and had thrown back his head to let loose a roar of pure ecstasy as he unleashed his creamy load into her. *"Mokrata!"* he yelled in his native tongue, as he pumped that seemingly endless load into her.

Kron men weren't accustomed or built for oral pleasures. Saghar didn't know the satisfaction of sweet, attentive lips working his cock. But they did such a number upon him that his eyes couldn't help but roll back into his head, forcing him to tear his gaze away from her. He grunted lewdly and she tasted that obscene flood of creamy seed stream into her mouth.

Just as it had been when Saghar had fucked her, the heavy load of virile cum dwarfed that of any man or elf she'd known. It flowed so copiously, she couldn't keep up with it, and it spilled from her mouth to drool down from the corners of her lips as his sac continued to empty itself.

She felt their combined cum flow all around her, dripping onto the bed, but it was so sweet. She coughed and sputtered as she pulled back from

Saghar's dick to swallow his load, closing her eyes as the torrent sprayed across her nose and cheeks. She gasped as she drank the seed down, her mouth opening and catching another stream on her out-hanging tongue.

Her cunny squeezed the other man so tightly as she whimpered, the pale elf covered in Kron seed.

It was so blissfully perfect, but when Ramtok lowered his head and looked to her with his fanged face all gaped, he looked shocked. His eyes darted between the two of them, and Aleena saw the sort of guilty look on Saghar's face as he diverted his gaze.

"Matron," came the warrior brother's startled voice. "You spurned his essence?" he questioned with confusion, and he tried to tug back, but those thick, rigid veins locked her in him some and he only succeeded in tugging her down the bed a couple inches.

"It is her choice," retorted the more slender brother as she still held his cock. There was clearly some cultural significance of the situation beyond her ability to predict.

She wiped the back of her hand across her mouth, though it did little to clean up the white mess on her face. Tilting her head she looked between the two, her brows furrowed in confusion. "Just this time," she said cautiously. "Variety helps bring spice to life, after all."

The larger brother looked confused by her explanation, but Saghar spoke up. "It is okay, brother. Elven ways are different," he said and gave a shrug of his shoulders. "You can go take a patrol around, while I start the food."

Even while she was a mess, the larger brother held her in place then plucked himself free to go get ready and do exactly that.

Saghar, however, kept his place and looked back to her after Ramtok left. "It is okay, matron," he said in a low voice. "It is just the nature of Kron breeding that all males contribute to the siring of a matron's brood. To spurn a male's seed from her womb is" — he struggled for the word, looking aside then back to her — "an act of extreme disregard. A way of saying a mate's cream is unworthy to help nourish the child a matron and her concubines make within her."

For all his cultural lesson, he never moved from her side, never ceased watching her. Never quite lost his erection.

She wasn't aware of how heavily she was breathing, but she felt a dollop of cum fall from her chin into her chest and suddenly realized how hot she was. How they'd set her on fire, and she took in a deep, cleansing breath.

"I did not know that," she admitted. No one had bothered to inform her much on the ways of Kron breeding, if only because of the intense taboo regarding it. "No offense," she added on sincerely, even though she knew he was excited by it more than anything, and her lips quirked into a smile. "Or should I apologize to Ramtok instead?"

The more slender brother — though still quite towering and muscular — cracked a wry smile then shook his head. "He will not understand," he said assuredly. "He is a troublemaker in many ways, but when it comes to the ways of mating?" He chuckled gruffly. "He is set in the ways of our people. Nothing you say could change his mind that you snubbed me in front of him. If you tried you might only succeed in convincing him you're an unfit matron instead."

The tall Kron watched her, trailed a finger up her breast, hoisted just a bit of his pearly white cream on a finger then lofted it to her mouth. "I understand elven ways are different, though."

"Quite a bit," she murmured before accepting his offering into her mouth, her tongue whorling about it seductively as she stared at him. It was a shame she wouldn't be able to taste the other Kron's cock, and she felt her body throb with the thought. Her breathing was still rapid, but as she suckled his cum from the rough digit, it held in her chest.

He watched her with such delight as she consumed his seed and lay there coated in it. Though at last, and reluctantly, he withdrew. "He will be insufferable for a while, thinking he is your chosen favourite." He bent forward though, bringing his face near to hers. "However, I know better," he said in a conspiratorial tone, just before he leaned in and kissed her cum-stained lips, tasting the salty tang of his own seed.

She pressed into him so passionately, even as her mind whirled and her body succumbed to exhaustion. Her grip on his thigh lightened until finally she lay back on the bed. The day had been exhausting and stressful, but the evening had been so delightful.

Until she managed to step on Ramtok's toes, at least.

As Saghar pulled back, he gave her a broad grin. "Relax, matron," he urged. "I shall prepare the meal for you. Rest and be at ease," he said in a soothing tone, moving off to the fire to tend to her other needs.

14

THE FRONT

he military camp was never quiet. The rattle of machine guns off at the front and the boom of mortars never quite ceased entirely. The Kron Confederacy, or whatever hellish name those fiends called themselves, would get daring if the Union forces ever ceased their firing. They sensed weakness like a starving animal, and conserving the precious explosives and ammo was one sign they were always on the watch for.

Some doubtlessly self-described cunning Generals and Marshals thought to use that to their advantage with somewhat regularity, though it never worked. The hordes on the other side of the trenches never seemed to dwindle, and always came back with more and more bodies to throw on the pyre.

The increased fire of the past day, however, made Sergeant Levek worry. He knew what it meant. The brass was planning an offensive. Doubtless because some fool young officer was now in a new position of authority and thought to make a name for himself by finding that breakthrough they all sought after, but could never find.

Despite what it would mean for his future, however, he knew it made for a prime opportunity to slip away, and beneath the dark skies he caught Caslian walking by the medical tents.

"Psst." He ushered her, grabbing her attention from that usual spot in the dim alleyway. It'd been a few nights since he'd saved her from those ravenous soldiers, and he did all he could to check up on her since.

It broke his heart to see her smile shyly as she glanced around, her motions so much more cautious than before. There wasn't the same exuberant greeting, the wide smile and the loud hello. Instead it was quiet, subdued, but still she never lost that appreciation and happiness as she looked at him.

The small woman moved towards him so quietly, her delicate limbs hidden in the plain, brown uniform. "Hi, Sergeant."

Adherence to the formalities of rank was abysmal at the best of times usually, but between them it was a growing familiarity that was the cause, not a dereliction of duty.

He was a tall man and his thick trench coat added some bulk to the swarthy man's frame. "C'mon." He motioned behind him, trusting she'd follow.

He led her on through the maze of tents and off towards the spot he'd found. Nestled amongst the clutter of supplies, the lumber, packed high, formed a hidden little square nook that he had to squeeze through a narrow opening to get to. It served as a solitary getaway in the ever-busy camp, and even muted the sounds of the gunfire. Only the stars and moon to light them up there.

As she slipped through, her pixie-like form fitting so easily through the narrow entrance, he smiled. "How've you been, Cas?"

She shrugged, and he knew it must have been a rough day, but that smile on her beautiful tan face never faltered. Her flaxen hair was still tied back in a bun, showing off the smooth lines of her jaw and her wide, hazel eyes. "How about you?" she asked, her sweet voice so quiet.

He almost shrugged his shoulders in return, but he knew he had to be more upbeat for her. That day he'd rescued her, something beautiful and special had died from the world despite his best efforts, and he wanted to make sure no more went with it.

"I've been thinkin' a lot, Cas," he said casually, reaching into his pocket and pulling out a tinfoil-wrapped bar. "Want some?" he offered with a wry smile. Opening it up, he showed it was chocolate inside. Rare, gritty, low-quality chocolate, that was as prized as gold at the front.

She nodded eagerly and reached out her hand, her palm facing up. She was still so fresh to the front lines, but she'd already learned that niceties were in her past. All that lay ahead was bleak, grim work and death.

And fear.

"Thanks, Levek," she said softly, moving closer to him. She hated to have any space between them, her arm brushing his. "Where'd you get it?"

Breaking off a small chunk, he then handed over the bulk of it in its tinfoil to her generously. With a bright smile he bit into his piece and shrugged his shoulders. "You don't live along the front as long as I have without learning how to get the rare things." He leaned back against the wooden stack and tilted towards her. He was a strikingly handsome man, and had managed to avoid the patchwork of scars most frontline soldiers got after any time in the fight. His smooth caramel skin and sleek dark hair complemented his southern look remarkably well.

She moved with him, crowding his circle as she

began to devour the chocolate, somehow managing to look like she was savouring every quick bite. "What were you thinkin' about?" she asked, her head tilting up towards him.

Despite it all, she remained so wonderful. The only spot of purity and goodness in the foul pits of the front. Levek wanted so bad to hold her, stroke her hair, and tell her everything would be alright. He didn't dare touch her unless necessary though. He didn't want to sully her with his own imperfections. His own baser instincts.

"Leavin' the war," he said as he chewed the last of his tiny chunk of chocolate. "I've been out here for nearly two decades," he said with barely a betrayal of how much that realization saddened him. His mind was on something more important anyhow: her leaving the war.

Her mouth dropped open and her head tilted, as if what he'd said shocked her. Perhaps it was his age, or maybe it was just the idea of him leaving the war, and she trembled slightly at his side. It took her a long time before she swallowed back another piece of chocolate, and somehow she'd eaten the entire bar in just moments.

"You... you wanna leave?"

Put like that, he didn't know how to answer it. He had resigned himself to a lifetime of fighting at the front. He'd do it until he died. Technically, once he reached the twenty-year mark he could apply for a discharge, but they always managed to come up with excuses to keep people on after that. Only those with connections got out. Ever.

Mulling it over, he chewed his chocolate thoroughly until done, then at last swallowed it down. "I'm nearly at that point anyhow," he said. "Discharge and all." He shrugged his shoulders. "I would've kept on forever though, before. Felt I could do the best here for my men. But then..." He looked to her, then away in an oddly shy manner.

But then her.

Her eyes were glassy and she blinked it away, instead managing a small, struggled smile. She wanted to be happy for him, even in the midst of her presumed abandonment. "That's... that's great, Levek. Then you can go feed a goat for me." She swallowed the lump in her throat, the precious young woman so forlorn and yet trying her best to support him.

He looked to her in time to detect her feelings, even in the dark of night. "There's only one thing," he said, pulling out a kerchief and wiping his fingers of any trace of the lingering chocolate. He managed to make himself appear calm and cool in the face of his raging emotions. The urge to fall to his knees and beg her to come with him.

Her eyes blinked again, avoiding him for the first time since she'd met him. "You've done your duty," she said, shaking her head, "anyone can see that."

With a chuckle, he shook his head. "That's not it," he said with a wry smile. "I just don't have any notion... any drive," he corrected himself, "to go it alone." He looked up at the starry sky, the sounds of machine guns and mortar shells exploding so distant to him as to seem from another world. "There ain't a world out there for me by myself, Cas. My folk are all dead or gone. And everyone in the world I know or care for is here." He looked down to her pointedly, his hazel eyes glistening in the dark of night.

Her hand brushed away a tear as she shook her head. "Levek, I can't leave. I just got here." Her slender body trembled and she paced from foot to foot.

"There's ways," he said to her, though, seeing her so upset, he bent down to her level. "Look, I ain't gonna leave here without you." His voice was reassuring, a smile forced to his face, because he hated to see her cry, no matter the cause, but especially when it was because of him. "I like you. I wanna look out for you, but..." He trailed off and looked aside, trying to think of how best to say it. "The thing is, Cas... this place is just hell. It's hell," he sighed. "You ain't meant for a life like this. Nobody was. But especially not you."

"But I have to be here..." She took a deep breath in. "Levek, I know I'm not gonna make it to two decades. I don't even know if I'll make it one, but I gotta try. My family's counting on me." It was one of the first times he'd ever heard her sound so dreary. So honest.

"If we run away, they'll find me, and then it'll be so much worse."

There she was, worried about others, and it broke his heart. He wanted so badly to rescue her, but her mind was on those she felt she could save.

"It don't have to be that way," he said, reaching out to brush a stray tear from her pristine cheek. "Anythin' could've happened to you out here, and I'm old enough ta be let off, so nobody'll question when we set up a ranch or somethin' somewhere and you're with me. They'll assume you're my wife and leave us be." He shook his head. "Ain't many women that serve anyhow. It'll fool 'em."

Her lower lip trembled. "If I'm with you and you're caught... if one of the other soldiers sees us... Levek, you should be free, but if you take me, you won't be."

"Don't say that. Once we're beyond the front and

the camps" — he shook his head — "they won't question it. I'll have somethin' to prove my discharge, and I look the right age anyhow." He forced a smile. "You don't have to decide nothin' now, Cas. Ya don't. I know ya only got here, and... and ya ain't seen the worst the front has to offer. Not by a long shot." He took a deep breath, trying to steady his voice. "But I'd like to get out of here with somethin' of value to hold on to. And I can't do that on my own."

He made it sound like it was about himself, but his prime worry was for her and her alone.

Her chin dropped to her chest. "When are you planning on leaving, Levek?"

"I told ya, I ain't gonna leave without you," he said and squeezed her shoulder. "But if we wanna get out of here with some part of us intact, we should go soon." He couldn't help it, he had to pull her in for a hug. He wrapped his arms about her and squeezed her dainty form, so ill fit for life at the front, and savoured the moment. "Take a few days, think on it. But for your own sake, Cas, don't wait too long, huh?"

She hugged him back with such warmth and compassion, it was hard to handle, and she nodded eagerly. Her head tilted up and she whispered in his ear, the backdrop of gunfire nearly drowning her out despite the protection the hideaway provided them. "I don't know if I can stay by myself."

Levek held her long after that, unable to say more. He struggled for the words, but they weren't coming to him.

It was the sound of the emergency siren wailing in the dark of night that broke their moment.

"Dammit," he swore out loud. "It's the call to battle stations." His men would be waiting for him.

"Be careful," she said as she stepped back, trying to hide the fact that she was still wiping away the salty tears from her cheeks. "Let's go save some lives."

He couldn't help but laugh at that. "Be safe, Cas. I'll return soon as I can."

Which might be never, a voice reminded him in the back of his mind.

15

THE SOLDIERS

When at last the two bandits were passed out from the agony, the Major gestured to the two Landsreck. "Take them to the cart. Aside from a few broken pinkies they have no serious injuries. Nothing to keep them from serving on the fronts anyhow," he said with a slight curve of his lips. The cruel torture of the two brutes had brought out something in him, Liena'sa realized.

The two soldiers dragged their unconscious bodies through the dirt on their way back to the cart. Despite their pale faces, they knew better than to utter a word against their superior's methods.

"They'd tell you anything to get you to stop, sir," she said lowly as the others left their earshot. "I think

I was getting ready to tell you where the hideouts are just to get you to stop."

It wasn't the first time she'd seen him perform such a thing, nor even the first time she'd seen that expression. The toothy grin that was so out of place on his stern, angular face. "Of course, Lieutenant," he said smoothly, not even sounding like himself. He slipped the torture device back into his pocket and stepped towards her. "We got the information we really need anyhow." He reached up, rubbing his fingers across her face until he was palming her cheek.

It bothered her a little, to know the pain those fingers inflicted, yet she leaned into it like a small kitten. Her wide eyes fluttered shut as she let her lips drop open. There wasn't the option for debate or disagreement. He watched out for her, and that was all that mattered to the half-elven woman.

"You liked that, didn't you?" she asked in a soft voice.

"No," he said harshly, yet again his voice filled with such uncharacteristic emotion, "I loved it." He grinned, pushing their bodies together as he grabbed her about the waist with his other arm, pulled her head to the side, and dove in, biting and sucking her neck in the woods. Such lust for her. She always knew it was there, but he usually contained it so well until the height of his passions, when he was hilted inside her.

It was a change of pace, something welcomed even as it mingled with her disgust at what he'd done. There was no pity or compassion left in the world, no place for it, and she understood it as well as any. Yet to know he had such sick fancies still struck a strange chord with her, even as she enjoyed his passionate vigor.

"I like it when you're like this," she gasped, and she meant it. Though she hated what it took for him to get to that point, she still loved his lust for her. For sex. For whatever it was he needed that she knew she'd never understand.

That mouth of his was so hungry, it nipped and suckled her flesh so roughly. It was such a strange dynamic they had. Since the fall of the elven aristocracy and the Union with the humans, elves — and especially half-breeds — had become second-class citizens of the Union. Yet he'd never held that against her.

As he pushed her back up against a tree and moved his mouth moistly up her slender neck to her ears, he bit and tugged it there. "I want you, Lien," he muttered in her ear in a gruff, lust-laden voice. She could feel his arousal press through his uniform and against her stomach as one hand came around and undid the buttons of her black tunic.

Her hand moved down his body, feeling him out as she wedged her fingers between them. She was usually so placid, so docile, yet his crassness had given her permission to do what she usually didn't. Her fingers rubbed him through his pants, felt out that firm cock, the outline of it so prominent.

Her pale flesh was reddening beneath her officer's cap and she couldn't open her eyes. She couldn't look at him, just felt him out. Holding him. Rubbing him.

It was enough.

As her earlobe snapped from his mouth he hissed into her ear, "Do you like seeing me work, Lieutenant?" Though the words were not in their usual formal tone. He used her rank almost as a tease instead, and as his cock swelled to her touch, she wasn't sure she'd ever felt it so large.

Her jacket came open, and he reached inside, yanked her shirt out of her pants, and went in to move across her pale flesh towards her petite breasts. He was hungry for her, and his steel-blue-grey eyes were wide and alight as he looked at the elven beauty before him.

A soft sound, like a whimper, came past her lips and she rubbed him a bit harder as she shook her head. "I hated it, Major. Every second of it." Yet she didn't hate his hands groping those pale mounds, tweaking her already hard nipples. Her back arched, and her hat knocked back against the tree, toppling to the ground.

He growled at her, though she couldn't tell if it was driven by lust or disapproval at her response. Though the way he gripped her breast tighter and moved his other hand down over her body, feeling her out as he went, suggested it did nothing to diminish his desires. "And yet you like what it did to me, hm?" he asked between licks and bites of her neck, his hand forcing its way down inside her pants and over her quim, a finger touching upon her slit.

"Yes!" she practically shouted, her behaviour so uncharacteristic of the tightly wound woman. She was already so wet for him that she was almost embarrassed, squirming under his touch. It didn't matter if she liked it or not, for it did something twisted to her body. Even if it was just liking how much her lover got off on it.

The husky groan he gave was of pure approval, his digit dipping into her, feeling her slick warmth. "My sweet, sweet Lien," he murred in her ear, and she felt the intricate care he made, tending to her slit with his finger like he'd never done before. The sweet tingle of sensations as he prodded her clit, squeezed her breast, and suckled her ear. "You still watched. Like such a good girl."

"I'll never abandon you," she promised. Even beneath her lusty edge, she meant it. It wasn't a simple throwaway promise between two lovers. It was a sincere pledge, and she went up on her toes as he glided his finger over her clit. That tiny nub was so tight and excited, and every rub of his hard finger made her sex throb.

Her head tilted back and her hair tangled in the bark of the tree, showing off the strong, angled line of her jaw. Her pale breasts tilted upwards, her entire body yearning for him.

He increased the intensity of his motions, biting at her exposed neck, but withdrew his hand from her breast. With his grasp free, he loosened her belt, then his, exposing his stiff cock to the spring air.

That grasp of his was so hard and cruel, but it was just his nature, not his intention. He took hold of her slender neck and twisted her around to face the tree. "I need to be in you. Now," he stated, and for the first time since he'd shown this darker side of himself, that tone of command had edged itself back into his voice.

Her forearms scraped against the tree, but it didn't matter. Her ass lofted in the air, her legs spread as wide as her fallen trousers would allow.

Her body was such a pale treat, that blonde fuzz topping her slit and helping to taint the air with the scent of her honey.

Her body was his to control and command, and she never forgot it. Yet when he'd snapped, when he'd acted like a real person without that stern demeanor and that careful exterior, she could fool herself. She could make herself believe that their relationship was based on something more than a trade.

With one of his long arms wrapped about her, his fingers still prodding that sensitive nub of her clit, the other went from her neck to her hair. He took hold of her by those blonde strands, using the bun she'd crafted it into as reins to hold her by as he slid his thick girth into her, hilting himself in one hard motion.

The satisfied moan he gave was more than she usually ever got out of him, and he bent over her backside as he began to pump into her pussy. His deep voice rich, he said, "When I catch that noble bitch, I am going to make you watch me repeat that scene on her, Lien." There was no mistaking the arousal in his words. "And then..." His words were broken off by another groan of pleasure as the slap of his groin striking her ass filled the air.

Her ass was so toned, her lean body always so fit from their work. There was no room for lazy people, and it had paid off for her in those smooth, strong legs and that lithe figure. She did her best to hide it beneath the officer's uniform, but it only made it sweeter to have her pinned to a tree.

"Yes," she hissed, for there was no fighting it. There was only enjoying the moment of raw passion with her superior officer.

Somehow Hendrik managed to keep rubbing her clit throughout his wild bucking, their two bodies slapping together so lewdly in the cool spring air. Their black uniforms covered most of them but for the crudely ground-together loins. "When I'm promoted for capturing that cunt," he said so crassly into her ear, "I'm going to fuck you in the Chancellor's office itself to celebrate." With that bit of bravado his balls slapped up against her so noisily as he thrust hard, and she felt him begin to tense inside her.

"Ah!" she half sighed, half screamed into the forest air.

His aggression, his needy passion was a release she desperately needed. It was a break from formalities, from cold cruelty, from the grinding slog of their drab, dreary lives. It was something pure, something that felt good and honest. She shuddered against him as he pressed her clit at just the right second, at just the right place, and she trembled against the tree.

Her cunny clutched him, milking him of his seed as he tensed within her body. Nothing was held back as he hilted in her, his balls tight as he spasmed in her warm clench. "Yess," he hissed at her, and her tightness drained him of all he had to offer, the tall officer's virile seed pumping in a seemingly endless series of spurts until his twitches of ecstasy at last ceased.

That just left the two of them, breathing heavily in the bandit's former clearing. Something happened then that surprised her all the more, and he kissed her neck one final time, then bit the skin before he pulled back. The familiar cloth from his pocket coming to cup her mound for the seed that spilled from her the moment his wide girth exited, leaving her gaping.

Her head dipped as she lowered from her tiptoes, her entire body feeling so warm and strained. She didn't want it to be over.

The crash back to reality was almost too much to bear and she moved back towards him, wanting to linger against his touch for just another second longer.

It couldn't be that perfect. She knew, of course. Theirs was an arrangement, and he was a serious man. Though as he tucked his manhood away and did up his pants, she felt a final trail of his hand upon the line of her hip and rear.

Something stuck out to her then too.

When he'd said he'd fuck her in the Chancellor's office after a promotion, it revealed two things: he planned to go both far and high. But more importantly to her: he planned to take her with him.

"Let's go," came his voice, gradually returned to its former official tone. "We've got to catch up to the men and set off after our prey. There's no way she's gone north, regardless of what those two fools thought."

16

THE REBELS

Travelling the wide expanse of the woods wasn't easy. The terrain wasn't even, and there was no direct route anywhere, Rosa was finding out. Everything was just an endless mire of trees, hills, rocks, and the occasional marsh. Worst of all, it only seemed to get worse the further out from the capital that she went with the stoic rebel.

She was better equipped for travel than most any, but despite all the preparations she had made, it wasn't enough to prepare her for life on the run. Just keeping pace with the athletic rebel was proving a near insurmountable task.

Night was falling, though she had a hard time telling, for the trees managed to keep out much of the sun throughout the whole of the day. "We'll rest shortly," came the blonde rebel's voice ahead of her, and he looked back and noticed how much she was trailing with a bit of a grimace.

Damn him, he still managed to be hot even with that look, she thought. *Even with the scar that blemished his striking features.*

Her nose crinkled as she struggled to keep up, but it was little use. She wasn't used to walking so much, so quickly, over anything but cobbled streets and marble floors. Every step made her muscles scream in protest, but she pushed on like a stubborn mule. The promise of rest was enough to make her try harder, however. Night had set in completely and she longed to rest.

"There's a clearing ahead," he told her simply. "We'll set up camp there once—"

He was interrupted by a howl that carried across the night sky. A wolf. Though its long wail was interrupted abruptly. The smooth sound of its cry was cut short and became garbled. The man froze in front of her. Completely still.

A chill ran up her spine and she held her breath. Even the stillness made her muscles spasm in protest, but fear kept her from making a sound, from moving. What could kill a wolf like that? She barely knew a thing about the wilderness, but for what she'd read in preparation. A bear? Could a bear do it?

She wanted to inch closer to him, to feel his strength at her side, for she was feeling so very weak and uncertain of herself. Even as her fingers touched her own knife, she didn't trust her ability to defend herself. Not out here. Not anymore.

Deathly silence, unnatural and long, took over. It wasn't until that strange, unearthly cry pierced the air that the world seemed to start moving around Rosa again. She saw the rebel before her cringe—literally cringe in fright!—and realized she had done so herself. Whatever had made that noise had some power of terror that neither could resist.

When he looked back to her, he was too pale, like the hearty man had fallen ill and begun to waste away in just such a short time. "We've got to run," he said weakly, but when he tore off at a remarkable rate she knew he was anything but. Fear drove his muscles and he took off at a speed she could barely fathom after the days of endless journeying.

Her eyes widened, for though she was frightened, she'd had faith in him. In his skills. He'd rescued her from those bandits, and the fact that he was running scared made her feel something she didn't know was possible.

Her legs were moving, but though she'd gotten used to walking at a quicker pace along the rough, forest floor, it was so different running. Adrenaline, a natural inclination to flee, flooded her, but it couldn't give her his grace and agility.

The trees rushed by them as they went, and he grew further and further ahead of her. She could not keep up with him, for all the adrenaline and fear that drove her legs on despite exhaustion also pumped through him. He was hardened by life and driven by terror.

They went on so quickly she did not even notice the branches that smacked her in the face and scraped her smooth, pale skin. There was no such thing as the option of slowing down, for though the night had returned to its eerie quiet, there was something she could simply feel.

It was a presence. It bore down upon her back with an invisible, crushing sensation at the same time it felt to her like the existence of a void. It was wrong. It did not belong in her world, nor any she could imagine.

Her mind raced, but when she broke through the trees to a clearing... she saw nothing. There was no sign of her guide, the man she hoped would protect her.

She was gulping for air, wheezing from the exertion, and her body simply wanted to drop to the clearing, to curl into a ball and hide. She'd tried to assassinate the Queen. She'd failed at that, and she'd failed at running away. Tears stung her eyes but she grabbed her weapon tightly and pushed herself on, trying to put distance between her and... whatever it was that made that horrific sound.

It was only by chance she caught sight of him as she ran, the glimmer of the moonlight upon a bit of metal—perhaps one of his weapons—betraying him as he climbed up into a tall tree at the edge of the clearing. She had no idea how he'd even gotten that far up, for it was far too much to jump and the climb looked to be more than she could handle even on a good day.

The growing sensation of that presence began to push her towards manic terror, however, and she ran to the tree. She found herself trying to ineffectually climb, and though there were no sounds to attest to it, she simply felt her pursuers were nearing.

He was so far up he was out of sight again, but try as she might, she couldn't get to where he was. Couldn't even make the first large branch. In her desperation she tried one of the smaller ones to leverage herself up, but it broke and tore into her leathers. She was probably bleeding from it, but her mind no longer felt like her own. She just had to get up!

There was no more train of thought in her mind. She was scarring up the side of the tree with her daggers as she tried to find purchase with them as climbing instruments. The centuries-old tree was marred by her failed attempts with great gashes in its bark.

The absence of sound was like a beating drum in her skull, terror like nothing she'd dreamt of filled her, but still she scrambled to get up. Then it all seemed to come to a head. She felt as if it was all over, and she'd surrender herself to the horrors of the beyond. Fighting was useless.

From out of the tree above came a hand, and it took hold of her bicep and pulled her upwards. That little lifeline enough to make her resume her fight.

With his hold, she climbed up into the tree. To one branch, then another. Higher still. And again.

She wanted to keep going, and very nearly grabbed for some flimsy branch that couldn't have possibly held her in her manic attempt to escape the unknown horror. He stopped her though, pulled her to his hard body as they rested on the thick limb. His hand clamped over her mouth, and his voice rasped in her ear harshly, "Stop screaming!"

Screaming? She hadn't realized she was, but when she stopped she realized her throat was sore and hoarse, more than she'd ever known it to be. She must have been screaming into the night ever since she'd lost sight of him, at least, for even when she'd had ash-throat infection had she not felt such hurt there.

All that, all that mortal concern swept away, though, as it—whatever it was—arrived. In that same silence it swept beneath them like a wave. She wanted to look to it, but he grasped her head and refused to let her look down. "Don't!" he hissed quietly into her ear. "Don't ever look!"

She could barely see him, her mania and tears blurring everything, and she clutched him like grim death. She felt something so primal thrumming within her, and her heart pounded against her ribs.

They were suspended above a sea of horror it felt, and all around she saw the trees move with its passing. It was the only sound, the only sign of its existence other than the eerie presence that prickled her scalp and made her skin goose bump.

It felt to her that if she just tilted her head down she could see it, perhaps understand what chased them. What nightmare haunted their journey. But he held her tight, kept her head from tilting down. She could see from the corner of her eyes him gazing up at the moon. And trembling.

He shook, his eyes wide and manic, teeth gritted as he kept himself staring up at the silver sickle in the sky. She knew instinctively he felt the same compulsion too. And fought it. Desperately. Whatever was below them, he knew—somehow—could never be laid eyes upon.

She swallowed and her throat burned with the effort, her lips parting as she stayed so near to him. She'd felt compassion for the rebels and their cause before. That was why she'd agreed to do what she'd failed to do. She didn't think it was fair that her life had been so pampered while they struggled and died in such numbers.

Rosa had given it all up to try to give them a shot, to equal their footing a bit, but for the first time she realized that was impossible.

There was no way for the nobles to live like this, to be afraid of things they didn't even have names for. They weren't equal. They could never be equal.

The rebels had every advantage, and every right to be in control, and she clung to him with a greater appreciation than she'd ever known for another person.

17

______

THE NOBLES

*I*t took the bulk of the day for Duke Samei Ellefor to get access to the Rensford manor. The shiny-helmeted Landsreck guard kept the compound walled off all day, putting the whole of the neighbourhood on high alert. Even with the diminished fortunes of the nobility, the death of one was still a tremendous affair.

Passing through the dark, ominous halls in his crisp suit, the Duke kept his head high. The soldier guided him into one of the larger parlors, and inside, he was surprised to see who was gathered. Or at least, he tried to act surprised. The Queen's own doctor stood by the side, but before him was the Queen's arbiter, a tall man with a severe look. He wore a brown suit with gold regalia upon it, including the chains-of-office.

There were no guards, but present was one genuinely surprising person. Duke Ellefor didn't recognize the young man, but he dressed like a noble, to be certain. The sour look on his face amplified the effect.

Most importantly, however, was his daughter. A whole day of being brushed aside and questioned on the death of the late Duke Rensford must have taken a toll, but she was a keen actress too, and so he went to her immediately and in a very rigid but fatherly manner put his arms about her. "Ahh, my dear girl," he husked. "What terrible tragedy befalls you so soon."

Her eyes were rimmed with red, and as soon as his arms wrapped around her form, she sobbed again. She'd changed into a simple black dress that suited her figure, and her fingers wound into the rich fabric of his suit. "I will never love again!" she wailed in protest before she sniffled and pulled away from him, swiping the tears from her cheeks.

That was laying it on a bit thick, he thought, but he patted her back and kissed her neatly arranged hair. "There there, child," he said soothingly. "You've many years ahead of you yet."

The other occupants of the room gave them their

moment, and Duke Ellefor looked to them. "She should return to the Ellefor estate for now, until she's calmed herself."

The sour-looking young man chimed in, "She's welcome to return for good as far as I'm concerned." He wore the uniform of a young noble who had just finished his term at the front. Or more precisely commanding troops who served at the front. Noble officers rarely so much as saw the frontline trenches.

The Royal Arbiter held up his hands, silencing protest. "The Queen recognizes that there is an issue of inheritance here to be resolved."

Samei's heart skipped a beat. The Queen was moving fast apparently.

Caprice's lower lip trembled and her brows furrowed as she looked over them all rather skeptically. "I've lost my husband, the man I gave my maidenhood to, and you wish to discuss business?"

The room of men all seemed to look a bit uncomfortable at her discussing sexual matters so blatantly. All but the sour-looking young man that eyed her skeptically, that is.

"My daughter has suffered enough, has she not?" he stated, arm still about his delicate daughter. "The tragedy she awoke to was harrowing enough." His mind, however, was on the Queen's Arbiter. Hopefully she was acting on his behalf, as he'd proven himself most useful to the ruler. As far as she knew anyhow.

The Arbiter quieted things again. "The Queen recognizes that the young Lady Rensford has sacrificed quite a lot for the two houses, to put an end to a long feud." That tone, however, shattered the Duke's dreams. "But to hand over the whole of House Rensford to her would be the death of that noble line, and so cannot be done lightly."

Samei's eyes shot to the young man and saw that he was no longer looking quite so sour anymore. Smug was the word.

"Pray tell," spoke up the consoling father, "does the Queen wish to break with millennia of tradition in this matter?" He was nearly trembling with rage, but he hid it well. He had to.

"This is my home, now!" Caprice protested, and her knees weakened and trembled. She looked so uncertain, so crestfallen. "We were just getting it the way we wanted it," she said of her and her late husband, and she looked far younger than her age for a moment. She seemed... diminished. "To lose him and our home and..." She sobbed again.

The dutiful father caressed her hair and squeezed her a little tighter. "There there, my child," he consoled, "we shall sort things out for you."

The Arbiter looked uncomfortable, doubtlessly

not caring to deliver such news in front of the emotional young woman. He cleared his throat and began, "On the contrary. The Queen recognizes that tradition is important, and must be respected" — and Duke Ellefor knew the "but" was coming already — "but every effort must be maintained to retain the lineage of House Rensford."

"Hear, hear," chimed in the young man.

"Out with it already," Duke Ellefor couldn't help himself from muttering out in irritation. Just spit out the Queen's little scheme already and be done with it, he thought.

Caprice ran her fingers through her long, dark hair. Her body felt so warm, her scalp prickling with anger and agitation. They were so close, so very close. They couldn't be refused, and her eyes glistened with fresh tears.

The Arbiter paused and cleared his throat, uncomfortable with the Duke's admonishment at first before he composed himself. "The Queen acknowledges the marriage of the late Duke Rensford and his wife Caprice, and should their blessed union have given issue and produce a legitimate heir to House Rensford, then all matters shall be considered resolved," he explained with a bright smile to the Duke and daughter, thinking it quite generous.

"However?" Ellefor bit out, knowing such a thing was not possible.

Caprice's hands went to her stomach, touching along to soft black stomach of her smooth flesh. The Duke wouldn't touch her; not like that. Not with any amount of sexuality, even at his most gruesome, and she swallowed hard.

"However," repeated the Arbiter, "should that not occur then the Queen shall have to intervene to see to the survival of House Rensford as a continuing column in the support of the Union," he explained cautiously, getting a broad smile from the young man. Did he know something? For he seemed too smugly confident to be that happy over the chance Caprice was not already pregnant.

"A wise woman, our Queen," stated the young man, paying proper deference.

"So that's it then?" retorted the Duke. "The future of my daughter and all her sacrifices shall be left up to the chance that a brief marriage has given issue to a child? And should that have failed, all her sacrifices would be for naught?" He couldn't help but let the bitterness edge into his voice. This was a dark betrayal to him. The Queen had no reason to think him anything but the most loyal of servants. No reason she knew of anyhow.

Caprice was at his side and too overwhelmed.

True fear had begun pulsing through her veins, but his sly daughter stood up tall and proud despite it all. "Then I will have faith that my husband and I conceived," she said, adding on brazenly, "we certainly attempted enough times."

The Arbiter looked until that point like he'd had about enough of the Duke's anger, but the lewd declaration of Caprice made him stumble. Though both the doctor and Arbiter looked abashed by her declaration, and her father feigned it, the young man, however, snorted in derision. He didn't believe her. How could that be? thought the Duke.

Clearing his throat, the Arbiter said, "In the meantime, the Queen urges both Houses to further their attempts at reconciliation." Then the presence of the young man was finally made clear. "Viscount Beren Rensford, should the widow Rensford fail to give birth to a legitimate heir to House Rensford, the Queen shall discuss how to secure you as the new Head of a future House Rensford in negotiations with the lady Caprice and House Ellefor."

The Duke was stunned. Who the hell was this young man to have gotten this shot at ruling such a major House?

"However," stressed the Arbiter loudly. "In the meantime, it would please the Queen most greatly if both Houses set aside their issues, and made another great act of reconciliation such as the marriage of young Caprice." He gave a confident smile, as representatives of both Houses looked displeased.

"What do you mean?" blurted out the Duke and Viscount, sparing each other a brief glare.

Caprice's face betrayed her annoyance and disgust at the young man, and she threw her head back, nose in the air. Attempt at reconciliation, indeed.

The Arbiter looked between Caprice and the Viscount. "The Queen shall leave that up to the imaginations of both Houses," he said softly. "However, it would please the Queen and the whole of the Realm to see another noble marriage between two once-feuding houses as a sign of continued cooperation."

The Duke was without words.

Caprice's face burned red, and she nearly lost her cool before she finally just burst into tears and fell to the floor. "I'm mourning!" she wailed, her body crumpled into itself.

The Duke comforted her, but couldn't help but notice that the young Viscount himself looked rather bothered by the idea as well. The nerve! The offense against Caprice made him so angry he nearly launched across the room to strike him!

"Until such time as a conclusion can be reached," broke in the Arbiter, "the lady Caprice and Viscount

Rensford shall remain here on the manor grounds." Suddenly the high security presence made sense to the Duke. "For the sake of fairness to all and to protect the future of both Houses, visitation shall be restricted until such time as a conclusion could be reached."

Caprice's head yanked up, and she glared at the Viscount. "Live with him?" Her voice was pitched high with disgust and outrage.

The Arbiter stiffened his spine and straightened his jacket. "So is the Queen's judgement. Her Royal Doctor shall check up on the lady Caprice in due time," he stated and headed towards the door with a bashful doctor in tow.

18

THE MATRON

*A*leena awoke in the predawn to strange sounds. Though she'd fallen asleep with one of her Kron mates, the other on watch, she awoke alone. In the dark of the cabin she could hear their two growly voices, low and muttering coming from outside.

Still, the fair elf was rather adept at sneaking, and a dark smile curved her lips as she began moving silently towards the two Kron. She didn't understand their sexual taboos, but found them fascinating nonetheless.

The fire was still going, and hadn't been left untended for long though it was kept low. Aleena made her way across the floor in absolute silence as she neared the door, their voices coming through the hard wood.

She picked it up mid-sentence from Ramtok. "...better than being a lowly dreck."

There was the sound of movement, perhaps one of them being shoved. "Shut up," came Saghar's response. "The Matriarch knows what she is doing. You're just too dense to understand her ways. Elves are different, brother."

A loud snort emanated from the larger Kron. "Didn't feel so different when she was milkin' me of my seed," he replied with some sense of pride in his words. "Felt pretty damn good and right, in fact."

Aleena didn't want to bring any ill will towards them, to turn their relationship into something other than it was. She'd been cautious of their jealousy, of the potential to hurt the strong trio she made, and somehow taking them both at once had been the thing to do it.

Her fingers moved through her white hair, her body still as nude as it had been when she fell asleep, still feeling Ramtok's cum between her inner thighs.

There was quiet for a moment, but then she heard Saghar move closer towards the door. "You keep tellin' yourself that you're a favourite. You'll be in for a rude awakening, brother," he said to the larger

Kron entering into the room as he was coming off his watch shift.

The elf couldn't help but be amused at the similarities of their two peoples. So different in so many ways, yet petty jealousy and possessiveness still made the blood burn hot. She leaned against the wall, but no longer was she trying to hide.

"I don't want this to hurt our likelihood of success," she admonished in a soft voice.

The towering Kron looked to her sharply, and she realized it was the first time she'd caught Saghar off guard since they'd set out. He had always been uncannily aware of the goings-on around him, which had made him such an asset in the initial leg of their journey.

"Matriarch," he murmured in surprise, shutting the door behind himself as he eyed her nude, pale form in the firelit room. He wore the simple white-fur kilt and cloak about his shoulders as usual, that hid so little of his chiselled physique. With some appreciation in his gaze he added, "Nothing gets past you, does it?"

"You'll remember I asked about jealousy," she said as she took a step towards him. "I didn't want to be the cause of any." Her body was lovingly caressed by the small fire, and the reddish-orange hue licked against her flesh. It made her small breasts seem more prominent, but more so, it highlighted the small of her waist and the roundness of her thighs and hips. She was a small woman, but the voluptuousness of her rear was something not many elves could claim.

Saghar was staring, but at last he broke his gaze and pulled off his fur cloak, casting it aside. "It is complicated, Matriarch," he said to her, his broad chest, less muscled than his brothers but still so hard, so strong, all bare before her eyes, its green-grey tone mixed with orange from the flames as he strode into the room a bit deeper. "No Kron woman would do what you did to me. Except maybe in mockery. How could I predict?"

"Mockery?" Aleena asked, confused. "Fuck, takes me more work to do that well than it does to screw well." She rolled her eyes up a bit and took a step towards him. "So what do I do to make things better between you two?"

There was a look of amusement upon Saghar's face, and he licked his thick lower lip as he watched her approach. "Our ways are different, Matriarch," he intoned, reaching a hand up towards her face and lightly touching her jawline. "But I enjoyed what you did. Enjoyed it... immensely," he said with something of a throaty growl, and she couldn't place it, but there was something a bit different about his demeanor. Almost... aggressive.

It was odd coming from a race so thoroughly controlled by their Matriarchs, but it couldn't help but make her stomach flutter with excitement. "Your brother seemed to like his part in it too," she admitted. "But neither of it means either of you are favoured over the other."

That kindled something in him, and she wasn't even sure what it was. His dark eyes widened, almost lit up, and he took hold of her shoulder with his other hand, brazenly pulled her towards him. "My brother is pleased to do his part in you," he growled out in response, simple and yet mysterious.

She didn't understand it, but her mind was becoming too hazy to care. She'd been curious and conflicted when she heard them arguing, but now that it was passed she remembered what had woken her. A dream that had made her pulse with need, and now that Saghar was touching her, it was hard to remember her worries.

Aleena was their Matriarch, whether she liked it or not, but in the deep of the night she had the same needs of anyone else. She licked over her lips, letting her head tilt to the side and her hair cascade down her shoulder. "You're pleased not to do that part, then?"

That made his lips curve into a rather feral grin. "Oh, it pleases me very much," he replied simply, and she felt his hard, strong hand stroke back along her pale jaw towards her ear, through her hair to her neck. "But I have been watching you. Observing," he said, pressing his bare chest to hers so that her teats nestled against his hard muscle. "Tell me, Matriarch, elves breed differently than we Kron, do they not?" And he lifted a brow in curiosity.

"We do most things differently," she agreed as her eyelids descended, her breath pushing past her lips faster. Her heart raced against her chest and her nipples stiffened against his hard flesh. "Our bodies are different."

He hunched his great shoulders and head, bringing himself a bit closer towards her as he spoke. "It must be something special then, for no Kron Matriarch would ever spill a mate's seed like you did when she had only two to fertilize her brood." Aleena could feel the swell of manhood beneath Saghar's kilt rise against her. "You have different ways... and I think perhaps" — he licked along the seam of his lips — "you chose to do things a different way with me because of that. A special way," he reiterated.

"Who's to say I just didn't want a taste of you?" she asked, but her voice sounded so foreign. It sounded smaller than she'd ever allowed herself to sound around him, and she knew it was her lust. She wanted him — and his brother — very badly.

It was a horrific taboo she was breaking, but she wondered if that only made it better for her. It felt like she was spiting her people for their lack of acknowledgement and her hand ran along Saghar's arm. "Who's to say it had anything to do with children?"

She could feel his heavy breathing wash over her as he slid a hand down her side, the other on her neck. He felt her out, came down to her round rear, then squeezed it tight. "You were taken with desire," he husked in return to her, and that thought seemed to drive him a little mad with lust of his own, for he lifted her slender body up by her rear and forced his lips to hers in a passionate embrace of tongues and mouths.

She met him back with even more hunger as her arms wrapped around his thick, Kron neck. She felt so small and so powerful with him at the same time, and as her thick thighs parted to wrap around his hips, she was reminded why. He was far bigger than any elf she'd been with, and the difference in their flesh tones was something twisted and exquisite.

Saghar hadn't the bulk of his brother, but he was not short on strength, and he pressed her nude form up against the wall, sandwiching her in between the wood and his own hard muscle. His tongue delved into her mouth, and he felt her out, stroked her bare, pale sides and ground his dick against her through his kilt.

He continued it for some time, until finally he broke the seal of their lips and pulled his kilt down, letting that thick shaft bounce free. His eyes met hers then, and he stared at her with wanton desire. "Show me something else," he said with a dark husk. "Show me more perversions, Matriarch."

Her eyes glinted with passion, but she so badly wanted to simply fuck him. Yet at his urging, darker things boiled to the surface. "We'll do as I please," she reminded him, but her words were breathless as her naked body ground against his.

Her sweet scent filled the air, and her nails dug into his neck. "Take me to the bed."

Something about him then reminded her of a chained beast, he looked almost ready to rebel in his lusts for her perversions, but he obeyed at last. With a reluctant motion he pulled her from the wall and carried her over to the bed, laid her out there then climbed atop it on his knees, his massive girth jutting out proudly, so thick and well veined as he loomed over her, stroking her legs. All the while his powerful chest swelled with his heavy breathing spurred on by desire.

She didn't think she'd last very long in her need, and yet she regained that control of herself, of the situation. She was a beautiful woman as she lay on the comforter, and her thick legs spread wide. Her scent wafted more thickly into the air, and her hands slowly ran up her own body.

"Watch," she murmured as her own eyes shut closed, and her fingers pinched her nipples, tweaking them roughly. She let them go for only a moment before she grabbed them harder, pulling the pale pink buds up and drawing her white breasts with them. A moan escaped her, and she repeated the motion.

"Now you," she commended, relinquishing one of her nipples as she continued to tease the other to such a state of stiffness.

Saghar watched, and very simply he reached out and repeated her motion. He had no problem replicating it, though with his rough, strong hand the squeezing and playing was much harsher, much more stimulating in its own way. "I know how to stimulate my Matriarch's tits," he said, twisting and toying with that stiff bud in a skillful manner as he loomed over her fair body.

She laughed, or at least, she tried. It came out as some deep groan of pain and pleasure and amusement. "How am I supposed to know that?" she groaned as her back arched into his hand. Pleasure spiked through her, and tiny panted breaths marked the air. "There's only so many things to do with two bodies."

He brought his other hand to her, and both of his great palms kneaded her breast flesh, teased and toyed with her pert mounds as he leaned over her, nearing her face. She could see the look of lust mixed with something else there. Frustration? Desperation? Aggression?

"You did something special with me though," he said in his growling voice. "You chose me to breed first, and then you tasted my seed." He licked along his lips as he so skillfully, eagerly worked her teats. "What elvish secrets do your actions hold?" And she could practically taste it then. He wanted to believe she had some higher purpose behind her choices. Perhaps that she had chosen him between the two brothers for some special bond.

She moaned and writhed beneath him as her mind became more and more fuzzy. "Tell me what else you do to them. To the other Matriarchs," she pleaded. He was working her into such a state and already her thighs were wet with her thick juices. She was so horny for him, for his brother, for whomever would fuck her the best. There was no hidden reasoning behind that. She just needed to feel that passion, that pleasure once more.

It was definitely frustration that laced his voice then as he continued to work her breasts, and buck his hips in such a way that his thick cock ground against her mons, through her patch of pubic hair. "They enjoy us to suckle them. To lick at their folds before mating," he explained in his strained, gravelly voice. "They sometimes make us touch each other for their entertainment before making use of our bodies themselves."

The Matriarchs certainly knew how to throw a party, and Aleena's body ached for his. She was worried that Ramtok would catch them, and that she wouldn't be able to get off before she had to negotiate the deal with the bandits. She'd never been so lust filled and pent up before, and he just kept teasing her higher.

"Fuck," she cursed, "Fuck!" Aleena sat up and looked at him, her eyelids descending in her need. "When we have more time, more privacy, I will teach you everything…"

Something warred in the large brute, but lust and something more won out. A slight crook of his lips took over, though there was a smidgen of doubt on his broad, handsomely alien face. "Very well, Matriarch," he growled and then took hold of her chest, positioning their two bodies so that his brutishly wide cock pierced into her slick quim, forcing its girth on into her tight, waiting canal with a lewd grunt from him.

Aleena cried out and bit down on her lip to silence the sound of pure pleasure. He filled her so wholly, his cock rubbing along her canal every inch of the way. She twisted her body beneath his as her legs wrapped around his back.

It was too deep, and a flash of pain went through her, but it was exquisite. "Yes!" she gasped and then bit down on her lower lip once more.

Saghar pressed her down into the bed, his two hands palming her breasts as those fingers curled about her chest. He began to pump his length into her tight depths, and she felt it then. Her dutiful Kron mate was fucking her with that tinge of aggressive assertiveness, acting out in such a strangely uncharacteristic manner for one of his kind.

The loud slap of his balls as they struck the swell of her ass filled the room, and he grunted and groaned over her as he struck in with such skillful precision. Even amidst his lusty change.

The subtleties reminded her, in ways, of elven society. Just the slightest change, yet it meant the world, and yet she couldn't care at all for the moment. Instead, she focused on the sensation of his hard body touching hers. The way their skin felt, rubbing together. How his arms felt beside her biceps.

For how wrongly their bodies looked together, how taboo it was for her to do such a thing with one of his kind, the way his thick manhood pummeled her depths and plunged so deeply into her was pure bliss. He could fill her like no elf or man ever could have, and with the careful practice and training of a lifetime, he knew how to use that gorgeous gift supremely well.

His eyes were nearly shut as he bent over her form, the slap of their bodies filling the room as he kept up his fast, hungry pace. That dark savage of hers so eager to feel her, swelling with each eager throb of his manhood.

Their bodies were different, and they responded differently. She knew as her own body spiked with pleasure that he wouldn't last longer. Couldn't, maybe. It made her orgasm even more intense as she bit down on her lip and arched her back, forcing him to rub against her body in just the right way to make her toes curl.

It was like sweet, blissful clockwork. The moment her slick honey flooded that tight canal and coated his loins, he arched his back and buried himself into her as deeply as he could fit, striking her depths a bit jarringly as he unleashed that obscenely thick stream of virile seed. Her two Kron men were so fit and masculine, and they unleashed torrents of cum unlike anything a human or elven man could.

That sweet simultaneous release had him bucking and grunting atop her, spilling that seed into her where his brother had unleashed his not long before. Though Saghar's fingers dug into her a little too hard as he quaked with his earth-shaking release.

Her breath caught and her body felt alight with sensations as she writhed beneath her strong mate. She'd messed things up so much, promised more than she could deliver, but the sweet bliss he gave her made her forget about it for those intense moments.

As the hulking Kron finished his long climax, he looked down at her through narrowed slits as he breathed heavily. When he pulled himself free of her unbidden, letting that torrent of cum slide out of her, she was painfully aware that the dynamics of her new relationship were more complicated than she'd previously realized.

19

THE REBELS

The night seemed never ending. The tide of wicked creatures below passed Rosa and Marin by. Mostly.

Yet some remained. She knew this because she could hear the incessant clawing on the tree below. She could feel it resonate through the trunk and up into the limb of the tree beneath her.

Throughout it, however, he held her. The compulsion to look down at whatever hunted them was diminished, but still she felt that nagging curiosity.

"Don't," came his voice in her ear, quiet but firm. It was almost as if he could sense the curiosity about to overwhelm her senses. Or more likely because he felt it in himself as well.

Hours had passed, and still his strong arms and

legs wrapped about her, kept her in place. Kept her safe, from the things below.

And herself.

She couldn't sleep, and every time she came close to nodding off she saw things she couldn't name or remember, the things even her subconscious feared, and she held him a little tighter. Fear bound them together, and even though her thoughts were muddled with terror, she felt something change within her.

Something important.

That respect had grown through the night, and she finally felt she understood what the rebels had been dealing with since before she was born. Since before her parents and grandparents had been born. These things, these fears and dangers that had shaped their lives, and she understood she could never be one of them. She couldn't help them anymore. She was worthless baggage, yet he'd come back for her, and the awareness caused her trembling body to soften against his.

"How long will they linger?" she murmured.

Those were her first words since she'd stopped unknowingly screaming. It had been as if speaking, even whispering, had taken such strength of will and courage she didn't have to spare through the night, but then they spilled out. The feel of that ominous presence, she realized, had dissipated and she could be bold again.

"They're gone," he said, though she already felt it to be so. "For now at least." And she could feel the pounding of his heart through his chest and into her. He was strong, courageous, he had saved her despite the panic and terror that had crippled her, and even with the danger gone — or so it seemed — he held her tight and close. Strong arms around her midsection, though he no longer needed to keep her pinned, the urge to stare into the abyss gone. It was more like a hug.

Relief had made the desperate hold into a grateful embrace.

She slumped her head against him, wariness gripping her as she hugged him back, her body feeling such a deep exhaustion as it'd never known before. She'd been hiking through rugged terrain for days, but this was something wholly different.

"We have to keep going?"

The steady breathing in her ear was heavy, and he hesitated answering her. For the first time since she'd encountered the man, he was weary. Exhausted. He held her firmly and husked into her ear, "We'll rest." It was still dark, though she felt dawn must be approaching.

With his hard body reclined against the tree

trunk, and hers melted to his, he seemed to be climbing down from his terrified high. "Relax and rest, Rosa," he said softly. "We'll eat and head out when we're sure it's safe." Though even she knew it was mostly because neither of them was in any shape to move as they were and relief at surviving the night was too thick to throw away just yet.

"They can't get us here," she reassured them both as her body leaned into his, the leather straining against her form. As the fear drained from her, pain took its place, and she realized her face probably had more than a few gashes, and her clothes were torn in places.

Still, it didn't matter. She was alive. He'd saved her again.

She dozed off at some point, at least briefly. Though when she awoke it was to the sound of birds chirping, the feel of sun on her face. They were so far up there were few branches to block out its light, and she greeted the morning for once with true happiness.

Surviving such a harrowing experience, and finding herself in the still tightly protective arms of her saviour was the best wakeup she'd had in ages.

He stirred behind her, his two arms across her torso, one pushed up beneath her bust, and she felt it then. That awkward morning stiffness, so very male, pressed at her backside as he held on to her fleshy and curvaceous form.

Still asleep, he shifted just a bit against her, greedy in his unconscious state for her closeness.

She rested her head against his shoulder, and couldn't help but smile a bit. She lived. Her fingers laced into his and tugged him nearer, feeling so vibrant despite the lack of sleep. Despite everything else. It seemed like it all washed away, and all she was left with was the present moment, that feeling of awareness. It was as though she were a flower finally opening to bloom, and she simply enjoyed it.

Basking in the warmth of the morning sun, he squeezed her from behind and nuzzled into her long blonde hair. In a low, groggy voice he said, "We made it."

That might've been expected there, but instead of stopping he brought his head into the crook of her neck and nibbled her ear. All while he ground that throbbing manhood into her round ass with early-morning need.

She couldn't help but be confused, but at the same time... she felt it too. It was like her body wanted to celebrate being alive, to seek out sensations and pleasure like it'd never known before. She'd been so close to the void, the thing that she couldn't imagine, and now that she was in the world...

A soft moan filled the air between them and she clutched him more needily. No longer was it the warm, considerate hug. It was something of passion and desire. "Yes," she murmured.

Those strong arms of his were so comforting through the night, so pleasing come the morn. He squeezed her in one, pushing up her breasts in the process, the other moving down over her to her inner thigh. He nibbled and suckled her ear all while that needful cock swelled between their tight leathers.

She'd never been with a man before, of course. Her lot as a noble was to wait for her appointed day, when she cemented some alliance of houses. Or a trade between them at least.

"Was worried we'd never get our chance," he muttered in his gravelly, early-morning voice as he ground into her so purposefully. Getting that sweet friction of her body against his loins.

Her stomach flipped, and she nodded dumbly. She could feel him all around her, and her breathing quickened. He'd been so professional, so capable. It'd barely occurred to her that he might have felt some desire for her feminine curves, for her body. Her finger moved to sweep her long, blonde hair from the side he sucked, and her blue eyes fluttered shut.

"Is it safe up here?" she asked quietly.

Those strong hands of his were so comforting, so powerful. He squeezed her inner thigh and slid his palm in towards her sex, all while he continued to rock his hips and grind into her backside.

"Don't worry," he husked and suckled her exposed neck with his moist lips. "I've got you, Terrel." And as his hand moved up and took hold of her breast he froze.

Her mouth dropped open, and she stopped as well. Her breath held deep in her chest and she exhaled it with a low, "Ah... sorry..." Her face flushed and she felt stupid for even thinking he could have been interested in her.

More importantly, she wondered if that was all it took for her to want to just... rut. A near miss, a terror beyond reason, and a hard, handsome man needing her back. She bit in her lower lip, because she knew it was. She wanted to feel alive, and to share that joy with someone else.

He loosened his hold on her, taking his hands from her breasts and groin. He pulled back from her neck and cleared his throat. Suddenly the tight proximity a point of awkwardness. "Sorry," he muttered, "I was tired and... didn't realize..." He cleared his throat. "Thought you were..." His words trailed off, not forming any clear, distinct sentence.

"Yeah, it's fine." He had excuses and reasons. All she had was that bright, warm flush that covered her entire, pale flesh. She tried to scoot away from him a bit, to give him his room, but her embarrassment ran deep.

He helped her move ahead, and then he swung one leg to the side, getting ready to climb down. "We'll eat and get ready," he said lowly. "I've got some things in my pack I can share with you for now. We can't spare the time it'll take to go hunt something up today."

"Great," she said with less gratitude then she wanted. She was about to give it all up for him, and he'd rejected her. Rosa glanced up at the sky and took a deep breath before finally looking down the length of the tree, swallowing back her fright.

20

THE NOBLES

As Caprice gazed out at the rainy streets below, watching her father leave for his carriage, the Duke's last words rang in her memory: "Everything shall resolve itself satisfactorily in time, sweet child. Trust me."

It was nothing really, a simple platitude to the ears of the Landsreck guards that accompanied all visitors to the manor now. Though she couldn't help but sense — or was it just hope? — that it held some greater significance. Did he have a plan? For she certainly had zero chance of giving birth to the old crow's vile offspring. He'd never showed the slightest interest in her sexually during his tortures.

Caprice Rensford — for she still bore the old man's family name — was, by the books, a virgin in the terms of the nobility. None had taken that from her, and she'd never offered it to any. Though for once in the life of a noble lady, that was a detriment rather than an asset.

"You're not fooling anyone," came the firm voice of that severe Viscount, the old Duke's nephew, Beren Rensford. He had broken the spell of her reverie, the two confined to that spacious manor, making it seem like a prison despite its classic opulence.

"I can tell you're going to be a fabulous house-guest," she spat acidly at the window, not even doing him the courtesy of turning to face him. Instead she watched her father — her hope — leave, and the strange reflection of her own face was distorted by the falling rain.

The sound of his boots upon the carpeted floor were loud, for he dressed like he was about to head off riding despite their state being so near to house arrest. High black boots, grey trousers, and a high-collared white shirt that tried to hide the fact that despite his height, he was not a particularly bulky man.

"Guest?" he remarked, running a finger along the windowsill where some condensation had built up from where the cold rain met the warmth of their fire-heated manor. "This is my family home," he said confidently. "Soon to be mine," he remarked with absolute confidence. "All mine."

Caprice rolled her eyes. How could any one person be so obnoxious as he? "Well, that's what you think. Your uncle was quite devoted to me. He's probably spinning in his grave as you try to take from me what he gave so openly."

It was all lies. Hell, she didn't even expect him to believe it, but Caprice wasn't one to admit defeat.

Brazenly he stepped up beside her. He looked every bit the ideal Union noble. His dark hair cut short and in the court style, with his sideburns and bangs given this wispy curve that looked natural yet took careful primping to achieve. With his steel-grey eyes he gazed down at her with a severe look. "The late Duke Rensford wouldn't have slipped his dick in you to save his fortune. Certainly not to give it away." And the crassness of the words rolled off his tongue with the effortlessness of one of the vulgar proles that worked the factories or streets.

Her face screwed up in disgust and anger, and she turned from him. "You're disgusting," she hissed. She was still in that black dress, her mourning outfit, but she was a still a beautiful young woman. Vibrant, with fresh skin and smooth hair.

But she bore the hatred of the Rensford family through her deceased husband, and even though she was grateful at the time that his tortures stopped at sex, now she lamented it. It could have been so easy.

The Viscount looked so young still, hardly older than her judging by looks, for he still bore some faint traces of freckling upon his cheeks when she looked long enough. Which was rarely.

For his youth and vulgarity, he didn't explode at her outburst. He continued in his self-assured manner, sounding so confident. "I would've thought you'd adopt a more conciliatory tone," he remarked. "I have to admit, it disappoints me some." The cocky prick smirked. "I figured you'd be working your ways upon me by now to preserve what you could of the estate. Yet instead..." He simply trailed off, a look of wry amusement upon his face.

"Yet instead I know how wrong and vile you are. The thought of being forced to spend time with you makes me ill, knowing how different you are from him." She brought her dark eyes back to him and narrowed them. "You're nothing but a leach."

He had seem so unfazed by everything that occurred. Taking it all with that harsh stoicism. Yet at that last remark, she saw it: she'd upset him. "That goes to show how little you knew him then," he retorted to her darkly.

Without pretense, he leaned in, a hand upon one shoulder as he gripped it tight and twisted her about to face him, to stare into his harsh gaze. "Your little charade might be enough to fool some others," he said in a raspy, low voice. "But I knew that rotten old villain better than anyone. Anyone," he stressed with a narrowing of his eyes, those cold eyes of his trembling with something. Anger? Fright? She couldn't tell, except that strong emotion broiled behind his facade. "He'd sooner be rid of his manhood than slip it into a woman."

She desperately hoped he couldn't see that flash of understanding pass her gaze as she tried to yank his shoulder from his grasp. "What a heinous accusation about my departed husband!"

Her attempt failed though, for he was strong, his grasp large, and he held her in place with seeming ease. He might not have been a bulky man, but there was muscle and sinew with power on that tall frame of his.

"Continue your little act if it comforts you," he remarked with a cocky smirk again. "Though it won't change a thing." Without warning he brought his free hand up and grabbed her face, clenching her jaw between his thumb and fingers, twisting her delicate stalk like neck back as he glowered at her. "But just you keep in mind that never was I a leach, you failure of a high-class hooker." His words were nearly spat out. "Nobody has ever earned such station and wealth as harshly as I. Don't you dare forget that."

Her eyes widened in anger as she tried to push him away from her, desperate for some space. She felt no shame for what she had done, no pity for what he insinuated was done to him. She deserved this house. Her father deserved this.

"Never touch me again!"

The Viscount let her go, but only after letting her futile struggles continue long enough to make it known it was by his will alone she got free. "We'll see how that tune changes," he remarked, standing tall and sternly, as if nothing so intensely inappropriate had just occurred between them. He straightened his shirt and looked to her. "When you've been in here long enough, and realize there is no hope for getting your payment but through me..." He smiled unevenly at her, walking about her towards the door. "We'll see."

She was seething at him as she spun around, her face red with anger. "And when they find I'm pregnant with your uncle's child, you'll know true pain!"

21

THE FRONT

The front was always punctuated by the sounds of warfare. The rattling of old machine guns, the poof and boom of mortars. Though to be at the very first line of trenches during an actual battle was something else altogether.

Sergeant Levek cowered in the trench, just as all his men did. The whistle of approaching ordinance shrilly rang out and they all knew what was coming.

There was no light, the clouds above them blocking out everything. Not that anyone was aware of whether it was day or night anymore. The enemy had contraptions, cruel devices that were alien and terrifying to the men and women of the Union. Rockets that exploded and released harsh smokes that stung the eyes, made one break into a fit of coughing, and blotted out the sky for days when used en masse.

More than that though, they could slaughter indiscriminately with a direct hit. Not that the things were precise. The whistle of their approach was part of their effect. They were so long in coming, and you never knew when or where they would land. It tore an individual's guts up inside.

Levek tried to shift his mind from that crushing anxiety, tried to think of sweet Caslian. Though it didn't work. Worry consumed him. He'd been away from her a while now, and had no way of knowing how she was faring.

The wait ended abruptly, the area lit up as the rockets landed. Each strike a hissing burst as the barrage of their landing caused the trenches to explode. None near him then... the scream came up from one of the lines behind him.

A cacophony of horror filled Levek's senses and it was so deafening that he didn't notice right away that a rocket had landed in his own trench. It had dug into the dirt before exploding and so the casualties were light, but his men watched in horror as one of their comrades' flesh melted before their very eyes, as he flailed and screamed in agony.

There was nothing to do for him, they all knew. They could only watch as they hunkered down, or force their gaze away as the wiser ones managed. Such horrors were not meant to be witnessed by anyone.

As the cries died down, their comrade-in-arms dead, some of the men stirred, anxious to move from the reek of burnt flesh and excrement that permeated their stretch of trench line. Levek placed a hand upon the closest one's shoulder and pushed him back into place.

It didn't take long to understand why, for that symphony of shrill whistles rose up into the dark charcoal-and-red-clouded sky, growing every higher. The next barrage on its way.

Levek thought, *I hope she's okay.*

22

THE MATRON

Saghar and his brother both reported back into the long-cabin at the same time, the two burly Kron looking battle ready. "They're coming from the east" stated Saghar, and his brother simultaneously said, "West."

Looking to one another, they then changed their story. "They've got us surrounded and are approaching, Matriarch." The two large, brutish-looking men in their armour and clothes looked not particularly disturbed by this, though Aleena knew much was at stake. The bandits coming for the trade could be a huge problem for her.

But it was just the next hard step in a march of many, and as she pinned her hair up in a ponytail and covered it with the fur-lined hood, her shoulders squared. She looked professional, and dangerous, the pale elf covered head to toe in white leathers and furs with daggers strapped to her hips.

She was a beautiful woman with her exotic features, and her green eyes moved from one brother to the next. Briefly she wondered if navigating the trade with the bandits could possibly be any worse than trying to figure out the Kron and their strange customs.

"You know what to do," she said as she moved past them and out the door.

The brothers simply nodded as she vanished out the door by herself.

She stood alone as the ragged-looking bandit leader approached from the tree line, his ratty furs draped about him and covering what was once an old military trench coat. The standard wear of most every bandit.

With two large men at his side, he approached her with gun in hand. An old long-barrel rifle, tied and repaired numerous times by the look of it. "We're 'ere for our stuff," he said in a harsh voice, his black beard shorter than Aleena would have figured, almost neatly trimmed. "Let's get this over with."

"All business." Aleena smiled. "Fine by me." She

was short for an elf, but the piercing green eyes were intimidating. There was something about her facial features that seemed almost feline or predatory, especially when she seemed pleased, and she straightened her spine.

The leader of the trio paused before the door and looked around. "No tricks," he stated. Then looking aside at her, sizing her up briefly, he added, "We know ya got fellas workin' with ya. Don't think of pullin' no surprises." With that his two flanking guards pushed around him and opened the door, making way for them both to follow with their clubs in hand.

"Hey, you're the man with the gun. I know better than to bring my knives to a gun fight," she said amiably as she let them brush past her. She ignored the heavy thudding of her heart in her chest, and the rush of annoyance at the paranoid and impoverished. These were the people who would help her, after all.

Whether they knew it or not.

Entering into the building, the bandit Chief and his two guards looked about, no sign of Saghar or Ramtok anywhere. Though the crates of supplies waited there, same as before.

The Chief gestured towards the crate — "Open it" — and the two men went to work prying the lid off.

While they laboured, the wary Chief cast a curious, dark gaze towards Aleena. "So these northern fuckers are recruitin' elves now, huh?" He remarked and shook his head in amusement. "Never thought I'd see the day." And the tall man rubbed his hand along the wood under barrel of his gun.

"My hunch is that they wanted someone disposable," she said thoughtfully, her eyes staying focused on him mostly, even as she kept her sights on everything around them as well. "I guess you're quite dangerous?"

She could sense the gears turning behind his dark eyes as he turned away and peered around the length of the cabin. Whatever dark aspirations he had, or whatever chances he was thinking of taking to rob her blind. "Does that warrant an answer?" he responded as the two men pried off the lid and he went over to inspect the goods.

Her lips quirked, and she shrugged, folding her arms beneath her small, leather-clad chest. "I won't pump you for answers if you don't like." There was just the slightest hint of innuendo, of teasing to her voice.

While the Chief went about inspecting the goods with more dedication than she'd have hoped with her not-so-subtle innuendo, the other two men had eyes glued to her. One even cocked a wry, toothy grin at the fair-skinned elf.

The Chief however, pulled out a gun and inspected it with some look of disapproval on his face.

"It's all there," she said, though her gaze moved to the one smiling at her, and her lashes descended in a flutter for half a heartbeat. "All in good order, too, I trust." She was getting antsy with them taking so long, and she knew it wasn't going to end well.

Ignoring her words, the Chief bent over the bin again, and she heard him pushing more of the guns and supplies aside. He laid his gun down, and then with an outraged growl he declared, "The fuckin' crates are bottomed with rocks!" and he grabbed for his gun as the other two men brandished their clubs immediately.

Aleena's eyes narrowed. "Fucking traitors," she hissed under her breath. "No wonder they didn't want to be here. Hey now." She looked at the three men. "Killing me is what they want! They're the ones that packed this, I'm just in the middle," she said without reaching for her weapons. Her body prickled with anger and adrenaline.

Growling out his words, the Chief said, "Tie her up, we'll take everythin' we can and leave the rest in ruin." Though before he could even finish saying that a large hand reached down from above, grabbed the barrel of his rifle, and slammed the butt of it back into his face.

The other two froze in their tracks as they watched their Chief fall back onto the floor, a large Kron descending from the ceiling, draped in white furs. They were startled into silence, the bestial-looking brute the last thing they expected, especially in such a manner.

Though as one went for Aleena, Ramtok descended from above with a loud crunch as he landed upon the man, sword singing in the air as he slashed out at the third. The strike slashed across his throat, but that did not prevent the man from emitting a terrifying sound from his blood-spurting gash.

She sighed, as if the carnage and ruin was a minor annoyance, and she moved towards the Chief. "It shouldn't have ended like this. I'm not your enemy. Apparently they hate me even more than they wanted to rip you off." Aleena lamented the truth in that statement as she bent down and checked his pulse.

The Chief was still alive, and she could feel his blood still pumping beneath her slender fingers. Though outside she heard it: the first crack of fire. The bandits were using their weapons, and it seemed they included a handful of guns at least, though none of the bullets hit the cabin. She knew then the diversionary setup of fake-guards that were really branches and wood beneath tarps had worked.

Ramtok took out his own rifle, and Saghar lifted the bandit Chief's. "We must fight," came the guttural voice of the shaman as his brother smashed out a window and took aim, firing a shot before anything more could be said or done.

"It always comes down to that, doesn't it?" Aleena grabbed the two wood-handled pistols from her boots and moved towards the door. "No survivors, except the Chief," she ordered in a hushed tone. It still held all that powerful command, however, and she knew they'd obey utterly.

She was the first to move out, and with grace beyond that of any normal elf she bounded to the cover of the trees in a mere moment. The crack of gunfire rang out and her sensitive ears drew her to it, the first bandit she sighted standing over one of the pretend-prone bodies and prodding the stack. The last thing he saw was the bramble of sticks beneath as she took him out.

She could hear some cries of alarm go out, and knew it must have been one of the brothers showing himself, the bandits not expecting to see the Kron there. The human bandits had all run from the front to escape fighting such beasts, after all.

The next bandit she crossed was more fortunate than the last, though as he pulled his rifle to bear towards her, she closed the gap and slapped it away before pushing her own pistol up in under his chin and firing.

The messy affair dragged on, and by the time her two Kron approached her, the gunfire long silenced, she was peppered in specs of red. "That's all of them, Matriarch," intoned Ramtok, rifle across his broad chest.

"You're sure?" she said as she looked around her. Pure white stained with red. It was pretty, in a morose way. She felt almost dizzy as the flush of battle drained from her, and she quickly began thinking of her next step.

Ramtok nodded his certainty. "I'm sure, Matri-arch." Though Saghar looked a bit distracted as he peered around him, gun in hand in place of his usual staff.

The noise of combat was over, and already, slowly the sounds of the forest were creeping back into her surroundings.

"What about the ones that set us up for this, hm?" she asked as she walked into the cabin once more. Her face felt hot and pricklish, and the familiar exhaustion began to coil through her body. She didn't have time for such pleasantries, however.

This was going to be harder than she hoped.

The brothers followed her in, looking about cautiously before shutting the door. Saghar spoke first, however. "They set us up to take the brunt of a bad deal, Matriarch. Either they're ready to pounce in and kill whoever won, or they're nowhere near here."

Ramtok grunted his agreement to that sentiment.

"I don't really like that first choice." She looked at the crate, her eyes falling to the Chief once more. "So I guess the question is, which one of us does he hate more?"

Aside from the large, swollen bruise on his forehead, the Chief lay there looking for all the world as if he were just slumbering.

Behind her, Ramtok said, "Either way, we should get moving soon, Matriarch."

"Agreed," said Saghar. "They might be content for us to deal with the backlash of their scam backfiring, but we shouldn't take the chance."

Her hand struck against the Chief's face, the sound filling the room. The back of her palm struck the other cheek, and when finally his lashes began to flutter, her voice was that of a woman in control. "We were both set up. Your guards are dead. We will return you to your people, however, and you will tell them of how charitable we are."

The slowly awakening man seemed to take some time to soak in her words, his eyes rolling in his head before he looked up at her with a bit of a glare. Though once he saw the two Kron behind her, she saw shock and fright replace all else.

"By the pits!" he cursed in awe at the sight of those two brutes. "They set us up in a trap with Kron?!"

"The Kron are mine. They didn't know about them, but now you do. The people that set you up were human, and the people that are trying to help you are us."

Saghar and Ramtok were unconcerned with the man as they kept watch around the cabin, though the Chief slowly seemed to regain his wits and she saw something other than shock and fright fill his eyes.

He glowered at her, hard and venomous. "Those fuckin' snow-wanderers set me up for a big rip-off," he growled, and she knew that look — though directed at her — was meant for someone else. "My people won't stand for bein' ripped off. Not after we did fair trade with them for years at great cost!"

"So wouldn't it be nice to get back to them and warn them before any more of 'em get killed? Take what you can carry, but we're moving fast," Aleena said as she stood up, holding out her hand for his.

"We'll get you back in one piece, and you'll get your revenge."

The fur-dressed man took his time, eying her, then her offered hand. At last he took it and moved back up onto his feet. "They'll get what's comin' to 'em," he growled out angrily, and she swore she could hear his teeth grinding even as he spoke.

23

THE FRONT

It had been Private Caslian's first serious engagement at the front since she arrived, and though she was not in the fighting, the stream of injured and maimed soldiers brought much of the reality back to her. On the second night of the enemy assault, one of their rockets that had travelled far enough back to hit amidst the medical facilities managed to light up one of the tents in an explosive ball of flame, the likes of which she'd never seen before.

Green fire shot into the night sky, and not a soul made it out of the tent alive. "The rockets do their worst when they touch on fabric of any kind," one doctor explained to her. "The flames consume clothes and tents and sizzle for ages on the skin."

She'd seen enough of that since to know it for fact.

Without realizing it, she had been staring at the carnage in the tent. It was then she noticed that one of the burn victims on a stretcher-bed was with Levek's unit. Berel was his name, though there was very little left of him to recognize. It was only that one eye that darted around frantically that drew attention to the deep blue that made him stand out amongst the soldiers under Levek's command.

Her stomach churned and her heart beat faster as she moved to him. Her hands were hardened and her face looked older than when she'd first arrived, and ever since that day Levek had protected her, she'd known fear. Caslian had managed to push it all aside, to focus on the positives in her life, but she felt something even deeper than horror.

There were no words for it. It was as if all the worries that kept her awake at night had come at once, and her hand reached for Berel's. "It's okay," she tried to say, but her voice was so weak. So foreign. She wanted to scream at him, to demand where Levek was.

How she managed to push it away once more, she had no idea, for her knees quaked and her breath was shallow. "It's okay."

Berel's one remaining eye went to her immediately at that touch, at last focussing his gaze for more than a split second. "Hey, you... you're..." He struggled for the words. "I know you," he managed after a delay.

"Yeah, you do." Caslian smiled, trying to look as bright and cheerful as always. Every day robbed her of a little bit of that joy, but she fought so hard to keep it. "Looks like you made it out alive," she added on, her thumb rubbing against his flesh.

Perhaps the strangest thing about him was how unblemished and normal the one side of his body looked. More so than the scars of the other even.

"Did I?" he responded, his eye flickering around again. "I guess they'll send me home... right?" he murmured, his attention seeming to fade again already as his eye reverted to darting about.

Her hand squeezed his, and she choked back her tears. "Yeah, I guess so." She forced a smile, and the young woman with her hazel eyes and tanned skin knew she could fake it well. She'd had a lot of practice. "Look, you just rest up, okay? Hey... Was Levek with you?"

"The Sergeant?" he replied with some confusion, his eye flickering faster. "He was... he was right beside me when it — " He broke into a coughing fit, blood coating his lips as he lurched from his position for a moment before settling back down and closing the one remaining eye.

Quickly after that, the doctor in charge came up to her. "Go take a break, Private." His voice was hoarse after working the day away and now late into the night. "You've been up longer than I have, and it's settled down now."

"I'm fine," she said, but her stomach felt like someone had punched her, and her hands trembled as she stepped back from Berel. "They need me." She was insistent, but the moment she swooned she knew there was no hope for her staying. She couldn't see straight, and her eyes were burning.

"That was an order, Private." And with that the doctor simply walked away, and Berel lay there, eye shut, looking unconscious.

There was no arguing with a superior's command. Didn't take a veteran to understand that. So with shaky hands she had to tread out into the night, the cool air tinged with the strange odours wafting from the front, the strange smoke still coating the sky and making it chillier than it should have been.

Her own bunk was far away; she'd been moved after the flood of injured came back, to make more space near to the medical tents for the dead and deceased.

With her blurry vision, she swiped away the tears that threatened her as she started moving. She didn't even know what direction, but she didn't want to go far. Maybe if she just paced around the tent, she'd find him. He was probably just busy, trying to clean up his people. Take care of them.

"He's fine," she said to herself, but her voice sounded so strained.

The voice that greeted her muttering was familiar, but it wasn't Levek's. "Well, thanks, sweetie."

When she peered up, she saw that she had wandered between two stone structures for housing some munitions. Some of the rare buildings were actually made from something other than tarp or wood. And the large, uniformed man that approached her from one side blocked her in.

There was no moonlight to illuminate him, so he was but a dark silhouette to her. Tall, a bit bulky in the shoulders and arms, he didn't wear his hat, just a tattered and worn trench uniform that frayed in several places along his outline.

"Huh?" She stopped, her hands going behind her back as she stood primly. Her flaxen hair was pulled back from her face and her outfit was as clean as it could get, given the circumstances.

"Sorry, ah... sir? I was just talking about one of the infirmed." Had she eaten yet? She couldn't remember, and the fact that it had occurred to her then was strange. Her stomach felt so tight she wasn't sure she could eat, even if she tried.

He stepped in closer to her, so she could smell the scent of vodka off him as he leaned against the stone building to her left.

"Yeah, I hear tell yer a real carin' sort," he said, reaching out with his free hand and touching a stray bit of hair that had escaped to her shoulder. "Ya make a lotta men feel real good about themselves, they say. And I gotta say I'm a bit jealous." The stranger's voice was so dry and husky as his eyes gleamed in the day down at her.

Her heart felt like it was in a clamp, but she smiled regardless. She always smiled when things got tough.

"Well, I think you're lucky you haven't had to come my way. Most of the men I see aren't too happy to see me."

Something was wrong. He was wrong. She glanced around her before taking a step back away from his hand.

"Have you seen Sergeant Levek?"

It didn't work, however, for he grabbed hold of her shoulder and wrenched her back into place. "Hey now," he began stepping in to her. "No need to be like that. Yer boyfriend ain't here anymore." He pushed against her, pressing her towards the wall as another voice came from behind him.

"What's goin' on?" It came through the dark of the night as she was pressed between the vodka-stinking man's hard body and the concrete at her back.

She felt paralyzed. She had nightmares about the night Levek had protected her from those men. Was this man one of them? Caslian tried to swallow, but her throat was too dry and no moisture would go down.

"I need to get back to work," she managed to squeak out.

She was such a delicate woman, so petite and innocent looking. The weeks she'd spent in the war, though, had stolen some of her brightness away, no matter how she struggled.

"Hear that, bud?" said the first man before her, his hand moving across her shoulder towards her neck, rough fingers feeling her skin. "She wants to get to work on us." And even in the dark she could see his uneven smirk and leering gaze.

The other man came up beside them both casually. "Shit," he said. "It's her." It was like those voices were coming back to her out of her memories. Out of her nightmares of that day.

"Damn right, it's her," the taller one stated, his

other hand moving down over her, feeling her through her ill-fitted uniform.

"We've been lookin' for ya a long time now, ya know, honey?" said the stockier man who'd just joined them, and his strong grasp went straight for her loins, pressing to her quim so hard through her clothes without the slightest bit of pretense.

"Stop!" She struggled against them, but she felt so frail. It was hard for her to even see and her head felt like it was pounding. Her blood was boiling as they grabbed at her so crassly and she tried to knock them away. "The doctor's expecting me!"

The first man's hand went about her neck entirely, his strong, calloused grasp choking off her throat, silencing her by force. "Shut the fuck up!" he spat out at her angrily, his temperament soured immediately. "Ya got any idea how long we've been strainin' our drawers over you, ya sweet lil' piece a meat?"

"Real long time," crooned the other man in his lower tone of voice, his thick digits groping at her sex so crudely still. "Musta wanked myself dry a dozen times since thinkin' a yer tight lil' body on my prick," he said with a lick of his lips.

Caslian tried to blink away the tears that burned her eyes, but her body felt like it was boiling over. Fear, anguish, rage... it all coiled within her as she felt that powerful hand squeeze her delicate throat. Still, her foot thrashed out, her fingernails digging into the man's uniform.

Her weary flailing against them was futile though. They were both built so solidly, and the first man slammed her against the concrete by his grip on her throat in punishment for her outburst. "Damn lil' bitch just ain't wantin' to be nice with us, eh, bud?" he remarked, pressing an arm and a leg against the wall with his body.

"Real shame," added the second, who kept her other limbs pinned as he began to undo her pants and belt even as he continued to so roughly rub at her slit. "I was thinkin' each time I beat off what a sweet time you an' I would have, hun." The breeches she wore nearly fell off the moment the belt was removed, so oversized for her small frame. "Damn, if she ain't the hottest thing I ever laid eyes on," he said as if in a dream, feeling out her lower body with only her underwear to protect her.

She made tiny sounds, pleading and begging, but they just came out as soft rushes of air. His grip was too tight on her slender neck. She was sure he would kill her. Collapse her throat and leave her there. Her parents had already mourned her — that was her send-off before coming to the front lines — and there was no one else who would care.

Except for Levek.

Tears streaked down her tanned cheeks as she shook her head, but her body was beginning to feel numb. As if it were no longer hers.

The feel of a cold knife blade on her skin brought the sensations back, but she could barely see it as the shorter man cut off her undergarments. "Here," he said, balling them up and then stuffing them in her parted mouth. "Wish't we could put her pretty mouth to better use," he sighed dreamily, returning his hand back to between her thighs, able to grope at her now-naked labia.

"Good thinkin'," said the first man, and he released her throat. She was finally able to suck in air through her nose again, but they only continued with their sick actions. "Nors'll be pissed," he remarked, undoing the buttons of her tunic. "He said he'd never jerk it again until he'd had a slice of this angel, and he don't even show up on time." He laughed, finding it hilarious as he freed her chest to the cold air.

"Please," she tried to muffle around the material, but then clamped her jaw together, as if that would save her. As if anything could save her as she pleaded at them with her eyes. She wanted to crawl up into herself, to hide from them. From the world. From this war.

She was so small compared to them, like a doll they were playing with more than a woman. Levek, she pleaded. She wanted so badly for him to save her, yet at the same time, she didn't want him to find her.

Part of her knew that if he did, there would be bloodshed.

As she tried to make some sense of it, the two brutes continued. No hesitation as they tore away her shirt and stripped off what remained of her clothes. Caslian was laid totally nude against the cold concrete wall, and that larger but shorter man continued to grope her with such enthusiasm, finding a breast in one palm.

"Oh shit," he muttered.

"What is it?" said the taller man, already undoing his own belt as he pinned both of her arms above her head with his free hand.

"Oh man... oh fuck," came his enthusiastic voice. "She's a fuckin' virgin. I told ya!" He nearly shouted so loud it could've awoken the camp, though the other man struck him in the back of the head and he muttered excitedly in the quiet, "I told ya, she's a fuckin' angel."

"Lemme feel," he insisted, and she felt the contest of hands for her cunny, pushing the thicker digits away as the first man prodded that thin sheath of her hymen. "Well, I'll be damned, he said, and she could see the gleam off his teeth in the dark night. "Oh, baby," he said, leaning in towards her ear, his voice harsh and hoarse. "I ain't never gonna forget poppin' yer cherry."

"The shit you are!" the other man said, obsessing over her, the two looking almost ready to fight it out over her body. "Y'know there ain't nobody wanted this beauty more'n me."

"And you can have her after," intoned the first, as she heard the jangle of his belt, his pants coming undone. "Treat her all sweet if ya want, I don't give a shit."

Caslian's knees trembled and she kept trying to back away, to stop feeling their hands all over her delicate sex and her smallish breasts, but there was no escape. Instead, there was just the cool concrete behind her and it kept knicking her tanned flesh.

She could taste herself on her panties, but she didn't dare relinquish them. Her face burned as she held back a cough, her throat aching from his brutal treatment.

She wanted to go home. Back to her family.

Even back to the medical tent, to helping people in trouble.

Yet there was a sense of inevitability. Levek had warned her, hadn't he? That she needed to get out. That she needed to run away from this all, but she'd been too proud. She was serving her people, and that was so important to her.

During her own inner turmoil they'd decided their order. "On the ground," commanded the taller one, and together they dragged her onto the well-trodden sod, the cold earth against her back as they spread her out like some long-sought platter.

"Don't fuckin' ruin her," complained the larger as he pinned her shoulders down.

"Now how could I ruin such a perfect beauty as this?" remarked the other with his cruel smirk, and she could barely make out the shape of it as he knelt between her knees, cock in hand as he bent forward and began to prod his crown against her. "Damn, you are pretty," he murmured to her as she felt that slick, precum-greased tip stroke against her, press into her tenuous maidenhood.

Her body was so tightly wound, her muscles aching with tension as she looked up at the burly man with pleading eyes. This couldn't happen to her. Not by these men.

She was supposed to be safe, as safe as she could get on the front lines. She was protected from the enemy — though not their munitions — but something like this wasn't supposed to happen to her.

These were her brothers. People she was supposed to be able to count on. To trust.

She tried to clamp her legs shut, her pelvis

thrusting into the air as she sought to escape his hardness.

It was too little too late though, he was already betwixt those slender legs of hers, and the other man had her two arms pinned with one hand as he reached down and groped her petite chest with the other. The gleam of lust in his eyes was so obsessive, not like the cruel desires of the man who then shredded through her innocence with one hard stab and a loud, "Ahhhh!"

He seared into her, and she screamed around her panties. Anguish and panic coursed through her body and she thrashed on the ground. It was no use. The small woman was pinned between two men, held in place so securely.

Even with the material in her mouth, her cries were heartbreaking. She was so scared, so sad that these men would hurt her in such a personal way. She could only see through a haze as her head thudded with pain. She tried to squirm back, into the arms of her second assaulter, just to get away from that all-consuming pain low in her belly.

So as that tall, cruel man gave her a few sharp pains more to remember him by, the other put his arms about her head and neck, keeping her own limbs pinned beneath a leg. "Hey, she likes me," he said, kissing her cheek messily and shushing her softly. "It's okay. It's okay, now it's your and my turn."

"All yours, bud," he said, wiping off his dick on her pants and slipping away to take her arms in his place.

How did her body feel so tender and limp? She could barely even fight, shake her head no. She was just relieved that the cruel man was done with her, even though she knew her ordeal wasn't anywhere close to over.

Everything about her felt foreign and strange, like something was deeply wrong.

They moved around her body in that dark alley, and she could only watch as that thick, strong man undid his own trousers, freeing his own manhood. "Oh, honey, you have no idea how much I need you," he said, lowering himself down to her battered and used slit. He was breathing heavily as he leaned in towards her face. "I think I kinda love you," he said before he pressed that thick knob into her slippery quim, pressing it in deep with a deep groan of satisfaction.

This wasn't love.

She knew love. Affection.

It surprised her, though, that in her darkest hours her thoughts had turned to Levek and not her family. Perhaps she'd mourned them, too. Now there was only him, and she knew he'd never be able to treat her like this.

If he was still alive.

That thought, that single moment was what made her begin to cry in earnest. More than the pain of losing her virginity, or the fear of being accosted by the two men. More than her terror and rage. It was the thought of never seeing Levek again.

It was hard to say if that made it easier or harder to bear the thick, strong man rutting atop her. For despite his pleas of obsession with her, of loving her, he was hardly gentler than the first man.

"Fuck," he cursed. "Fuck yer so damn beautiful." And he pawed at her face and breast as he pumped into her again and again, forcing messy kisses around her stuffed lips. "I've been dreamin' of a perfect girl like you all my life, and now yer mine," he said in a groan, his dick throbbing so wildly inside her as he rutted her like a immoral animal.

She wasn't his.

They could do what they wanted to her, but she'd never be able to commit herself to such a selfish and cruel man. There was a piece of her that not even they could touch. Not with their hands or their bodies or their cocks.

She lay still, too exhausted to fight them. It was over anyways. She had lost.

"Such a perfect lil' pussy! Oh gods... oh gods... never felt so good!" Each sickening refrain signalling another surge of thick seed as he emptied his loins into her too.

It was surreal when he was done, and she was used by them both. She could hear a loud noise in the distance and both men began to jump. "Shit," they both cursed, but when the rain began to fall they realized it was just a storm coming.

"Toss her shit," commanded the tall one, though he didn't wait for it to be followed. He gathered up her clothes into a bundle in his arms and gave it a throw off over the roof of the building beside them. "Let's get outta here!"

The larger man pulled out of her, looking down at her reluctantly as he gave her breast a final, almost tender stroke. "I'll find ya again," he said, as if that promise would be reassuring.

Though as the deluded one did up his pants, the first one knelt beside her, grabbed her hair hard, and hissed between his teeth. "Don't fuckin' say a word to anyone," he threatened. "Or this'll just be the start." And she thought, for one split second, she knew what "this" was. It was the horrible violation she'd just suffered. What they had robbed her of. But when that knife cut across one side of her face, she knew better.

The pain blinded her. It was like time stopped for a moment. One second she was wondering how they expected her to stay quiet when they threw away her clothes, and the next there was nothing.

Just agony.

Her head felt like it was going to split in two, her eyes already searing from the gritty tears, but that was nothing. All of it was nothing. Everything else melted away to only leave room for that one, singular focus of him tearing into her skin with that blade.

She didn't hear them scurry away into the night. As she lay there, her body split in agony from her head down across her torso, the burn of the raindrops — tainted by some foul reagent from the rockets — seared her wound and there was only pain.

24

THE REBELS

Days of travel through the forest. Endless walking over uneven ground was exhausting in a way that Rosa was totally unaccustomed to when she set out, but her calves and thighs had hardened from the journey in so short a time already.

The quiet rebel, Marin, led the way as always, bringing them through the woods and then into a strange part of the forest. It took Rosa a while to realize what was wrong with the picture. Everything was so green, and covered in vines, but it wasn't trees that surrounded her, she realized. They were buildings, or mostly what was left of them. A wall here, a part of one there. Piles of rubble all about.

And everything covered in moss and vines so that it blended into the forest seamlessly.

She paused and felt her muscles go taut as she looked around, her brows knitting. "What's this?" The blonde noble had never seen anything like it before, and it was almost like walking into a fairy tale from her childhood.

Evening had not yet descended, and the sounds of life resounded about them. Birds and crickets filling the area with their chatter, the noise of some larger animal she couldn't place off further into the heart of the strange ivy-ruins.

The rebel stopped and turned back towards her. "It's your destination," he said, gesturing up and around with his arms. "Welcome to the City of the Outcast," he stated with a crooked smile. She could see how it was once a city, but to call it that then...

Still, she didn't screw up her nose like she wanted to. She was just relieved to be there, to be surrounded by some kind of civilization. "Do *they* come here?" she asked before realizing she'd balled her hands into fists, just at the thought of those things she couldn't look at.

He didn't answer as such but curled his fingers in a "come here" sort of manner before turning and leading her on through the ruins. Despite what he'd said, the journey didn't seem at an end, for he took her on quite a trek, the old city seeming large as she passed by some former buildings that still managed to extend up a few stories high. Though still, no sign of inhabitants, other than the noise of birds and insects.

At last he took her into one of the structures. It wasn't even one of the more remarkable ones, a small thing, with three walls still standing, and much of another. "Here we go," he announced, brushing aside some hanging ivy and opening an inclined cellar door in the floor. "Shut the door after you," he told her before moving down the incline.

She looked at it skeptically but did as she was told. It was becoming sort of a habit now, truth be told. She was so eternally grateful for what he'd done for her that she couldn't think to try to push him away once more. It was a miracle he'd come back for her at all. He could have left her to her own doom too many times for her not to respect him.

So together they descended down, and all went dark the moment she shut that door behind them.

Panic nearly set in, but before she could react she felt a hand reach out and take hers. "This way," he said to her softly, and guided her along. The passageway was smooth stone by the feel of it scuffing her boots, but she had no idea where they were going. All was dark to her, and he didn't bother lighting a torch or anything.

Twisting and turning, at last she heard something: the sound of stone grating on stone. Then things changed. He led her into a whole other world. An upside down world, it seemed.

She stepped out into what was apparently the inside of an office building. Old and worn, bereft of those things that made it fit for offices, but so similar in style. "One last climb," he told her, leading her on down some stairs. It was there she got the chance to peek out an open, glassless window and onto the city below.

It was like a miniature version of the capital, submerged beneath the ground. Lights emanated from below, where an old railway track still remained, so similar to the one back home. The brassy metal still shining in the dark. People bustled or milled about, and the sounds of it reverberated through the place.

She never expected anything like this. Her eyes widened and her mouth dropped open with surprise, and she felt excited for the first time since she'd taken on the contract to kill the Queen. "This is amazing," she whispered, afraid to draw attention to herself.

Marin pulled off his hood and shook his chin-length blonde hair free. "C'mon," he said with a slight smile for her on his strikingly handsome face, "there's a lot more to see." The climb down the stairwell was long, but compared to the journey she just made, it was easy. At the bottom a pair of large men dressed in old shorts and breeches greeted the rebel with a smile and a slap on the back.

"This one's with me," he said gesturing back to her. "Another wayward soul brought to sanctuary."

They eyed her up and down with interest then stepped aside. "Leave it to Marin to bring in the pretty ones."

"You just say that because he brought you in," replied the other guard.

Rosa flustered, but she dipped her head down and let her blonde ponytail fall into her face. She felt anything like pretty. Her legs ached, her stomach felt tight, and the leather outfit she wore was too tight in some places and too loose in others. It had fit perfectly when she'd had it custom made for her.

Marin laughed at the two men. "I'll catch you two at the tavern later." Then he checked for her to follow him as he headed off into the streets.

It took a while for her fascination with the strange, underground town to wear off enough for her to realize the buildings were mostly askew, positioned at odd angles, and though everything was maintained, and buttressed where necessary, some seemed to have suffered damage at a time long ago.

Though as she watched a brass trolley, loaded with materials, hauled along the tracks by a pair of oversized lizard-beasts her attention was stolen away again.

Her head tilted to the side, and she stopped, staring quite rudely. It wasn't until she realized he was getting ahead of her that she trotted after him, her voice louder than she intended. "What are those?"

Taking a moment to realize what she meant, he looked to the lizards as they scurried on ahead along the fixed track. "Oh, pack lizards," he said. "I guess you don't see 'em very often further west than this," he acknowledged and led her on.

As her mind reeled with the odd sights and sounds, she began to notice the strange dichotomy in the humans and elves she saw. There were some very pale ones, and others more healthily coloured. It dawned on her that those paler inhabitants probably rarely got out of the underground city.

"I'll take you to meet the town's leader," he said to her, the two nearly side by side again. "Or, at least the closest thing this place has to a leader."

"Are they going to punish me?" It was what she'd feared since he saved her. That he'd play the role of the saviour, of the man that had got her through this ordeal unscathed, only for her to be more strictly punished by those he followed.

He furrowed his brow and looked at her with confusion. "Punish you?" he asked. With a shake of his head he said, "They aren't going to punish you. They didn't even know you existed until the scouts up above must've seen us coming." He smiled just slightly, a bit sad perhaps. "This isn't a rebel town, Rosa. This is just a haven for the outcast. There's no rebellion here, just surviving. Thia wouldn't allow it."

That name immediately rang a bell. For what young literate of the capital didn't know about the bawdy tales of Thia, elven seductress, printed on cheap papers and distributed to every nook and cranny of the city?

Her nose crinkled and her head dropped. She wasn't even welcome with his kind, and she didn't know why the realization bothered her so much. She had to be with the people that took anyone, she supposed, and she inhaled deeply.

"So this is, like... the best I can hope for, huh? Bottom of the..." She stopped herself before saying something she'd regret. "So this isn't your home?"

He simply looked ahead, taking a while before he shrugged his shoulders and responded. "As much of a home as I have. We don't settle down in one place for too long. But I have ties here," he remarked, and she noticed that he was guiding her towards a large marble building. It looked like it was a government building in times past, but now was painted and given life and flair beyond anything the Capital could've dreamt of.

"It's a good place," he added. "About as good as it comes. And don't show that attitude to Thia," he remarked disapprovingly of her sulking. "She has no time for someone looking their nose down at her domain."

"Yeah, I'll be good," she promised, rubbing her bicep with some embarrassment. "Just isn't what I expected. What will I do here?"

Marin shrugged his shoulders again and brushed some of his hair back, betraying his half-elven nature. "That's something you'll have to work out on your own. Maybe Thia can help, but," he remarked with dark humour, "she's even less forgiving of inconvenient scruples than I am." He stopped at the entrance. "I know you don't want to sell sex, so you want my suggestion?"

"I asked for it," she said, her face feeling so warm. Her skin was pale, like most of the other pampered nobles who wasted their life away indoors and under parasols, and every time she blushed she hoped it wouldn't show.

He took a moment, pondering the possibilities before answering. "Go to the tavern. There's a spot there where they're always lookin' to hire folk for various things. Always dangerous things. Costly. Never easy." He shrugged his shoulders. "That's your best bet, I'd say."

She nodded, and almost looked happy with the "assignment." It was something that used her skills, her abilities. The ones that had failed her not long ago, but still. It was better than... She stopped her thoughts, thinking about the rumours and stories about the woman she was going to meet.

"So... Thia is... *the* Thia?"

He turned and briskly trotted up into the building at a quick pace. "The one and only!" he called out.

25

THE NOBLES

Caprice's wait for her father to visit through the secret entrance in the library was agonizing. The time spent with that overbearing Viscount was wearing on her. The lack of freedom, the anxiety and doubts...

She lingered in that old library, staring at the false shelf where she knew the secret entrance lay. Where was he? He should have been there already!

Her own thoughts were rattling about in her head so frantically it took her a while to hear the scratching at the entrance. The pushing and futile movement. "Daddy?" she murmured, getting up and moving to it. She rested her ear to the wood and heard the movements on the other side, of someone trying to push the entrance open in futility.

What was going on? She pulled back and her eyes darted about, and it was then she noticed it. It should have been apparent to her sooner, but she'd been so consumed with her worries! Nails had been driven into the secret passage, sealing it shut tightly. They were driven in so deep she couldn't conceive how she could get them out without risking detection, and the inevitable attention of the Landsreck guards.

Worry ate at her, but it was then she saw it. Through the very narrow space along the floor a scrap of paper was pushed through. There was barely room for it, and the writing was made with a pencil, the kind carried in a pocket to make quick notes, the handwriting familiar but obviously hurried.

Child,

There is more going on than we realize. The Court is full of rumours that if we do not find a resolution with the Rensfords, the Queen shall pursue a case against us for the death of the Duke.

We've grown too powerful too fast. We have made many new enemies.

Destroy this note.

It ended there.

Immediately she began tearing it into pieces, and her heart pounded in her chest. He was supposed to come with solutions. Answers. She crumpled the splintered note in her palm as she walked quickly out of the library. What was she supposed to do? Walled up inside this mansion with a man no better than her late husband?

Still, she would never cry. Not over this. Not over any of it.

26

THE SOLDIERS

*T*he outpost was about the finest of its kind, which is to say it was worn, barely more than makeshift, and poorly planned out. Though it sprawled larger than most, owing to its proximity to the main supply lines for the front. Altogether Major Kelifron estimated it held up to a hundred troops, with the possibility to hold a division if necessary.

No place ever held its maximum capacity of troops though. Not for long, at least.

It was part civilian trade station, part military outpost in practice. The empty bunks were rented out to traders to recover some costs, and the locals and merchants valued the safety that came with operating safely under the watchful presence of the Union troops.

What should have been a wall around the place, however, was little more than a ramshackle series of broken barriers, poorly maintained. For in all the Endless War there had not been a single major break-through at the front lines that had jeopardized anything this far in the rear since the nearly mytho-logical early years. A wall would only serve to keep out bandits, but no bandits would be foolhardy enough to directly challenge the state so.

"There's no excuse for this," spoke the severe Major to his adjutant as they passed through the entrance, his piercing eyes soaking in the ill-prepared nature of what could've been a fort with a bit more due diligence. "We have to be kept at the ready. They may not suffer a Kron attack, but there are other dangers closer to heart." He cast a brief look to Lien-a'sa on her horse as the pair rode in front of the other two men, who were busy back mending the cart and staking out the road.

She thought better than to argue as her gaze met his. He was quite attractive when he was upset. She hid her smile well, though, and gave him a stern nod in return. "A little time and effort would go a long way. They have no pride in their work."

The half elf was nearly as severe as him, with her fair hair tied back tightly and her clear blue gaze. Her jawbone and eyes were sharper than a human's, and those pointed ears gave her away to any who cared.

"It's about that and more," he said to her as they headed in through the miniature village of tin-sheet-roofed homes and buildings, the sound of the little makeshift marketplace in the late-afternoon sun carrying to them. "A state of readiness keeps the men sharp, feeling purposeful. It places a feeling of awe, security, and fear in the people. Instead, they see us looking weak, lazy, and vulnerable. Oh yes, the bandits won't take advantage of that. They know that though they might take a quick jab at us through such installations and succeed, they'd be tracked down later and made to pay. But what of those who don't fear reprisals, Lieutenant? What of those who need what we hold here more than they feel they need their lives?"

It was a test question. He did that to her routinely. Put her to the test to grade her insight. Hendrik Kelifron was never satisfied with performance, not truly. There was always better to be achieved. It's what made him such a great survivor.

He had a point that few ever would think of. Including herself, if she was being honest. Her gaze moved forward, thoughtfully, as she stared over the ears of her horse. Lives were cheap. She knew that as well as any. Even she'd lived longer than most, and she was still a babe according to some.

It was as if she was seeing the world through new eyes, and she tried not to dismiss it. There was no reason for her not to scoff, to laugh him off. There was no group more cohesive than those few that routinely got themselves killed just to make a point.

"It never hurts to maintain an air of strength," she finally agreed.

As they approached the stables, the Major dismounted without waiting for aid, the spry officer moving and taking the reins before going to her horse and doing the same, entirely ignoring the dirty stable hand. "Why do you think the rebels do things like throw their lives away on fool's errands like assassinating the Queen, Lieutenant?" Was it another test question? No, he answered for her. "Because they fear the power of the state. They feel in their hearts anything more would be foolish and doomed. They peck at the body of power because that is all they can envision."

He could make such thoughtful gestures, letting Liena'sa off her horse before guiding the two to the army-reserved slots near the end. "What happens when we stop maintaining that air of strength you just spoke of then?"

"They peck harder," she responded, staying near to him. Even for someone of her station, she was cautious around outsiders. He was, in many ways, her protection. Her security.

"Though I think the fact that the assassin failed bodes well. It will be even better once you find her."

The look he gave her as he straightened his uniform was of disapproval. She'd failed that test question, she realized immediately. "They dream bigger, Lieutenant." He led her on, giving the half-asleep stable hand a kick in the shin. "Tend to the horses there. And give it your best." The harshness of his tone brooked nothing less than that.

"Y-yes, sir!" he said, scurrying off, leaving the pair to continue their journey.

"They dream bigger. And as for the assassin? Her capture won't solve anything, or help anyone... but us," he remarked sternly, striding towards the central station as if he were going to tear it down with his bare hands once he got there. "But in this case, that's enough."

"Yes, sir." Her brows furrowed in the centre as she easily kept his pace. She was used to it by now. "But if those like her understand they'll fail and get caught, wouldn't that keep them in line? For all but the suicidal, I mean."

"Or," he responded, "it makes them realize that a better hope rests in acting together for once. Trust me, Lieutenant. I know how they think."

27

THE REBELS

here were a lot of people waiting, though not what Rosa would've expected.

The building seemed to serve as the command hub of the city.

And brothel.

It was teeming with scantily clad men and women, hanging on and taking clients to the various rooms of the place. It was jarring to see herself brought to so seedy an environment.

Marin didn't slow down though. He kept going, and after pushing through a thick, red velvet curtain, he opened his arms. "Been too long," he said as he approached the elven woman that stole all the focus of the room.

It wasn't hard to understand why. Even though

there was flesh everywhere, what she wore was both scandalous and modest considering the surround-ings. The gown reached the floor and was a smooth, almost shimmery material that Rosa had seen back in the City. It hugged her body and dipped terrifyingly low between her breasts.

As Thia turned to hug Marin, Rosa saw that it was even lower in back, revealing the line of her ass to the room. Rosa felt dirty just looking and dropped her eyes to the floor.

"It's good to see you in one piece again." Her words were genuine as she pushed back some of the blonde hair from the elven man's face. "I barely see you anymore."

After ending their warm embrace, Marin smiled to the lovely woman. "I know," he said softly, with more familiarity and fondness than she'd ever heard from the man. "Doesn't mean I don't think of you though," he remarked with a kiss on her cheek that touched the corner of her lips.

It was fleeting, but he gestured to Rosa. "And no doubt you've heard about my companion by now," he said.

"Of course," she said as she turned, her green eyes sparkling as they trailed up and down Rosa's figure. "Quite beautiful." Thia stepped forward, pushing the knotty ponytail off of Rosa's shoulder.

"You must be exhausted. I'd say with a little rest you'd be as perky as anything."

The noblewoman didn't back away, didn't dare insult the elven woman as she stared up at her. She didn't know how it was possible for one person to be so attractive. With her deep-brown hair and those wide, exotic eyes, she was beginning to understand where the rumours came from.

And that didn't even touch on the fact that her body was to die for.

Marin stepped in, a hand casually upon Thia's hip and waist as he whispered to her so Rosa couldn't hear. "She's not interested in working here," he said, knowing the disappointment that was likely to cause in the business-minded woman.

Thia's hand withdrew and she looked to Marin as if she hadn't heard right, a brow arching. "We'll discuss later," she said breezily as her gaze returned to Rosa. "Why don't we see about finding you a place to spend the night, get you a proper bath and we'll have a chitchat in the morning, alright, doll?"

Rosa nodded dumbly as her blue eyes went between the two curiously.

Marin gave a warm—almost dreamy—smile to the legendary woman. "Thanks," he said simply, though the word seemed to carry a great deal of weight. He turned towards Rosa and touched a hand upon her shoulder. "Hope you appreciate that," he said, though there was no way Rosa could appreciate the significance of it all.

Suddenly Rosa felt incredibly self-conscious, and she shifted in her leather boots.

"Thanks," Rosa said in return, taking in a deep breath. "You have no idea how much I could use a bath right now." Thia laughed, placing her hand firmly on the other woman's shoulder, and even though they were almost the same height, Rosa seemed so much smaller.

"I'm off to visit Terrel. I've not seen him in ages," Marin said, waving good-bye to Thia and blowing her a kiss. "We'll talk later."

"Ta-ta." Thia blew a kiss back, her thick hair looking perfect even as she moved. Every little motion seemed so practiced to make herself look as amazing as possible.

"Terry," called the elven mistress to one of the gentlemen who served the clientele outside the velveteen den, "take our guest to get cleaned up."

The young man bowed and did just that, escorting Rosa out of the room.

Her new guest was barely gone when Thia recognized the heavy footsteps reverberating through the marble floor. From behind her another set of velvet drapes pulled aside, and the towering hulk that emerged, appearing terrifyingly out of place in the refined hall.

"So that's the little noble your boy hedged his bets on and lost, hrmmmh?" came the growling voice of the massive, brutish man, his body coated in fur, his face wolfen. A half man, half beast. One of the lycanthropic breed of humans, dressed in but a leather harness and kilt as he loomed behind Thia.

"Mhm, and it seems she's too good to be useful to me, as well." Thia's red lips quirked. "We'll see how we can persuade her. She has a beautiful figure."

A deep rumble emanated from low within the monstrous brute's chest, and he reached out, placing a large hand upon Thia's hip, the sharp, dagger like claws threatening her waist with their pointed tips as he leaned down, nostrils flared at the elven woman's scent. "If she's not interested in working for you, my pet"—he licked along his fanged maw—"perhaps I have an even better idea for her."

Thia's eyes fluttered closed at his touch and her entire body went soft against him. "Oh, do tell, my love."

The black fur of the towering behemoth bristled, and his grasp about her waist tightened as he parted his mouth and nipped at the elven woman's neck. "It can wait," he said in his bestial voice, his other clawed hand coming around and resting on her thigh as he tugged that beautiful dress up her leg. "But I can't any longer."

She smiled and nodded, her smooth skin and fine dress at his mercy as she pressed into him. "Then we'll have to see to urgent matters first," she agreed, and her palms moved to the back of his hands. He was so strong behind her, and she knew there was no saying no. Not that she ever wanted to.

His knees bent, and it brought the misshapen man closer to her height as he leaned over her back, pushing her towards the nearby countertop. The sounds of sex permeated the place, even back to the elven mistress's lavish office, though the heated breathing of that wolf-man as he bent her and pulled her dress up over her ass, exposing the swell of flesh, was strangely out of place. Though with the way his throbbing male need pressed through his kilt and against her, there was no mistaking it for anything but the heavy breathing of desire.

She had no shame as she pushed back against him, her voluptuous body displayed for him as she spread her legs. Her arms braced her weight against the counter, but she knew it wouldn't be enough. Not to take the brute of a man behind her.

Her bare slit already glistened with need as she pushed herself up on her tiptoes, wriggling back and forth against his hidden cock.

It didn't remain that way long however, for a simple flick of his thumb loosed the leather kilt about his hips, and it fell away promptly. Revealed beneath, the heavy, enormous length of throbbing, veiny cock pushed up between her legs. It didn't spring with the intensity of a smaller organ, for with its heft, the weight of that blood-engorged member gave it a slow rise as its heated flesh touched her wet slit.

A low growl rumbled in her ear as he ground himself against her sex and angled his own hips, eager to have the elven woman that was every bit as beautiful as he was monstrous.

She was known far and wide for her skills and abilities. She'd sold herself to men that were handsome, charming, rich. Men that promised they'd take care of her, that gave her intense orgasms and devoted touches.

Yet the hunger she felt for any other man couldn't compare to her need for the beast. For his huge cock and dangerous claws. No human, no elf could promise to do to her what he did, and her smooth slit was soaking wet with her lust.

To say he speared her honeyed cunt would've been false. He practically bludgeoned it with that broad, flared crown of his, battering her labia as he forced that gargantuan girth into her narrow, elven cunt.

With each battering buck of his hips, he let loose a snarl or a growl, his claws digging into her pristine flesh as he forced his throbbing, veiny shaft into her with an urgent need that was nearly heedless of his monstrous strength and ferocity.

She screamed and her sounds mingled with the other moans of her brothel. He was exquisite.

No man could cause her pain like he could, not just by fucking her. She felt like she was being torn apart, and her legs spread wider to try to accommodate him. It was fruitless, however. The only thing that would help him impale her fully was brute strength, which he had no lack of.

"Yes!" she cried, but it was filled with anguish. "Fuck!"

As he forcibly crammed more of that inhuman cock into her womanhood, she could feel the twinge of pain as each throb of desire in him flowed through its length. He bucked harder, plowing deeper into her by sheer force, grunting as his broad, muscled chest puffed out, his shoulders back as he rutted into her.

His heavy balls swayed as he managed to force her narrow canal wide enough to thrust.

"Oh fuck. Oh fuck." The prim elf was, by all appearances, a business woman. Stern. Powerful. Being pounded by the beast behind her, though, stripped it all away. It left her in ruins, exposed for what she truly was. Her cunny was flooded with arousal, puffy and swollen for his attempts to impale her, and even the thick honey that welcomed him wasn't enough to make it much easier.

It was exquisite.

The battering of her puffy folds, the abuse of that needful quim by his brutish savaging. She was slammed to the counter again and again, her legs left as wobbly stems as his claws dug into her flesh and he pounded his climax into her with a thunderous bellow that reverberated through the halls with each spurt of virile seed.

She was left haggard and panting, feeling so full of him, of his cock, of his seed.

As they both came down from the high of their quickie, and before he even had a chance to pull out, she gave a soft moan. "So tell me of your plans for Marin's present."

28

THE FRONT

Caslian's face was bandaged up as she sat cross-legged behind the medical tents, facing those endless rows of supply crates, coffins, and makeshift structures. Yet despite the care she'd received in the clinic, her face still stung.

"The tainted rain got into it," she recalled the medic on staff saying in his practiced voice. "The Kron must make those rockets special to do just that, because once that smoke gets into the rain clouds and the drops seep into a wound... it never quite heals right. Ask any number of men and they'll tell you." And he scratched a small, open sore on his own forehead, that she'd never noticed before beneath his bangs.

It had been dwarfed by her own new facial scar, however, which was deep, bright red, and promised to never heal. She had to dwell on that, alone, behind the tent. A permanent mark to remind her.

That, more than anything, was what she didn't understand. She could rationalize their need, their carnal use of her, even if she would never forgive them for it.

But to harm her in such a malicious way, for no reason at all... She had to force her fingers to stay away from probing it, from touching it, but every time her face screwed up to cry, it burned the wound. Instead she simply stared ahead, reflecting on the cruelties of her own comrades, and fought the urge to end it all.

Caslian had never been a malicious girl. Her parents had always taught her to see the best in everyone, but there was nothing in them.

That was the only thing that kept her hanging on, though: the foreign need for revenge. To see them as hurt as they'd hurt her.

She was so lost in her own misery that she could've missed it, that sound of shuffling booted feet. The heft of a much larger man moving towards her on the well-trodden, dry dirt.

Her recent experience would never allow that to go unnoticed though.

As a medic and private, she was not given a pistol to carry. She had to make do with a personal knife that was given out to all conscripts as that dark silhouette rounded the corner, approaching her from a dozen meters away.

Her fingers wrapped around the butt of her knife and she was still surprised that her vision didn't burn and blur over. It was the type of thing that might have made her lose it at one point, but no more. Tears were another weakness she couldn't afford as she stood and steadied herself. "I'm armed!"

The man paused in the dark shadow of the afternoon sun that filtered through the slow-to-dissipate clouds.

He was hunched and uneven as he stared at her, a hobbled man? Not one of her attackers, no. Couldn't be. The fates wouldn't conspire to make such vile humans suffer so soon. They were not so kind.

He shuffled closer again, but before she could cry out a second time, the voice that carried out was so familiar. "Caslian?" So familiar, but so strained and weak compared to the last time she'd heard the man.

"No," she whimpered, and her hand dropped to her side. There was nothing she could do to stop the tears as she struggled with her inner turmoil. She wanted to turn from him, to run, to never have him see what they'd done to her.

She wanted to spare him that pain.

And at the same time, she was drawn to him. She had lost hope for him, and it knitted her guts that she thought about ever giving up on Levek. Her kinder, more selfless instincts won, and she moved closer to him.

The swarthy man came to her out of the shadows and threw his arms around her, dropping the crude walking stick he carried to hold her. "Cas," he breathed out into her hair as he clutched her delicate body to his. Even in the pain and excitement of the moment, she couldn't help but notice how much gaunter he felt. He had been gone so long!

It felt like she was on fire, but it didn't matter. Not then. Everything about her ached, but she pulled him into her, her delicate frame meeting his. It was almost uncomfortable with how thin they both were, but the fact that he was there outweighed everything.

She let the knife tumble to the ground as she squeezed him, and cruelly her wound pained as her face warped with joy. "Levek?"

The long-absent Sergeant clung to her no less tightly than she did to him. "I worried I'd never see you again," he choked out, his voice so raw and harsh compared to how it had been. "My boys, Cas... all of 'em... but I held on, for you. I had to get back to you. Keep my word. All that mattered to me." His sentences were so chopped and forced, and she realized his voice wasn't weak, it was injured. His throat damaged by something that made talking hard.

"It's okay," she shushed him, hands running down his arms. "You don't have to say anything."

It was as if that rage and anger she'd been holding on to for so long just dripped out of her and in its place was simple relief. She felt like herself again, filled with warmth and affection for this man. Her fingers clung to him.

Levek disentangled from her just enough to be able to drop to one knee, bringing their faces closer together as he embraced her again. Though for that brief moment she got a glimpse of him, that smooth, dark face, gaunter, but unscarred. He'd made it back in some ways better than she'd survived staying behind.

"I heard, Cas. I heard and..." He squeezed her so tight. "I'm sorry I wasn't there."

The idea that people were talking about what happened to her made her stomach churn, and she pulled back away from him. The idea of thinking about it while being touched by him...

"I can't," she whispered, and her open wound tingled with painful sensations. "It doesn't matter."

He didn't hold her there, but he didn't want to let her go, she could tell that much. The tears in his eyes said more. "If we stay any longer, this place'll destroy us both, Cas," he pleaded with her in his strained voice. "It'll crush our souls if it doesn't kill us first."

"That's what the front lines do to people." Even she was surprised by the hardness in her tone. "You should have just left me, Levek. Got yourself out of here."

He took her hands in his, and she felt the strange feeling of broken or missing fingernails. "Come with me," he pleaded. "Come with me now, while there's still time. While there's still some of us left worth saving, Cas. Please." His eyes were so wide. So pleading.

She didn't feel like there was anything worth saving, and her head dropped. Her flaxen hair brushed her cheek and it made her itch. "They'll just do it to someone else. Unless I get them back."

Levek's hands nearly slipped from hers, and he stared in quiet bafflement. The depth of his shock and sorrow written in that mourning gaze.

"There'll always be men like them, Cas. There... there is nothing for us to do to stem the flow of their cruelty," he said with some shred of weak hope to his gravelly voice.

"I don't care about men like them. I care about them!" She could feel her temper begin to rise again, the force of it making her knees tremble. She'd always been such a calm and optimistic person, but they'd taken what she was and twisted her. "They didn't have to cut me! Or throw away my clothes! They told me not to tell anyone, but they took away everything I had that could have kept their secrets 'cause they don't care. They know everyone knows, and they don't care."

There were tears in his eyes, and his hands shook. "Cas..." He tried to speak, his voice failing him then. "Don't let them take your innocence from you." And she realized he didn't mean the innocence that most meant when they spoke of young women like her. "Don't let them rob you of your goodness... taking a life, any life is—" He broke off with the strain.

Her jaw tightened and she felt like her throat was being choked off. Even still, the idea of disappointing Levek cut through her. She hated those men with such passion, but to know that it was hurting the man she adored was even worse. Her body trembled and she took a step back away from him, because she couldn't bear to be near to him. For a moment, a brief, fleeting moment, she hated him.

Hated the fact that he was back, that there was someone who cared about her. Someone she could disappoint.

She loved him, she realized. She'd thought him dead, and now he was here in front of her and all she could think of was how much she hated to make him upset.

29

THE MATRON

Aleena didn't know what to make of the band of raiders. They were not what she expected. They did not look scruffy and world weary as the ones at the cabin had. At least... they hadn't when she first arrived, but after the buzz of their initial arrival with the Chief, it started to seem to her as if more and more of them were looking as she would've expected: hairy and wind blasted.

Was it just the few oddly ethereal ones that stuck out at first, pushing the others out of notice?

It was hard to say.

Though one thing was for sure, the look they were giving her and her two Kron was mixed, but almost all amazement.

"We were betrayed yet again by those Kaliak

dogs!" bellowed their leader, who had not so long ago tried to kill Aleena.

One of the raiders called back, "Is there no depths of shame to which we won't subject ourselves beneath these usurpers?"

Disquiet rippled through them all in their assortment of furs, though still she noticed a great deal of eyes upon her as they conducted their little gathering.

"No!" replied their leader. "I say we are done being conned by them! They drove us out of our lands long eons ago, and now have the nerve to cheat us out of trade deals for the fruits of our own heritage! I am done being the voice of reason and calm with them!"

He was worked into a fury, she could see, but from out of the crowd—damn, she could almost not make out a single smooth, beautiful face anymore!—a voice arose. "What of the woman and those... Kron you brought back? You bring outsiders in unannounced?"

The uproar to that was confused, curious, not entirely angry.

"She and her minions spared me. They were tricked by the Kaliak same as we. And revenge is to be theirs as much as ours."

"But she's not of our kind!" came the voice again, though she couldn't see what one exactly.

"You know in ancient times we worked side by side with the elves!" retorted the leader.

"Until they betrayed us too!" came the response from out of the crowd as the source emerged. A young, almost fae man, the sole beautiful one of the lot, with skin fair, eyes black, and long, wavy hair of white. He didn't hide himself. Not at all. And that was enough for her to put the pieces of the puzzle together.

Aleena had always been obsessed with the past of her people. As heir to a noble lineage that was all but wiped out, she had long dreamed of reclaiming what was hers. But more than that, she had studied the dead histories, even beyond the beginning of the eternal war.

It was said in the ages past, when the elven throne still reigned in its northwestern corner, that they had allies of their own. One was a mystical race of shifters. They were spies and even assassins for the elven court, because they could change their appearance without aid of magic—not that magic existed, of course—and she realized she was now looking upon one of them. A whole hidden clan of them in fact!

"Not betrayed," she had to say. "We were victims of betrayal then, as I am now. And with the elven throne crushed, our empire fell beneath the boot heel of the humans."

The pale elf was short for her kind, but the way she stood—she hoped—made her seem larger and more powerful. She had a practiced way about her graceful motions, and she took a step forward. "They hoped your leader would kill me, or I kill him. Either way, they would have one fewer problem in this world. I'd say that's enough for a temporary truce."

Shifters such as these had once bowed before the elven throne, having no rulership of their own. She could see some glimmer of the past in their eyes as they stared at her, the anger mostly diminished, even in the black eyes of that one fiery upstart.

He turned his gaze upon their Chief. "And what then? There are too many of the Kaliak for us to conquer or claim all their lands for our own. So we strike back for our revenge and... what?"

"Revenge shall have to be enough... for now," replied their leader, and that seemed to be enough for most of them as they cheered and picked up their weapons.

Aleena couldn't help but smile.

This was turning out better than she could have hoped. They'd be thirsty for more after this, and if she played her hand just so...

Aleena spoke quietly to the leader, "I know the

one that set us up, but only just, and he has no love for me. I can take him though, should you provide enough distraction by killing his men."

The dark-haired Chief gave her a firm nod. "It'll be done."

30

THE NOBLES

Perhaps most grating of the realities of her imprisonment was seeing the young Viscount actually socialize with the guards. The shameless nerve of the man, to consort with the lowborn so brazenly, currying their favour with some offerings of comfort and treats. Smiling and sharing jokes with them.

She spied as he shook one of their hands before they returned to their duty post. He turned about and caught sight of her, a wry smile on his face as the door shut behind them, leaving them alone.

"Ah, good morning, young miss Ellefor." He purposely used her old family name, striding down the hall towards her slowly.

"Good morning, child Rensford," she bit back

before she remembered her plan. Well, the one that required her to be, at the very least, marginally kind to him. Though as she looked over him with her skeptical gaze, she even wondered at that. It was a long shot, no matter how she treated him, she decided, but that wouldn't deter her.

"I see you're making good friends with those you'll..." Her teeth grabbed her tongue. *Play nice, Caprice,* she chided herself. Her entire life had been filled with nothing but scorn for those not of her circle, however, and it was proving more difficult than she'd initially thought. "I presume you want something of me?"

The stately-looking Viscount in his velvet vest with silk shirt beneath gave her a mildly amused look. "Me? Of you?" he remarked in exchange, lifting a hand to idly stroke over his cravat as he looked her over in turn. "Well, I suppose some pleasantries are in order. Being family and all in the technical sense... for now, that is." He smiled to her. "I trust your evening was pleasant then?" he said in a questioning voice.

She'd spent most of her night primping herself and bathing, finding the entire thing to be even more dull than usual as the hours dragged on. The fine gown she wore was as scandalous as ever—she would not let him make her ashamed of her body—

and the tight, black corset pressed her breasts up and made her emerald necklace slip into the crevice.

"I must say, being a prisoner of someone who despises me has never been more fun."

"Mm," he began, showing no sign of being afflicted by the same disposition that he inferred his uncle had as he took an eyeful of her bust. "I imagine it's quite a step above your last period of captivity. However brief it might have been," he said to her. "Though until the time is up or you simply give in and admit you'll never bear the offspring of that wretched old monster, we're both stuck here."

"I'm told patience is one of my many virtues." Caprice smiled at the man, but even that couldn't disguise her tempered rage. She wanted to be free of all of this, to be able to live like a Queen. To go to balls, and drink of the finest wines. "And what are your plans today? To torture me with your disbelief?"

It was strange how fast it happened, he leaned in towards her, his one palm slamming to the wall over her shoulder as he spoke to her quietly in a low voice. "Knock off the pretense, little princess. We both know the truth, so save your theatrics for those who might have a shot at buying it. Alright?" Though the way he said that in his dark, ominous voice as he towered over her so menacingly made it sound like a command. Not a question.

Her dark eyes widened as she stared up at him, mouth agape. She managed to recover quickly, tearing her gaze from him and looking, instead, under his arm. She felt her body tremble with fright, and she cursed how much that old bastard had shattered her nerves. Her neck and back were so tense, but still she refused to cry.

She was still prideful.

Looming over and around her, so tall and powerful, he spoke to her casually in that low voice. "What makes you so stubborn, hm?" He brought a hand up, the backs of his knuckles grazing her cheek brazenly. "Do you think that when this is all through, that the Queen will still give you some portion of the Rensford estate and it'll still be worth it?" He gave a cold smile. "That won't happen, child." And that word so echoed her father. "The Queen won't see a sliver more of power go to your family. Not now."

"And what, you wish for me to admit a falsehood and have you evict me like some common... whore?" She crinkled her nose, using his own word. "And I told you not to touch me," she added on, her voice hard. "You only wish to try to run me out of here."

The cold young man didn't heed her words. "Oh, I expect you to resist. You'd disappoint me if you didn't," he said with a smile, those knuckles of his brushing over her flawless cheek some more, back towards her dark hair. "A struggle just makes the victory that much more satisfying to savour. You just don't seem to know what you're doing. Holding on a prayer perhaps?" he remarked with an uneven smile. "Shame, you're a pretty one. Especially as far as eligible princesses go," he remarked with amusement.

Her jaw tightened as he pawed at her and her resolve wavered. She'd been bluffing about so many things, hanging on the hope that given just a little more time, she'd come up with a plan. A solution. Something that would make her father endlessly proud of her.

"I know what I'm doing," she lied once more.

"That's a weak lie," he responded in that dark, low voice of his, so calm now despite its ominous tone. "You don't. You don't have the faintest clue what you're doing on your own." He tilted his head slightly, eying her with his cold grey gaze as he took a lock of her dark hair in his fingers behind her head, the other hand tracing along her jawline toward her mouth. "Was it the mother that made you so reliant on the instruction of another? Father?" And his lips curved into such an amused grin at that. "You need a big, strong daddy to tell you what to do?"

"I told you not to touch me. Who was it who taught you not to heed those protests? Your uncle?" Caprice's body tightened, for even as she was saying it she knew she'd crossed the line and would pay for it. It felt so good, though, for the briefest of seconds.

The grim look that crossed his face was terrifying. His hand went from her face to her neck, and he clenched her throat shut in one hand as he glowered so hard at her. "You should have got on your knees and begged me for your chance at getting out of this with something to show. You should have prostrated yourself and fought, not been a snide little bitch who was too full of her own ego to make the slightest effort to hold on to this." He ground his teeth and glared. "You're weak. Soft. And worse yet, you aren't even clever."

She couldn't come up with a retort as his hand tightened around her, but she didn't struggle against him. She wouldn't. Feeling his anger was almost cathartic in a way because of how she'd had to hold back her own rage.

Still, as her face began to redden, her hands lifted to his arms, grabbing onto him.

"You've lived a pampered existence," he spat out bitterly, unperturbed by her struggling. "You think you suffered because you spent so short a time with that piece of shit. But you don't know what suffering is, you little bitch. You don't know what it is to have to work for your successes every day of your life." As her face turned so blood red and her lack of air became a panic, he let her go abruptly. "If you had the slightest idea, you'd have seen me as a generous opportunity."

She coughed away from him, her delicate body trembling under that tight corset and her eyes watered from lack of breath. When she finally managed to get some breath into her lungs, her gaze narrowed at his. Her pale hand went to her throat, rubbing along the silver chain that the emeralds hung from to try to soothe her pain. "I saw how thrilled you were to have me here. I couldn't imagine doing enough for you to overcome that." He took hold of her hair with his other hand, pulled her into an upright position by it, tugging those strands against her scalp as he forced their gazes to meet again. "You see? You're weak. You give up so easy. Like the pampered little porcelain doll you are," he remarked, and then she heard it: true distaste on his voice. It wasn't the anger or sternness of before. It was almost disappointment instead. And as his eyes trailed down over her well-presented body, there was no longer the desire of before.

The pain prickled her scalp and she rose up on tiptoes, her house slippers doing little but making her feel precariously off balance. The fact that he could see through her, down to the things she denied about herself, was like salt in a wound, and her breath quickened as her hands dropped to her side. She pressed the palms against the wall behind her as she stared at him.

"You'd have me beg only to feel the joy of refusing me," she lamented, and she was reminded of just how right he was. She hated to try anything if there was a risk of failure. Of being unable to save face.

The young Viscount leaned in so that he was but a couple inches from her, barely any space between them at all. "I'd take more joy from you than that," he remarked, but it wasn't meant to be reassuring. The darkly lecherous look on his face said he had more thoughts than simple refusal. Though his fingers curled her hair tighter in his hand, and she felt herself near his face because of it. "But not from a weak-willed little doll." He had hovered a hair's breadth from her lips, but abruptly he pulled away and relinquished her hair. "There's not enough fire in you to make it interesting," he said, turning and walking away.

"I'm not weak. I lived with him, didn't I?" She had no idea why it bothered her so much, but it did. He'd bruised her pride, her ego, and dug his claws into her cunning. She felt raw and exposed, as if she couldn't keep anything from him, and it was like bugs crawling on her.

All she got was a derisively singular laugh from him as he receded down the hall. Her time with the old man must have been so short compared to what he likely endured.

"You should be grateful!" she shouted past him before collapsing down in a heap, her corset digging into her breasts and ribs. Her ego kept her from running after him, from begging him for his blessing, but her hope had dwindled. What now?

THE SOLDIERS

"Furthermore, Captain, I want to see this place got into shape. Once your men are done searching the surrounding countryside for my targets, they'll start to get the walls and fortifications into place." The Major was in no mood for disagreement with a subordinate, not after the shabby state he'd seen the camp in.

"But sir, my men are hardly construc—" The portly officer was cut off immediately.

"But nothing, Captain. Your men need discipline, to keep them ready. We are in a war for our very right to exist, and we face opposition at home as well as from across the trenches."

As the Major gave his speech Liena'sa saw a messenger come up the stairs and head towards the office, about to interrupt. She knew better than that, however, and blocked his way, keeping Kelifron from having to break off his speech.

"What is it, Private?" she insisted sternly.

It caused the young man to halt and stare at her with some confusion. "I've got a message just delivered," he said breathlessly, having run up the stairs with his own growing size impeding him. "For the Major," he explained, holding out the sealed official envelope of the state. It must've just arrived by official courier to the base.

Liena'sa took it and waved her dismissal. The fair half-elf woman was used to Kelifron's moods, good or bad, but she knew better than to break that seal. Instead, she went back to his side and waited for a pause before handing it to him.

"Issue the orders, Captain." He ended his stern lecture abruptly, sending the rotund man off down the stairs. Still wearing the expression of the severe, intimidating superior officer, he looked to Liena'sa. "What is it?" he asked, taking the envelope, and plucking a letter opener off the desk.

He took out the letter and she could see the most minute flicker of change in his expression as he saw what was sent. The Major was not easily surprised or perturbed.

"What's wrong?"

Very calmly, Hendrik took the letter over to the Captain's desk. There he unshielded the lamp and lit the corner of the letter on fire, taking great care to spread the flame and burn the whole thing. "Our prey has gone to ground," he said. "They don't know where, but I can find out."

How many places could one scared woman hide? Liena'sa's lips turned upwards as she walked after him. "I don't doubt that. You're quite resourceful."

His gaze turned to hers, hard and demanding. The complement rolled off him simply because his mind was turning, and it wasn't the time for such things. Oh, he could use her for his enjoyment, but not when there was work to be done.

"Go get us some civilian clothes for us both, Lieutenant. Something worn and travel ready. We're going to go after our prey, down and dirty."

"Yes, sir."

There wasn't even a flicker of disappointment across her elven features as she turned to do just as ordered. There'd be no point in it.

32

THE REBELS

*L*ife beneath the surface of the world was strange and busy. The people there were always moving, day and night, as neither had much meaning beyond the sun. It kept the secret city safer, Rosa was told, to have the place active around the clock. It made it less vulnerable to surprise.

Though the people there were never still, she found her own journey to have come to a begrudging halt. Everybody had a place, a use, but Rosa had yet to find hers, and she knew patience was not endless. In fact, she'd already been granted more than she reckoned others typically got.

So she began her day again by heading to the tavern once more. The place was always busy, the gruff and world-worn travellers there the type that were always involved in over world missions of trade, raiding, or worse.

At the bulletin board, her distress at seeing no new postings melted into quiet curiosity. She noticed it again then: the strange fungus that seemed to grow on most everything in the underground city. It coated the cavern walls. It coated the buildings. With a poke she felt how strangely spongy it was.

Her reverie was broken by a low, strange voice to her side. "It sops up all the noise. Keeps all our ruckus from bouncin' off the cavern walls until it crushes us all." And with a look she saw the visage of a large figure by the end of the bar. Clad in ragged leathers, he was no man. At least, no ordinary one. The thick, brown fur that poked out of his collar and sleeves revealed him for one of the wolfkin.

She couldn't help but scrunch up her nose a bit, though she'd been trying to reduce her apprehension of the nonhuman among the city.

Still, years of hatred was not easily undone.

"Well, that's good. Not dying. Is there seriously no one in this place that needs anything done?" Each passing day made her more and more aware of her likely place in this society, and she couldn't stand the thought of it. Yet at the same time, the idea of going back into the forest was unthinkable.

Death was better.

Reclined against the bar on one elbow, the bestial man raised a glass of ale and drank before answering her. "Plenty of job notices there," he said, and true enough, though none suited for her, or that she hadn't already been rejected for. "More still, if ya know who ta ask," he added as he dragged his wrist across his maw, wiping it clean. "What're ya lookin' for anyhow?"

"A way to earn my keep that involves more than s —" She bit her tongue. She was supposed to know better than talk ill of that kind of work, but she'd been conditioned to loathe it. That was for people who didn't have her skills. "I can fight."

The tall brute eyed her curiously, as if disbelieving her statement at face value, but he nodded his acquiescence to her claim. "Not many volunteer to go up and fight if they can avoid it. It carries a short life expectancy for most. If yer caught it's back to the front, which is worse'n death. It's undeath, waitin' for the end," he said, his curious, inhuman gaze staring off as the glass dipped in his hand.

It wasn't going to be the front for her. She knew the risks she was taking, and it almost seemed laughable to her that she didn't want to stay beneath where she was safe. All she had to do was sleep with random people.

But that wasn't what she wanted in life.

She wanted to be useful. To do something that she could be proud of.

She wanted to make a real difference, to atone for her failure to assassinate the Queen.

"Well, is that why no one bothers advertising it?"

The wolfish grin he gave her before downing more of his ale spoke of his amusement.

"Raiders who last form tight-knit groups. They don't recruit openly, most of the time," he said in his alien voice, deeper than a normal man's, harsher. "But it's a shit life too, miss. Ya risk a lot, holdin' on for those brief moments you get ta come back here an' rest between missions. But all the while ya tryin' ta relax and live, that tickin' clock won't shut up in the back of yer head. S'why so many of 'em blow all their earnings at the 'Town Hall,'" he said, referring to that large brothel she'd been brought to on the first day. "They get less time here, but... makes it more worthwhile for 'em."

He shrugged before draining his glass.

Her lip twitched and her arms folded beneath her chest.

"But they do the shit jobs no one else can do, because they need to be done, right? They're, like, the protectors of this place, in a way."

"Raiders?" He screwed up his face then shook his

head. "Nah, that's the guards you mean. The raiders and guards are two completely different groups. Don't much like each other either. Though there's a lot of former raiders among the guards... an' more than a few shamed former guards among the raiders." He shook his head and said, "The raiders bring some supplies that're hard to get. Can make 'em popular with the right folks. But everyone kinda fears 'em, because there's always tales of how far some of 'em go to get their stuff..."

He let that hang there ominously as he brushed his clawed hand off on his leather jerkin.

Her dark brows knit as she stared at him. She felt so out of place at times, like she didn't have a clue about the world at all, and he certainly wasn't helping. "Well, as far as I can see it, then, this city needs both."

"True enough," he said. "Though I wouldn't tell either of them that," he added with a slight grin that exposed a few fangs. Brushing off his two hands, he sat up straight and offered one out to her. "Faze," he said.

Her lip curled again as she glanced to his clawed hand, hesitating a moment before accepting it daintily. Her noble customs were hard to break, even in this place. "Rosa."

The hesitance did not go unnoticed, and the large

beast of a man took a deep breath and sighed just a bit before squeezing and shaking her hand carefully.

"Not much of a fan of my kind, huh, Rosa?"

"Don't take it personally." It was a bit harder than she intended, but as she took her hand back she stood a bit straighter. She was still in the same leather outfit she'd arrived in, and she'd been keeping her hair pinned back out of her face in order to seem more professional. "You just kind of look like someone that could bite my face off."

The toothy smile he gave was hardly reassuring on that front, but he said, "A pretty face like that, now why would I ever wanna bite that off?" He patted the stool beside him in invitation. "What's yer poison, Rosa?"

"I doubt my 'poison' is available here, so whatever you're— Whatever most humans have," she corrected herself as she moved to the seat and slid onto it. Her legs crossed at the ankle, but it strained the leathers and she stopped fighting it, instead hooking her feet behind the wood.

"Two ales," he said to the bartender, sliding the coins across for the drinks as they were put down before them.

"Y'know," he started up again, speaking to her more personally now that she sat beside him. "Our peoples aren't so different. They say there was a time we were once like you," he remarked, lifting his ale. "Well, not exactly like you, I'm sure," he added with amusement. "They say long ago, before the war even began, we were nobles. Part of the royal bloodline of the humans."

She scoffed.

"Who's they? One of your kind?"

He looked amused at her disbelief.

"Our elders," he said. "They still wear the insignia upon their armour to this day," he added with a nod. "We were cursed though. They say we were exiled unjustly, and struck with some dark curse that made us look like I do. And it's carried with us ever since."

"Cursed by who? Who could do that to a race for, like, eternity?" She didn't believe a word of it, and she felt her pale skin begin to redden with anger. She was desperately trying to quell it, but he was hitting a sore point with her.

He shrugged his shoulders.

"We were just a family back then. Was ages ago, after all. An' since no human'll breed with us, we've continued on as we are." He eyed her in her near rage. "Ya don't buy it, huh?"

"Of course not," she hissed. "No one has that type of power." She grabbed her ale and began to drink it, if only to try to calm herself down, but it didn't work.

"Besides, with how many of you there are, it couldn't have just been a single family."

To her surprise he slapped her on the back and broke out into a fit of laughter. "Yeah, I don't buy it either," he remarked with amusement. "Little too far-fetched even for a pup, I think. Though it's kinda funny seein' those puffed-up wolven princes stridin' around in their fancy, old-fashioned armours."

Her lip turned up in one corner. "I can only imagine." The idea of such a beast walking around in court finery was funny, in a sad and pathetic way. She paused before downing the rest of her ale and pushing the empty mug away. It tasted like swill to her refined palate and she clucked her tongue trying to rid herself of its lingering aftertaste. "This is what the humans here drink?"

"It's what everyone drinks," he said, finishing off his own following her, not to be outdone. "Ain't the best, but it's better'n what you can get in most places. I should know, I've sampled some from all about. So how desperate are ya for work?"

She paused, her hands going to her knees.

"I'm desperate to do something worthwhile."

"Desperate enough ta work alongside a mangy mutt?" he asked, a toothy smile on his furred face as he watched her.

"Depends on how mangy."

He stared back at her blankly for a while, before breaking into another good-humoured fit of laughter. "Careful, ya might hurt some feelin's I didn't know I had."

"It's good to learn new things about yourself," she retorted, and for some reason he was making her feel more comfortable. Maybe it was just that he wasn't taking himself so seriously, because his face was quite serious enough for her liking. She was trying not to stare at those long fangs. "What were you planning?"

"Planning?" he said with some surprise. "I don't plan. I do." He thumped his chest a bit in amusement. "I run letters, packages, shipments. I scout. I got connections with some groups inside an' out of this city, so I'm the go-to guy for a lot of go-between work. Earns me a decent livin' without near so much danger as the raiders."

"Who do you deal with up there?" she asked skeptically. It sounded a little too good to be true.

"All sorts," he said with a shrug. "When traders are missin' a caravan, they come ta me ta scout it out and see what happened. When someone needs ta get word ta family outside, I take care of it. I got connections with some wolven units, so I some-times trade 'em contraband for a few of their things too. I got a thrivin' lil' business goin' here. A lil' too thrivin' for one man. Even one wolf-man," he joked.

Her eyes narrowed as she stared at him, her head tilting to the side.

"Did someone put you up to this or something?"

"Put me up to it?" He stroked his chin. "No, but I was tipped off about ya, if that's what you mean. Madam Thia herself," he said, sounding like that was quite the ringing endorsement. "But even the word of the world's favourite harlot don't mean nothin' if Faze don't talk to the candidate himself. So here we are," he said with a sheepish smile.

She wasn't sure if she should be touched or impressed, but she was. "So this was some type of... interview or something? Is that what it's called?"

He chuckled gruffly. "Somethin' like that, yeah. I ain't never worked beside no one before, so I'm a might particular over who I'm gonna choose, ya understand."

"Well, I'm glad I started in by insulting you and your people, then."

With another guffaw he slapped her back again.

"Yer rough around the edges, I'll give ya that. But I do need someone who can be serious and focussed. This job is a lonesome one mostly. The, uh, insult part though... we'll have to work on that."

"I don't mind being alone," she reassured him,

straightening her back against his constant rough-housing. "And I can be quite serious. And focussed. I can do this."

"Well, we'll see, huh?" He smiled unevenly, though even the lighthearted beast's merriment had a tinge of menace thanks to those fangs. "First things first though, I'll have ta show ya the ropes. Take ya on some practice runs of my biggest job. That's the one that's most regular, also be easiest ta break ya in on, so you can run it yourself when I'm busy."

"Fine," she agreed. "When do I start?"

33

THE SOLDIERS

ajor Hendrik Kelifron looked like a whole other man in the civilian clothes Liena'sa got for him. The brown vest and coarse cotton shirt didn't fit him as snugly as his uniform, but it was both jarring and somehow fitting to see the man in the worn civilian clothes. He looked natural in them, yet she still couldn't help but think of him as the stern, hard-nosed superior officer who dictated her fate.

With both hands he vigorously mussed up his own hair, giving it a more natural look, in contrast to the usual. He let his eyes drift to hers in the office mirror. "I have something for you," he said and pivoted about towards her.

It was both excitement and apprehension as she watched him stare at her. Her own movements were still controlled, but she was trying to look more casual. It didn't come easy to the woman, since she let her guard down almost as rarely as her commanding officer.

"Oh?" She felt grungy and dirty in the simple clothes she wore, the dark brown making her appear more washed out and tired than she felt. It certainly wasn't as flattering as the outfit he wore, though perhaps she was biased. She caught herself staring at his physique before her gaze returned to his. "Is it something that makes this outfit look good? A torch, maybe?"

He reached into his new shirt and pulled an old cord from around his neck. It had been hidden, out of sight, though she'd noticed it on him before as he changed or the two had gotten naked on rare occasions.

"Not quite," he said, reaching into the tiny brown satchel attached to it. What he pulled out couldn't have been more surprising to her. The tiny little ring was not extravagant and, despite its age and the secret source he pulled it from, could not have been very valuable in material terms. Not by the standards of anyone but the poor, that was.

"Lien," he said softly, reaching out and taking her hand, "you will be my wife." He slid the ring onto her finger, and it was only her own daintiness that allowed it to fit.

She wanted to blow it off, to accept it as part of her cover. Their cover.

Yet the way he spoke to her make her heart pound and her breath hitch. She tried to swallow, but her throat felt constricted, and the softest of smiles flirted with the corner of her lips. Even her unflattering clothes couldn't make that gaze she gave him seem like anything but meaningful.

"Gladly," she managed before clearing her throat, embarrassed.

It was human custom in the capital to give a ring, but then she was half human. He smiled to her in return, surprising her yet again as he cupped her cheek and leaned in, kissing her lips softly.

He had a way of making her head spin, and that gentle, tender kiss managed it more than anything else.

"We're on the run," he said to her softly, explaining their cover carefully. "We fell in love against our families' wishes, and as punishment, I was expelled from their home. With nowhere to live, I lost my factory job, and so was eligible for conscription. But I can't live without you, so we are making a run for shelter somewhere."

"I buy it," she whispered, hungering for more. She didn't know when this thing with him changed from being a habit of survival to something more honest, and that scared her. She didn't realize how hard she'd fallen for him until that moment, and she wanted to throw everything aside. To revel in the feeling.

But they had a job to do, and her palm glided up along his hand. "Lead the way, husband."

He smiled genuinely. It had to be genuine. She'd never seen such warmth in his expression, and it was as if every ounce of the harsh officer in him had melted away as he gazed at her with his steely eyes, filled with emotion.

"I'm Roland Malik, you're Lura Malik." He leaned in, kissed her lips again, slow and longingly, suckling her upper lip awhile before moving to kiss her forehead then embrace her. "And I love you madly, my wife," he added in a low murmur, almost too soft to hear.

There was no purpose to him lying to her. To slipping into his role so readily in the privacy of the room, and her hands went to his back and squeezed.

They were both so stern, so matter of fact. Even their trysts had been harsh.

Maybe that was what they both liked.

"I love you," she murmured back.

"C'mon," he said, still talking so casually, so unlike him. "Need to find someone who can lead us to refuge."

THE NOBLES

The servants had prepared a lovely meal for dinner, the candles lit as the weather outside remained dreary and dark as it had in recent days. Though the most priceless part of it was when Caprice saw the Viscount enter the room and pause with surprise at seeing her there for the first time since their joint housing.

It was odd to see the dashing noble caught so off guard, but he recouped and made his way to the head of the table as usual. "How curious," he remarked simply, unfolding a napkin and draping it over his lap as he pointedly looked at the food rather than her.

She was done up in the same overzealous manner that she always seemed to be. She hated to be seen—

even by him—looking less than her best, and the teal corset nipped in her waist and emphasized her breasts, as usual. She gave him a smile, but it was the look of noble restraint.

Her glass was already filled with a dark, red liquor, but she hadn't drank any of it, instead waiting patiently for him.

"You look well rested."

"I am," he remarked, serving himself from the generous setting of food before them rather than having one of the servants do it for him. "It's my first time in so cozy and lavish a setting in quite some time," he stated, beginning to eat and sparing her nary a glance. "Along the front even the officers don't get much in the way of luxury."

"I had assumed you just liked the fashion," she admitted as she began to cut into her already served food. "It suits you." Her stomach clenched, but she fought the urge to take a sip of her drink, to ruin this so soon.

"That it does," he responded, and truth be told, he fit the style well. His trim figure cut an impressive image. With his hair and severe looks, he looked every bit the image of the ideal officer, portrayed on war posters and murals across the well-to-do sections of the city. Most members of the court would've found it too gauche to imitate the style so closely—an obvious grab for respectability—but it simply suited him so well, it seemed the style was made for him.

"You would know all about that though," he retorted, his eyes on the window as he ate. "You never seem to wear anything that isn't well fitted."

"I'm surrounded by beautiful things. I'd rather not stick out like a sore thumb." She ate slowly, trying to draw out the pleasantness. To see if she could do it.

It was hard.

His gaze slid to her, the steel grey so cold as he watched her across the table. "Somehow I doubt that's what it's about," he remarked, cutting off another piece of his steak fillet and eating it in quiet enjoyment.

"Taking pride in your looks isn't a bad thing," she said, her voice going as cool as his eyes. "I like to look nice."

He nodded his head in quiet acceptance of that.

"Would you take such pride in them were yours not so naturally beautiful to begin with though, I wonder," he mused aloud as he watched her, his expression softened just a hair.

"I imagine I'd have to work harder, in that case." Her eyes fluttered to him, her arched brow raising slightly. She reached her hand for her wine, quickly noting that it trembled, and she instead laid it on the table.

"Mm," he responded simply as he ate, watching nothing but her now. "Is this your new effort then?" he asked across the table. "Are you trying to climb your way out of the hole you're in at long last?" The question was not even malicious. Oddly enough he sounded simply curious, in his own way.

"I'm trying to make this more pleasant." She cursed her fair flesh and the fact that she knew she was blushing. Grabbing the stem of the glass, she brought it to her lips and felt more secure having drunk something. It soothed her rankled nerves, just the act of it.

He didn't respond right away, but after wiping his mouth, he very casually said to her, "The meal would be exponentially more pleasant if you opened that corset another inch or two down the middle." It was amazing how he could say something so vulgar with a straight face, watching her so placidly as he took his own wineglass and sipped. "Do it for me." And those words sounded like a military order by comparison.

She gasped and nearly dropped her drink, her dark eyes going to his. She looked like a deer in headlights, as if that were the least expected thing he could have said.

"You're not... serious?" she asked, a bit of that stern hardness coming back to her own voice. "I'm not a whore, despite your assertion, so if you're trying to prove something to yourself, well, you're wrong."

With a slow, meticulous movement, he lowered his wineglass and placed it back upon the table, dabbing his lips with the napkin again.

"It would improve my disposition," he remarked. Then in his ominously low voice he added, "I said, do it for me." The words were a command, and with the way he gazed at her, he seemed intent that she would not disobey him.

Despite her daring outfits, and her good looks, not another man had gazed upon her breasts. Besides her father, that was. She shifted in her seat, growing more flushed under his constant stare, and her breath quickened, those heavy mounds rising under the press of her corset. "Look, I just want to try being friendly."

He resumed eating, his casual demeanor a bit unnerving with what he was demanding. "Undoing the strings on that corset an inch or two would go a long way towards making me a friendly, amicable man. Now do it. I won't say it again." He raised his brows and peered across at her as he popped another bit of his steak into his mouth, waiting expectantly as if for some fascinating reveal.

Instead, she moved out of her chair. "I'm not going to degenerate myself in front of you, obeying you simply because you think my refusal is weak." Her hand went to the glass of wine and she drank it back, her meal hardly touched. "A weak woman would have said yes to you, and begged you for a place in this manor as your lapdog."

"Convince yourself of that all you like," he remarked to her, flippantly. "But we both know at heart, this is the coward's way out." He looked to her and said as if it were the simplest thing ever, "All I asked for was a bit of breast on display for my enjoyment. Not even a teat. A simple sign of willingness to try"—he gestured to her chair—"because the chitchat certainly wasn't enough of a try. I've done worse than chitchat with those I've barely been able to resist strangling for their crimes."

Her eyes narrowed, her fingertips running the length of her chest, from left to right before she put the empty glass back on the table.

"I've committed no crimes," she said, and she was convinced it was the truth. That old man deserved what her father did to him, and she would have done it again, even knowing she'd gain nothing from it. "I'll be in my room." She could feel the anger rising in her, and she began to breeze past him when he grabbed her, yanking her body so hard she went toppling into his lap, as he had planned it.

Her hand jostled the table as she held on to it, trying to get off of him, but he squeezed her wrist so tight in his grasp, there was no escape as he stared into her eyes.

"Here I was hoping your appearance here was a sign you'd found some fire for life inside yourself," he remarked, letting his eyes roll down from her face to her chest. He reached for the front of her corset, and tugged the strings there, doing for himself what she had refused to obey.

"You know nothing about what I have a fire for." Her words were filled with fury as she tried to hold that thick, teal fabric together and failed. It had been done up so tight that it was an impossible fight without both hands and a lot of concentration.

She was so exposed to him as the corset began to peel away and she squirmed in his lap, desperately trying to free herself.

For the first time since she'd met the unpleasant young Viscount, she watched as his face broke into a genuine smile as she struggled upon him. He enjoyed it. He liked watching her resist him, and he kept her there as she felt his loins stir beneath her.

"Maybe you do have some fire in you after all,"

he remarked, keeping a tight hold on her one arm, refusing to give it back. "And for that, I'll let you spend the remainder of the evening with me in the study, being friendly as can be. We can even discuss the news," he remarked with some slight amusement.

"Screw you," she hissed as she continued to squirm, but it was only causing that fabric to move further away from her body. It threatened to expose her, and she was fighting one measure of lewdness with another. Her head pounded with the frustration, and even the liquor couldn't calm her nerves from this outrage.

The throb of his male excitement beneath her had grown as she tried and failed to fight him off.

"Such a saucy mouth," he remarked with a smile. Then, abruptly before it all fell apart on her, he said, "If you come to my study tonight, I'll be very friendly. Promise," and he let her go, no longer holding her in place atop him.

She scrambled up, holding her corset closed, but it already showed so much of her to him. Her pale flesh along her midsection, her belly button, those inner clefts of her breasts, it was all revealed as she looked to him in astonishment.

It felt like she was walking into a trap, and she tried not to stare at his lap, but she couldn't help it.

His uncle had made life hell for her, but never had he done something like that. Caprice was, for the first time in a long while, stunned into silence.

Without covering his lap or attempting to hide the rather large bulge in his black, pressed pants, he resumed eating, as if nothing untoward had just occurred.

"Come to my study later," he said again. "We'll put those lips of yours to use. And talk," he remarked without a hint of a smirk or wryness. There was something there, something familiar as she watched him. It took her a while, but it occurred to her: her father. The officer's fashion, the calm control. The fire of anger when incited just right. He was similar in so many respects to her father. Not the least of which, his good looks.

She took a step back, feeling dishevelled even though her brown hair was still in place, and the rest of her outfit was properly fitting. Her dark eyes went a bit glossy as she moved past him, fumbling with the strings at the front of her corset.

From one torturer to another.

35

THE FRONT

The food at the frontline camps was far from enjoyable, yet compared to the rations they gave those down in the trenches, it was near palatable. Levek at least enjoyed the warmth of it, having snuck off with his tray to go sit in the private little area Caslian and him had frequented. He had to get his health back up and store some food for the getaway, all of which meant somehow weaselling more food out of the system than they ever conceivably allowed.

The warm beans and ham, however, he ate then and there. He couldn't even make himself wait for Caslian's arrival. The two had to split up on their way to the hiding spot, so nobody would suspect their plans.

So it was that she saw him, crouched in the hidden nook, almost back to his old self, health wise, savouring the rather unimpressive fare.

Sometimes she felt like they'd somehow switched roles. That she'd gotten hard where he had become more needy for affection, but she knew it wasn't true. It was just another barrier she'd erected to try to get herself through this time.

She'd so quickly given up on revenge, now that she had something to live for. Someone to protect.

Caslian was sure that Levek couldn't live without her. That he'd only lived because of her, and she wasn't willing to force him to risk that.

Instead she smiled as she came around him, sitting cross-legged. Her festering facial wound burned, but she ignored it. The pain was so constant it was hard to do anything but live with it.

He smiled up at her, bright and sunny despite it all. He didn't see what was done to her, even the wound that lingered on her face. He just seemed enlightened and inspired by her presence, as if she were the same old Caslian.

"I was thinking..." He glanced back towards the two exits through the little shelter of coffins. "I know a guy on the kitchen crew. I could bribe him with some cigarettes, and he could drop a package of good, easily carried food into one of the refuse bins."

He chewed another mouthful, grinning pleasantly at the thought.

"Will he get caught?" She settled in and began picking at her food, though she wasn't hungry. She just didn't want him to worry. She was back to thinking of others first. Her inherent goodness was so hard to quell, but when she was alone, the rage would overwhelm her. He was her safety net.

He shook his head.

"Stuff goes missing all the time. Impossible to pin it on any one person. Unless it gets out of hand the COs just shrug their shoulders. Not worth their time." He let his fork rest on the plate as he stared down at the small remaining bit of food. "Cas... we should go. Tonight." He hesitated, but added, "They are gonna send me back out again soon."

She just nodded. He'd already convinced her, though not with his words. It was her seeing how broken he was, how much she knew he was afraid. For her.

He had long ago given up on himself, but never on her. Not for a moment.

"I'll get the food and then... then I can come meet you here." He looked over to her, a mix of hope and fear in his eyes. She knew he didn't want to ask his next question. "Can you get a first-aid kit from the medical tent to take with us? We... we don't know what might happen during our escape. It could save our lives."

She simply nodded once again. They were already risking their lives by even talking of escaping. Truthfully, it didn't frighten her like it once had. She wanted to keep going, but only for him.

She smiled through the dark thoughts. "Leave it to me. If I'm not back, leave without me."

"Ain't gonna happen," he said, forking up the last of his pork and beans into his mouth as he gave her a big, goofy grin. Though there was no doubt that he meant it. "If you aren't there on time, I'll come for you. Wherever you are." He shrugged. "If you get caught taking a med kit, you explain that a soldier in the alleyway asked you for help. You lead them there if they wish, and when there's nobody there... you explain you must've been conned."

"I'll get it." The least of her worries was getting caught. Every time he'd seen her she'd forced herself to seem stronger, but she never went anywhere without her knife. She never stopped hearing their voices in her head. She never stopped feeling them over her body.

She never stopped being afraid.

"C'mon, the faster the better," she stated with finality.

36

THE MATRON

Aleena helped lead the makeshift alliance, standing side by side with the leader of the shifters, Britus. Her two Kron followed behind her, lingering close as her devoted bodyguards.

A hush was through all those gathered, for though the lost tribe of shifters were more than her three, they were far less than what the Kaliak huntsmen could field.

The other man that had opposed her aiding the attack watched her suspiciously the whole while.

"What? Do you have a problem?" she said, sick of feeling his eyes bore into the side of her skull.

"Yes," he said simply, standing tall and thick like a bear of a man. "You put your trust in the wrong sorts. And now we have put our trust in you. It is a mistake on both of our parts," he said, not angrily, merely in quiet resignation.

"Save the doubts for after the battle is done, huh?" she said, focusing her gaze back ahead.

"I am Vicalus, and the well-being of my people rests with me. Doubts are almost all I have now," he said in a morose tone.

Aleena arched a brow at the man curiously.

"If you're the leader, then why is Britus in charge?" she asked.

"Because he is the war chieftain. And war is all we know anymore."

"Tough gig," Aleena said, the group of them moving through the snow as they approached the Kaliak village.

Britus gave the hand gesture to come to a halt and everyone stilled. It was night, and there were no sounds of birds or life of any kind. Only the sound of life extinguished, as one of the forward scouts took out a Kaliak guard.

The dead man gave a cry, but it was only short and carried not far enough to reach the village.

The stage was set then, and Britus turned to them, the group huddled about, numbering only a couple dozen.

"We strike fast, hit them hard. No prisoners, we light their barracks on fire and get out. With any luck, we're done before their main forces return from their patrols."

His hard gaze travelled along the assembled.

"It has been a long time since we gambled this much, my kin. Let it not be in vain. Go with caution," he stated.

Aleena and her two Kron thought it hardly a worthy war cry. All the same, it began the battle.

The group moved in on the village, their nimble feet moving over the snow covered ground quickly and relatively quietly. Dawn was still an hour off from full breaking, the blue hour still casting its haze, and they were set to make use of the dimness.

To the pine-log wall they went, and down toppled one of the guards at the gate. Then the group of attackers surged forward.

It was not Aleena's battle, not really, but after the betrayal she was excited for a bit of revenge. Her and her two Kron shared more in common than either realized.

Separating from the pack, Aleena and her men took a different route, catching another patrolman before he could sound the cry. Her daggers made quick work of him with but two plunges.

As the door to the outhouse swung open, a shocked woman gasped as Ramtok struck her in the belly and winded her, right before finishing her off.

It was not a glorious battle, but that wasn't what it was all about.

Revenge had little to do with honour.

The three of them continued their circuit along the interiors of the pine-wall toward the barracks of the Kaliak when a loud shriek sounded into the night, alarming the locals. Things had instantly got more desperate.

The trio moved quicker, rushing towards their destination, arriving just in time to meet with Vicalus, leading his people.

"Where's Britus?" Aleena asked.

"He's dead," Vicalus said grimly and without hesitation. Just like that, and an ally had fallen, with no time to even pay a moment's respect to the dead. That would come later, for their people.

"We must hurry," he added, "and light the barracks aflame. We are out of time."

His statement was quite true. Saghar and Ramtok watched as lights lit up the windows of the houses and doors began to open. The village had at least four hundred people, and even without their guards, they would easily be enough to destroy their raid.

"Britus has the torch and tinder," Aleena said.

Suddenly Vicalus looked mortified, as if he'd done something quite wrong.

"We are running out of time," Saghar gruffly

informed them, pulling out his own flintstone as his brother tore off some fabric and began to form a torch.

Vicalus snarled and pushed into the barracks with his people, the dozens of shifters making haste inside.

"What are you doing?!" Aleena hissed at the leader, watching as the locals gathered makeshift weapons, mainly ice picks and spears for hunting. "You'll trap yourselves in there!" she said, though Vicalus paid her no mind.

Ramtok and Saghar looked to her, continuing with their work, lighting the torch and appearing perturbed.

"Inside you two!" Aleena cried, knowing their escape was likely already cut off.

No sooner than they rushed for the door, the shifters were quick to shut it behind them. They slid the bar across and locked it.

"Just the two were in here?" Vicalus asked one of his recruits coming from the second floor.

"Yes. The lookout post above is clear. I can see no way of escape," reported the shifter to their new war chieftain.

Aleena saw that in addition to the two guards killed in the barracks, however, that one of the shifter's laid dead too. An inauspicious start already.

"Dammit! We're trapped here! There's no way out," Aleena said, storming past the shifters towards the stairs.

"We'll find our way," Vicalus said with a sneer. "Where are you going anyways?"

"To look for myself," Aleena said, climbing the wooden stairs and on up to the ladder above.

It took her no more than a moment to climb to the top and up out of the hatch, looking out at the village and the snowy fields and forests beyond. True to the report received below, she saw no way out.

The pine wall was too far from the barracks to make it in a leap, and already the townspeople were clamouring around. By the hundreds.

37

THE REBELS

*R*osa had spent a great deal of time trekking through the woods and wilderness the rebel, Marin. Trying to outpace her pursuers and hide their tracks, it had made for a great initiation into her new chosen career path, she was realizing.

Following after the large, bestial Faze wasn't too different from chasing Marin, except in a few crucial aspects.

"What's the difference between bein' hungry an' horny?" Faze asked with a broad grin on his face, another one of his jokes on its way.

Being a courier-messenger seemed to lack the grace she imagined being a raider would have. Though she had to confess that Faze was far more personable than

Marin had been, which was impressive, seeing as he was a wolfkin. Or wolven, as they preferred.

Whatever he was, he certainly wasn't what she expected from one of his kind. Though that never stopped her from being guarded with him at all times. That was just playing it safe, she assured herself.

Rosa rolled her eyes at him, but it was good natured. At least he smiled, and laughed. That was more than she ever got from Marin, certainly. And definitely more than she got back with the other human nobles.

"What's the difference, hm?" she prompted him.

It was obvious that the large, furry man-beast found his joke absolutely hilarious because he wouldn't stop grinning like a fool.

Faze let the moment drag on long before he spat it out. "Where you put the cucumber," he remarked at long last, his mouth hanging open as he let out a guffaw of great amusement.

Her brow raised, but she couldn't help but try to hide her smile. She wasn't used to such crassness, but somehow he made it almost endearing. Perhaps it was his own enjoyment that gave her such delight.

"Come up with that one yourself?"

"Nah," he confessed without hesitation. "Heard it

from one of the bar wenches back in town," he remarked. "Pretty good though, huh?" he asked as he led the way, the sky overhead turning orange as evening approached.

"Yes, well. I just had no idea you were into that type of thing," Rosa replied with a flip of her blonde hair over her shoulder.

Ever in good spirits, the beast-man chuckled.

"Wasn't sure what a cucumber was at first, we don't eat that vegetable stuff if we can help it. But then she offered to show me," he explained as he stomped along with surprising quiet for his size. That was, aside from his noisy guffawing.

Before she could retort, he stopped, lifted his muzzle to the air, and sniffed around. It was a curious sight, seeing that beast, so much like a man, yet in so many ways exhibiting behaviours like the wolf his fur resembled.

She knew better than to continue on ahead and instantly grew quiet. Whether he simply needed to find a new way or he found trouble, she wasn't about to chance it. There were too many dangers in the world, and simply thinking about that which had terrified Marin so made her tremble.

She never wanted to run into whatever they were ever again.

Faze took his time but then headed off in a different direction.

"Gotta watch out," he remarked to her over his shoulder, speaking much quieter. "There's all kinds of mischief you can run into with this sorta work, I'll tell you. Luckily a good nose helps," he said with a wink and a tap of his snout.

"Yeah, well, good I have you along, isn't it." Her shoulders were tensed, and she forced them to relax. They could take care of themselves, she reassured herself as she followed after him.

"You'll have ta learn how ta do this on yer own though," he cautioned her. "But don't let that trouble ya none. A keen sense a smell might seem like an advantage, but it just means you'll have to rely on other senses more. Besides, ya won't be yappin' out here by yerself like ya are with me, so ya won't be in so much trouble if you do get close to some soldiers or… trouble."

The trouble went unnamed.

"Yeah," she whispered, barely audible even with their silent movements. "How much longer will I have you with me?"

Faze looked back at her, opened his maw to speak, but then froze. He sniffed at the air again, though looked far tenser.

There was barely a breeze at all, so he bent down

onto all fours and sniffed at the ground. It was then that Rosa looked around suspiciously and noticed a curious series of gouges in a nearby tree.

She inched towards them, both of her hands clasping her daggers tenderly, like a comforting blanket. Her leather didn't even creak with how supple and well-crafted it was, but her breath held instinctively. She forced herself to breathe out her lungful of air as she studied the strange marks.

They were too big to claw marks. Or so she hoped. The gouges deep and wide. The furrows that were raked into the tree didn't seem to resemble the mark of a blade or axe though, so... something natural?

She pondered it until something finally dawned on her: one of the noble crests she remembered from her days in the Court was of two fighting elkeer. Mighty beasts that resembled elks, they were savages that used their great horns and crushing hooves to hunt all sorts of prey unlike their more docile cousins. It was said they marked their territory by tearing apart trees and rocks with the antlers they bore.

Rosa stepped backwards towards Faze, her eyes darting around them urgently as she moved to tell him. She'd never seen one in real life, and truthfully, she didn't hope to start today.

"Elkeer," she murmured under her breath, looking at her companion intently. He'd definitely know more about them than she.

The crouched wolven lifted his head and looked about to question her on it, but then his eyes fell on where she had just come from. He saw the markings, and looked quite surprised. No, shocked.

"Oh shit," he muttered. He grabbed her shoulder, gave her a light shove, and began to run with her. "Let's go!" he hissed to her.

She didn't question it, or him, simply sprinting at his side. Apparently he did know more about them than she...

It terrified her, the thought of being alone in these woods with their unknown monsters lurking within them, but she'd never admit it. Not to him, not to Marin, not to anyone. Even as she ran for her life, she knew she'd never back down from this challenge.

When the bellowing cry of the elkeer called out, however, everything felt shaken.

It seemed to make the whole forest rise up in terror. Great flocks of birds could be heard ascending into the skies, and she swore she could hear other soft footpads coming from all around where before had been silence.

Though once she heard the heavy pounding of the elkeer itself, there was no noticing anything else.

It was like the march of hell's armies itself was after her, and the ground shook beneath her feet.

"Don't stop, whatever you do!" called Faze to her, the large wolven running half like a man and half like the wolf he resembled, intermittently using his clawed hands to help propel himself along with his loping gait.

She was so grateful for the "practice" she'd received with Marin, but even then she remembered that he'd had to save her. Help her into the tree...

Yet with those marks, with the rumours and myths she'd heard, she knew a tree couldn't protect her. Not from this beast.

Her lungs felt like they'd explode as she pushed herself faster, her legs burning in agony. Yet still she ran, the forest passing her in a blur.

Rosa had not dared to look back. The ground-quaking stomps of the beast behind them were enough to let her know it was too close for comfort. The bellow of its cry sent the trees about her shaking, causing a shower of pine needles to fall down upon her, like a million pinpricks against her skin.

Night was falling fast, though it seemed to take so long with her heart-pounding race. Though as the blanket of darkness descended, she swore she could detect some odd noise in the trees, like a sort of unearthly chittering.

"Do you hear that?" asked a panting Faze.

Rosa thought she might simply faint, but she wouldn't allow herself the pleasure. "Up a tree!"

She would rather take her chances with the elkeer sending her tumbling to her death than to see those terrible, terrifying things that had scared Marin so.

Letting loose another of its bellows, the mass of unearthly noises grew louder, as if approaching from all sides. The coming storm nearly about to consume them both whole, it felt like.

It was as she tried to select a tree to get up in that the big wolven grabbed her in his arm. "This way," he hissed needlessly, as he carried her completely.

It would've been an amusing experience, if not for the situation. Though as he rushed forwards, she saw a curious and terrifying sight.

The great elkeer stood a story tall itself, and its antlers added another to its height. Though unlike its shrub-eating cousin, it had a mouth of fangs and a predator's eyes.

She never would have thought that great, menacing beast would be the less ominous sight before her, however. For even though she couldn't make the things out, a swarm of formless black creatures came at it from behind and to the side. They jumped at it, clawed, bit, and let out their hideous cries.

It was so familiar to her, and she felt her world spin as she stared into the heart of the abyss.

It was only the recently set darkness that spared her a closer view of the shadowed creatures, yet still her mind reeled.

The elkeer bucked, its gait off as it bellowed in anguish at the gnashing teeth and claws of the dozens of creatures that mauled at it, and the dozens more that joined in the fray with each passing second.

Such a mighty beast struggled valiantly, but she knew the inevitable.

As her world spun and she felt her mind slip from her, Faze pulled her into a burrow of some sort.

Darkness consumed her world, but it was a comforting kind. It was a worldly darkness. Not like the horrifying abyss of the creatures above that she had witnessed.

He pulled her to him in the underground hide-away and covered her mouth, forcing his own breathing to still.

While above she could hear the final anguished cries of the elkeer, the slowing stomps of its passage, until the final crash. The bleat it gave was pitiable, but the gnashing and clawing of those creatures... The sound of it seemed to eat at her brain!

Faze muttered into her ear, "Stop screaming."

She hadn't realized she was, but the moment he pointed it out, it only seemed rational to scream. The creatures were gnawing at her mind and devouring her from the inside out! The anguish!

And then her world went black.

38

THE NOBLES

Caprice lay in the soapy water, her hand swiping the salted tears from her cheeks. She cursed herself for her weakness, for letting him get to her.

Part of it wasn't even Beren. It was something else, and the feeling of the lapping water at her chest reminded her of why she felt so alone.

Daughters shouldn't be so fixated on their father. On how their hands felt, on their scent, on how they made their stomach leap, but as Caprice's cloth rubbed along her stomach, that was what came back to her. Her father bathing her on that fateful night.

It had been something she'd revelled in, teased him about, but now she was alone with a man that was so similar to him. Yet he inspired none of the excitement that her daddy did and she gasped as she felt where the cloth had wandered. She throbbed with need and pressed the warm material in harder, trying to quell it.

She hadn't decided if she'd go to the study, but something inside her screamed that she had to. That she couldn't be so stubborn that she sabotaged her own interest. Worse still... what if she sabotaged her father's interests? Would he still love her as he was rotting in a cell, paying for the crime she'd begged him to commit?

Her body rocked and the water lapped at her breasts, exciting the light-brown nipples further in the cool air. "Daddy," she murmured into the empty room, feeling her body coil before the inevitable lightning strike coursed through her.

39

THE FRONT

*D*awn was rising as the two soldiers made their way through the woods, travelling AWOL.

They had walked throughout the night without rest, at Levek's urging. Though one thing kept bothering Caslian…

"It was so easy," she said, muttering in disbelief as the sky began to slowly turn a greyish-blue.

"I can't believe it either," Levek said. "Nobody tried to stop us… there was… nothing."

Their pace was slower as the reality that nobody would be pursuing them sank in.

"But why? I was sure at least one man spotted us sneaking away," Caslian said, her weariness overpowered by her confusion.

Though Levek seemed to figure it out quicker, with his many more years of experience.

"They figure we won't last out here. So why waste their energy?" He asked, his voice rough and tired as they carried on through the trees.

The night had been uneventful. So close to the front as they were when they started, there was no life. No birds, no crickets even. It wasn't until they finally made it to the trees that they seemed to slowly escape the realities of the front.

"Should we stop for some rest then?" Caslian asked, but immediately her eyes were already drawn to something.

"What is it?" Levek asked.

There was very little left to see, but for the blood on the grass, and the broken and gnawed remnants of bones. But whatever it was, the creature must have been immense.

"What happened here...?" Caslian murmured softly in disbelief.

Levek, however, reacted less with curiosity and more with alarm. And panic.

His eyes widened and he stumbled away, looking manic as he stared at such a gory sight.

"What's wrong?" Caslian asked, coming to his side. He'd been on the front for so long, and had seen and experienced so many atrocities, so his alarm was more frightening than the sight itself. She didn't get an answer immediately though, just watched as his chest heaved and he seemed so utterly panicked.

"It was just an animal," she said, trying to calm him. "See? There's parts of an antler."

Though Levek was so petrified he couldn't move. He clutched at his head, tore at his hair as he struggled to breath. His panic was intense, the sight of blood and gore affecting him so deeply. It took Caslian so long just to snap him back to reality, let alone calm him down.

"It's okay," she said, looking into his eyes.

Her gaze slowly brought him back to reality, and not even her disfigured face prevented his fondness for her from bringing him around.

"Oh Cas," he said, putting his arms around her as she then cradled his head to her chest.

On top of everything else, Levek's tenuous new position only made their lives all the more difficult. They were both so broken, so afraid. Caslian was almost ready to give up herself then, unable to envision how she could shoulder Levek's psychological burden upon her own, when a sound startled them both.

It was grunting. A woman's grunting.

Levek reached for his belt and pulled out a pistol

he'd stolen from one of the commissioned officers at the front.

Though Caslian saw the way his hand shook so intensely, and wondered what good it could possibly do.

Once he pulled back upon the hammer and it clicked into place, however, the sound of the woman ceased.

"I'm armed," came a woman's voice.

"So are we," Caslian said, taking the gun from Levek's shaking hand and holding it herself with all the brief basic training skills she had.

Carefully, gun held out and at the ready, Caslian rounded a bush and pointed her weapon at the source of the voice.

There before her, she saw a disheveled woman, all in leather, only a pair of long daggers for weapons as she crouched beside a large, beastlike creature. He was human in ways, and yet not, with fur covering him and large fangs.

Caslian wondered if that was what had killed the antlered creature.

"Dammit! No!" the woman cried out, sounding so defeated as she plunged a dagger into the ground again and again in frustration.

Caslian found herself staring in utter confusion,

unsure of what the creature the woman was hauling was, and why she was so distraught.

"Just let us go, please!" the woman pleaded.

Levek stood and walked over to Caslian, placing his hand upon the barrel of the gun and slowly lowering it.

"We're not going to harm you," he said, his voice still not as steady as usual, but better than his panicked delirium but a few moments before. "What are you doing, ma'am?" he asked the woman.

Rosa wiped at her face with the back of her sleeve, crouched down, weary, cut and exhausted.

"My friend is dying," she said, looking to the large, furry monster of a man. "I need to get him to help."

40

THE MATRON

Aleena awaited the end with Vicalus and his people. Though unlike them, she didn't wait for it sitting down. She would not wait for death with patience and grace.

She paced, mostly.

"I don't want to die in some stinking, piss-drenched barracks as part of the last gasp of a lost people," she said, agitated and irate.

"Neither do we," Ramtok said firmly.

"Shut up, already," Vicalus said irritably.

"No," Saghar said. "If some of us charge out the front against the siege, while we light the back wall on fire with our torch, then perhaps we can buy time to escape."

It was a long shot, Aleena knew that immediately. Nothing burned that damn fast.

"And who'll do the charge, huh? My people? Ever the sacrificial lamb?" Vicalus said, balling up his fists with suppressed rage.

"Chieftain!" came the cry from above, as one of the shifters lowered themselves down, looking less like a man and more like a snake with how he did so.

"What is it?!" Vicalus said, his rage vanished as he looked on expectantly.

"They're coming!" said the man who had been watching from the tower above. "Their guard is returning from their patrols!"

With that, hope fled all those present.

What little opportunity Saghar's proposed plan offered melted away, and even the two Kron seemed a little flattened by it.

"We're doomed," Vicalus said, slumping down onto the floor before the hearth.

Everyone sank into depressed silence, until Aleena — still struggling to come up with some miracle plan — asked:

"From what direction?"

"What does it fucking matter? We're done," Vicalus said, falling sullen and into despair.

Aleena was brimming with rage at the man herself. Far from apathy, she wanted to call him out, tell the whole lot around him that he must've murdered Britus when given the opportunity, and botched the whole plan.

"West and North by North-Northeast," said the shifter.

That distracted Aleena from her anger.

"What? Did I hear you right?" she asked.

But Saghar was already moving off to the ladder pushing the shifter out of the way to make his way up and peer out.

"It's the Kron!" Came Saghar's cry as he ducked back inside the barracks, eyes wide.

41

THE NOBLES

The fire in the study gave a pleasant crackle, and the Viscount Beren Rensford sat beside it in his black velvet vest with red silken shirt and cravat. He looked strikingly handsome with the way the orange flame reflected off his skin and hair.

"Come on in," he invited without even seeing her in the dark hallway outside. He poured her up a glass of wine. "I won't bite."

She'd spent a lot of time recovering from her bath, and had fixed her hair into ringlets that cascaded down her shoulders. They bobbed as she walked, barefoot, over the cool floor. Her stomach was wound into knots, but she felt a certain relaxed calm as well.

With each step closer to him, however, that feeling began to disappear.

He was unpredictable. Cruel.

And he had no love for her.

He would use her and spit her out, only to laugh at her foolishness. Yet her shoulders were straight and her jawline was held high.

The navy skirt was longer in the back than in the front, and the emerald top could have clashed with it horribly, but somehow the two shades worked together. They made her look more grounded in the earthier tones, and she hid her sneer with a smile.

"Well, I wouldn't take that bet, for one."

He returned her smile with one of his own.

"Smart girl." He lifted the wine glass he had for her, though she noted the lack of a seat anywhere in his vicinity. "Lovely dress, by the way. I appreciate you going through the trouble of looking pleasing for me." And it was hard not to remember the scene with him just hours before in the dining room.

Her stomach tightened again, but she smiled graciously. She'd had her noble training, of course, but she so rarely cared to use it. She couldn't stand useless people, and bowing down to them was something she'd never been able to do, no matter how powerful they were.

She stood in front of him, strategically out of

arm's reach, looking down at him and feeling stronger because of it.

The young Caprice was beautiful, and she knew it. Her brown ringlets skirted across her fair, naked shoulders, and the emerald shirt was light and airy. It was a contrast to the constrictive corset, but her form was still so attractive even without the aid of the shaping device.

"So then. What did you have in mind for this auspicious evening?"

"Come, sit," he said, offering the wine glass to her, with no apparent place for her to take him up on his offer except the floor or his lap. "Let's talk." He looked so pleasant as he smiled to her, his own hair and looks neatly tended to in preparation for their meeting, she could tell. "I've even got a present for you. Something you'll like, I swear."

She smiled at him as she remained still.

"I don't think I'd take any of your bets, Viscount." Her dark eyes moved around the room, making a show of it. "And it seems there's nowhere for me to sit."

Caprice knew what he wanted, but her pride still kept her numb. She'd do this. Do what she had to.

That doesn't mean it should be easy on him.

The young Viscount parted his knees and gestured to the floor between them. "There's a lovely plush rug right there," he said, and true enough, it was a thick, old rug from some bygone era. An antique in its own right, but looking soft and thick. "Don't be shy now. Sit and take the wine, we've got things to discuss."

He was so inwardly smug, that was all she could think. Oh, his smile looked so genuine, so handsomely pure, but how could it be? He was dangling so much over her, it hardly seemed possible.

Her nose twitched and she regretted wearing the skirt she was in. It wasn't scandalous, but the front rose up and it was so billowy that sitting would be a task. Still, she gave him the same smile in return, but where his was fiery, hers was cool.

"How blind I must be," she said with saccharine sweetness as she let herself sit as gracefully as she could onto the soft carpet. Her legs went to her side and the skirt slid off her thighs, revealing far more than appropriate. Her slender fingers accepted the wine, and she lofted it to him.

"To his death, then."

He looked down to her there at his feet, crooked a brow just slightly then nodded.

"To his death," he repeated, taking a sip of his wine.

There was no rush to get to the point, and he let his piercing gaze study her, roam over her form.

"You're a beautiful woman," he said, taking another sip of wine. "You would make a lovely trophy piece for the arm of a powerful lord."

"And isn't that what I've always aspired to be?" A trophy. She was far more than that, she thought, but she tried to hide her ego with another smile. She was sat on a rug at a smug Viscount's feet. It was too late for pride.

The smiling fiend put his glass aside.

"I very much doubt that," he said, sitting comfortably before her as he took a small little box from the side table. "And perhaps you're even clever enough to attain more," he remarked. "Regardless, I got you a gift. Something special, that I think will compliment your beauty nicely."

Very meticulously, he opened the box and slowly pulled out a delightful little choker. It was black fabric that then dangled a fat, teardrop emerald in silver. "An old heirloom, one might say," he said as he let it twist in the fire light so beautifully.

Yet she was suspicious of any kindness. From anyone, not just him. Her fingers dug into the carpet as she pushed herself up to stare at it.

She took her time, dragging her tongue over her mouth as her dark eyes moved from it to him.

"And the catch?"

"None." He smiled down to her with a crook in

his lips. "And I mean it this time," he said with some slight amount of mirth.

Very slowly he bent forward, undoing the choker then leaning in close to her, about ready to place it around her neck. "Lift your hair," he said softly.

She hesitated before sitting up straight and letting her fingers lightly gather her curls. He could see as her thighs tightened, the muscles becoming more pronounced as they had to work harder to keep her balanced.

The care with which he placed that choker around her neck could only be described as gentle or delicate. His hard, masculine hands were tougher than what she was used to, but felt so strong. He clasped it shut, and it felt tight. Not enough to choke off her breath, but the feeling of its presence was unavoidable as it squeezed about her throat.

"Beautiful," he said appreciatively, touching the large emerald and affixing it just above her breasts as his fingers grazed her skin. "A gift to keep, regardless of what happens," he mused aloud as he studied her and the new item.

She felt herself flush, first in rage, then in embarrassment. Her tongue swept over her lips once more and her hand went to touch the delicate jewel. Her fingers lightly brushed his and she stopped, pulling away. "And what is going to happen?"

He didn't shun her touch, however. He lifted his hand and stroked his fingers along her jawline and over her cheek.

"There are several major possibilities," he said calmly. "You could be stubborn, and it all ends with you losing everything. You could play along but fail to impress me, and I lead you on until I grow bored and dispose of you. Or..." His thumb returned to her chin, then went up over her lower lip. "You please and impress me. And I claim for myself a beautiful and useful wife, who will ride my coattails to greatness... on her knees."

She'd been staring at him curiously until those last three words, and her nose crinkled. She didn't bow to anyone. Her petulance had gotten her into trouble in the past, of course, but not like this. Not when everything was riding on it.

"How do you think I could do that?"

"It's okay," he said, having smiled at her reaction. "You can be bothered by the prospect. I like that in you," he remarked with amusement. "It'll be especially fun to beat out of you." He said that with such an eerie calm, stroking her pale skin, her beautiful curls. "But not tonight. I promised to be friendly. And I always keep my promises, sweet girl."

"When I first met you, you looked like you hated me. Like you didn't have a singular interest in my existence. Am I really to believe that being put under house arrest with me has changed that? Or is it simply boredom, a way to pass the time for you?"

Her words were soft, but they still held the icy-hot anger that threatened her body as she tried to stop trembling under his touch.

He had the nerve to laugh at her.

"I hated what you stood for," he said with a caress of her cheek. "What you represented. An impediment to me, my future. Lazy decadence." He cupped her cheek and turned her face up towards his, locking eyes with her. "I thought you a pretty vessel, but dumb." He narrowed his eyes just slightly as he studied her, as if reading what she truly was in her own gaze. "Perhaps I was wrong though."

"I'm not dumb." It was defensive, but she didn't care. She'd be hard pressed to admit to such a cruel thing under his hard gaze. "So yes. You were wrong. I'm glad you can admit that."

He laughed just once.

"I haven't seen evidence of that yet," he remarked with another of his galling smiles. "It would be most convenient and fortuitous if I was on this count though." It was hard to escape the similarities. The warmth of the fire, sat at the feet of a man so alike her father. The way he caressed her cheek, touched her brown curls. The harshness was not like him though.

Her father rarely had anything but glowing praise and affection for her. "Beauty and brains are so rarely in the same package. And you've beauty to spare." His hand cupped her jaw and he guided her in just a bit closer. "I'm not going to impregnate you so you can try and pass it off as that old bastard's spawn," he said calmly. "Not, that is, unless we were married." He grinned just a bit, but it was a pleasant, playful grin in appearance.

His calm demeanor was driving her mad, and she couldn't help that her dark eyes narrowed at him.

"You insult me then tell me that we could be wed. You want me to be obedient yet say that you like that I'm not, only to threaten to beat it out of me. You're a contradiction."

He brought his other hand over to caress her thick ringlets as he held her jaw in place. "But tonight there's just friendliness, as promised. You want that, yes?" he asked, "You and I to be friendly to one another? It would make the night easier to pass. Be a building block for the future between you and I." He smiled so pleasantly at her.

"I wouldn't have shown up if I wanted to continue with things as they were." The memory of him grabbing her, of his eyes on her body made her flush and her fingers went to drag the light skirt over her thighs a bit more modestly, though the fabric instantly fell away. It was too slinky to ever do anything but fall from resistance.

She swallowed as his fingers touched her, and she thought, once more, of her father. "I'm willing to play nice."

"You're used to pampering," he said softly, those hard eyes of his soaking her all in, leaving nothing for her to hide, it seemed. "And I can give you that. But not only that," he explained to her as if laying out the details of his perverse plans to a child. "I can pamper you, but you'll serve me while you do it. I don't need just a wife. I need a willing accomplice. A submissive little princess with her own cunning." He retracted his hand from her jaw, but kept the other in her hair as he very slowly undid his pants, drawing her gaze to the bulge of his manhood.

Her throat constricted as she stared. Her lower lip drew in, and she began nervously chewing it, letting his words digest.

She didn't believe him. Not really. His kindness was a farce, and he'd never let her keep anything, but she was desperate. To protect her father's interest, she'd take the chance that she'd be left with nothing, embarrassed and perhaps worse.

She nodded, so gently as to nearly be invisible.

That was enough to draw a broad grin to his face.

"Good girl," he said, as if an echo of dear dad.

He withdrew his manhood from the confines of his pants, not yet turgid, but growing thicker before her eyes. His hand in her hair gently but firmly guided her in towards it, the scent of male musk wafting to her nose as the stunning organ swelled upwards under its own power, as if seeking her plush lips.

"You said you'd be nice, and you weren't lying then," he remarked approvingly.

She understood on an instinctual level what he wanted her to do.

Yet she was inexperienced, and her hands trembled at her sides as she followed his lead. Her mind was growing hazy and she wondered if it was fear that was making her so dizzy or if it was him.

If she was going to do this, though... If she was going to bargain with the cruel man, she was going to impress.

With the firm guiding hand of his on her head, he brought her mouth to his cock.

"There you go," he said, "open up." He gently but strongly guided her mouth down around him so that she felt the warm, throbbing member slip along her tongue and mouth. He grew there, throbbing to a new girth that pressed out against her teeth.

"Good girl," he said on a sigh, exhaling in satisfaction at the warm wetness. "I'll be gentle this night, as promised, so make the most of it to learn, pet." And his hand in her hair coiled its digits about her ringlets and began to urge her motions on, making her begin to bob her head.

She couldn't believe she actually felt a small bit of gratitude at his words with what he was making her do. He tasted foreign and the motions were unnatural and ungraceful. Tears stung her eyes as she thought of what she was doing, of what she was allowing him to get away with, and anger boiled beneath her pale flesh.

Yet there was the insistent tug and pull of his hand as he guided her along his shaft. He was using her more than she was fellating him, though the motions were mostly gentle but firm.

"Good girl," he said, reclined back in his chair, watching her through lidded eyes as his cock swelled to fullness, her lips pulled taut around it. He brought his other hand to her head, caressed her cheek then took hold of more of her hair. "You are a very pretty little princess," he said in his low, lust-tinged voice. "It would please me immensely if you proved adequate for my needs." He licked his lips, acting as if his infuriating words were anything but. "I could enjoy the sight of you stuffed with my dick each and every night for many years."

He repulsed her. His treatment of her, his

behaviour, it was all so vile. She wanted to jump from the floor, to flee from the room and simply wait out the rest of her captivity, but she knew it wasn't an option. She'd held on for some hope, some way that she could save her father without resorting to the Viscount's generosity, but too much time had passed.

Her charade would soon be over and they would be jailed. They'd lose it all, if she couldn't make this man see her worth.

Her tongue swiped across his cock, her mouth feeling so moist and hot. It was uncomfortable, and she was frightened.

Each and every swell of his shaft in her mouth was like a taunt. It goaded her as he forced her mouth and face upon his cock faster and faster. He was building towards his release, she knew, and gave a low groan of pleasure from her tongue as he let his fingers rub against her scalp in his grasp.

"That's it," he said in a husky groan. "So close... good girl, good..." He pulled her face down partway along his shaft one final time then held her there. She couldn't budge against that grip, and had to accept it as his girth expanded and the thick streams of salty cream shot from his bulging crown along her tongue and the roof of her mouth again and again.

Her feet kicked in protest, her hands digging into his thighs as that strange sensation overtook her. It wasn't like anything she'd ever experienced before, and the taste was odd. She didn't know what to make of it, of him, and her face was red with shame.

Slowly his member stilled, the last of his seed spurting out into her mouth as he breathed heavily. "That's it," he crooned huskily, hand still clutching her head. "Easy now." He retracted his shaft from her mouth very slowly. "Remember, good girls swallow it all down," he said as he slipped his well-shaped crown from betwixt her pouty lips.

She did as instructed, but she couldn't look at him. Caprice's eyes were blurry and her entire body felt like it was betraying her. She was so hot and it felt like there was something crawling under her skin. She needed release, some pressure put on that little bundle of nerves between her thighs, but she wouldn't let herself.

Instead she simply licked the seed from her lips and slipped down onto her haunches.

"Well done," he said at that, and he released her hair as he bent forward and kissed the top of it like a doting patron. "You didn't disappoint." And those simple words were said as if they were extreme praise.

She could still taste him on her, and her breathing was panted and shallow. Her heart pounded beneath her ribcage and she felt panicky, like she had to get out. To escape.

She pushed herself to her feet, stumbling as she regained her balance. Even without any shoes on, her knees were trembling and her muscles felt tight. She needed to get out.

The smug Viscount sat back and casually tucked himself into his pants. He smiled to her. "A wonderful start for our new beginning. And keep that choker on," he instructed with a flick of his finger towards her neck. "I'd like to see you wear it at all times. To know you appreciate my thoughts and present."

The thing had been so tight around her neck, it'd made swallowing his seed much more difficult than it had needed to be. And it still proved a constant reminder with that over-tight squeeze of her throat.

He shifted his shoulders, getting more comfortable in his seat.

"I'll see you at breakfast. Upstairs, just you and I."

She couldn't speak. Tears stung her eyes as she nodded and walked away from him, her skirt trailing after her in her speedy retreat.

Was this what her life would be like, now?

And in the end, would it matter at all?

Caprice felt like all of her pride had been drained from her, leaving her destitute and afraid. She could handle doing what he wanted, but she wasn't prepared to handle what it was doing to her.

Even before she got to the safety of her room she had to stop along one of the dark hallways and touch herself. To try to release that tension that was building in her.

42

THE REBELS

aslian used the medkit that Levek urged her to take to treat and bandage the wolven's wounds.

"I can't promise I know what I'm doing here," Caslian said to the blonde woman, working diligently. "I've never worked on one of his kind before, and I'm only a fresh medic myself."

"Please, just do whatever you can," came the desperate reply.

"Don't worry, we will," Levek said, placing a hand on the woman's shoulder, causing her to jump and pull away.

"It's okay," Caslian said, brow arched. "We aren't gonna harm you."

"S-sorry, not used to... y'know, soldiers of the

state being so… helpful," the woman said, cracking a forced smile.

Caslian gave a bitter, harsh laugh.

"We understand," Levek said, offering a sheepish smile and diverting his gaze from the bloody, wounded mess of the wolven.

He was doing what he could not to see the blood and gore, Caslian realized. Distracting himself by reassuring the woman.

"I'm Levek by the way. What's your name?" he asked warmly.

"Ro—ah, Laura," Rosa lied, brushing back her blonde hair. "So what are two soldiers doing out here in the middle of nowhere anyhow? If it's not to hunt down folk like us?"

Caslian and Levek looked at each other, surprised by the question in the face of the obviousness of the answer.

Rosa looked between them before it slowly dawned on her.

"Oh shit! You're deserters!" She said, eyes wide. "Sorry! I—" she quieted down, calming herself. "Fuck, sorry. I thought you were like… hunting for deserters, not…"

Levek chuckled and smiled.

"It's okay, Laura. Yeah, we're deserters. Cas and I are looking to start a life together. Somewhere peaceful. Somewhere safe," he said, smiling at Caslian's back with some tiny sliver of hope still in him.

"Speaking of somewhere safe, we need to get your friend to such a place. Quickly," Caslian said, rising up. "I've done what I can for him, but he needs more care than we can give him out here."

"Alright, lead on," Rosa said, hands upon her hips, ready to go.

Levek and Caslian just looked back and forth between each other.

"What?" Rosa asked.

"We're deserters," Caslian said.

"We have nowhere to go. Nowhere we even know of," Levek added. "I've not left the front in years... Cas is from the south coast. We don't know of any place."

Rosa paused, reality sinking in.

"What was your plan then? You can't live out here. You'll last no time at all," she said, looking between them.

Their eyes dipped a little.

"Shit," Rosa said, rubbing her mouth and chin. "Well... alright. Guess that leaves it to me huh? Only... there's only one place in this world I know I can go and be safe. And they threatened to murder me if I so much as hinted at its existence."

Caslian and Levek peered between each other in confusion.

"You can't very well carry the guy back on your own," Caslian said.

Rosa took a deep breath, her ample bosom heaving.

"Right. Well… okay. Off we go then. Guess you're comin' with me to the refuge," she said, bending down and grasping part of the makeshift gurney Levek had constructed while she fretted and Caslian healed.

"Wait… you mean… one of the outcast refuges?" Caslian asked, eyes wide.

"The underground city?" Levek added, apparently knowing more about it than Caslian did.

"Yea, that's the place," Rosa said. "So come on and help me get him there already. We don't have a lot of time."

Caslian and Levek finally felt a little bit of relief, that much was obvious as they grinned at each other happily. It was the first bit of good news either of them had had in weeks. Longer.

"We've got a place to go now," Caslian said, unable to believe their fortune.

Levek reached out and took her hand, squeezing it before moving to help Rosa with the rope and stick gurney.

"Well, let's not get crazy. They don't exactly like me a lot there," Rosa said as they began to tow the wolven's body. "What's the two lovebird's names anyhow?" she asked.

"Caslian."

"Levek."

"Well good to meet some decent folk out here, Cas and Levek. I'm Rosa," she declared.

"I thought you said it was Laura?" Levek asked, brow arched.

"Oh shit, I did, didn't I?"

43

THE MATRON

The Kaliak were battering at the door of the barracks, but already Aleena, her Kron and the shifters were huddled upstairs, with the stairways destroyed for some tiny modicum of added defense.

If the outraged mob didn't get them, then the army of Kron approaching would slaughter them all.

Vicalus hung his head into his arms, while the Kron waited behind, watching through cracks in the wood at the mob outside.

Aleena realized they didn't have much to be concerned about. Assuming their people won the day, they'd be freed, assumed to be prisoners.

Except then they'd have to return to the war, she

realized, and wiped that self-involved thought from her head.

"I'm going to head up and watch things unfold at least. More interesting then what's happenin' down here," Aleena said, climbing up the ladder.

More interesting it was, though only barely.

Dawn had broken, but little was happening. The Kaliak guards were returning to their city, the Kron were approaching, but it all seemed to happen in such slow motion from her distance…

Though as Aleena watched, she started to notice something.

The outlay of the terrain made the approaching Kron forces undetectable to the Kaliak. There was a ridge blocking their view.

She looked about the village, and realized: her post, the one she currently occupied, was the only one with a clear view of the Kron's approach.

She waited, waited. Watched as the two forces moved slowly across the landscape, until it became clear the Kron were where she wanted them… out of sight of the pine wall behind the barracks.

Ducking back down inside, she went to Saghar.

"I need you to do your plan from before. Light the back wall on fire so we can make a plan to escape," she said.

Saghar didn't argue, he nodded and gathered his things.

"Right away, Matron," he said, rising up the ladder with his makeshift torch and flint.

Aleena paced back and forth, waiting. The long, insufferable quiet only punctuated by the thuds of rocks and blows against the outside. Until finally...

Saghar returned down and nodded to her.

"What are you all up to?" Vicalus asked, growing suspicious, though sounding too depressed still to do much about it.

"Getting us out of here," Aleena said, climbing up to look at the back wall catching aflame.

She couldn't help but grin with excitement. Though her gaze was then quickly drawn aside.

The Kaliak guards were almost at the city, but something stood out more... the Kron were closer to them than they were to the village.

The Kron had the larger force, that much was clear, though a chunk of them broke off and began to move along the village wall. Right towards the front gate.

As Aleena watched the fire blow and fail to destroy the wall as she'd hoped, she glanced back to the battle that unfurled. There, the mass of Kron clashed with the guard forces, an out and out battle occurring. While aside, the second force of Kron made for the still open gates… and right in upon the throngs of Kaliak that had them barricaded inside.

"Well?" Vicalus asked hopefully.

Aleena had no good news, but she refused to give up.

She looked around, saw some of the weapons about the place. She noticed to one side, the military issue spades with the hatch blades on the side. "Everyone grab as many of those as you can. We're gonna hack our way out through the back while the two armies fight. Let's move!" She insisted, and immediately Saghar and Ramtok were in action.

The rest followed their lead and quickly, as Ramtok handed her a spade of her own, she ascended the stairs then began to climb down the roof of the barracks.

It was a steep plunge, but the snow piled between the wall and building made for something to brace her impact at least, and she leapt down.

By that point, the sounds of clashing forces from the other side could be heard, and Aleena waved the others down in a hurry before beginning to chop at the burnt wall.

There was no time to waste.

44

———

THE NOBLES

Caprice could not be more disgusted with herself or the situation, or so she thought.

Truth was, she had a lot further she could fall, and even she — deep down inside, somewhere — knew that, despite her sheltered upbringing.

But having serviced the Viscount's lusts upon her knees the night before, she was humiliated, embarrassed and outraged.

In the early morning hours she snuck from her room, ready to pry open the secret passage and make an escape. Talk to her father. Anything.

She simply knew she had to do something.

What she didn't expect, however, was to find the study door locked.

It seemed unnecessary after the nailing-shut of

the passageway, but that only made her all the more suspicious.

Her father had taught her a few tricks over the years, many of which she'd never paid attention to. But this one had stuck with her.

When her mother would lock her into her room at night, he showed her how to pick the lock so she could escape and spend time with him in his study without her knowing.

Taking a pin from her hair, she managed to work the lock open in very little time. Though what she saw on the other side surprised her.

The room was empty, but there, in the corner… the secret escape.

It was shut, but the nails were clearly removed from it. All it took was the usual force to slide it open and reveal the hidden passageway.

Dressed in a simple — albeit still silken and beautifully purple — gown, she made her way down the tunnel. Though as she got further and further along, she started to hear strange noises.

Caprice slowed and walked more quietly, calling upon the years before of skulking about her father's manor, avoiding her mother or caretakers.

As she approached the exit, it became clear it was the sound of talking coming from the other side.

Cautiously, she approached, through the open,

concealed door there and towards the door of the storage shed.

She leaned in close with her ear towards the glass, but away from the light the morning light shed.

"...hold tight for now. It won't be much longer," came a woman's voice she swore she recognized.

"This is tiresome political theatrics. How long must this go on? You promised me the whole of the house to rule over for myself, and now I find myself forced to tie myself to this woman. Who clearly loathes me, I may add."

That was the Viscount's voice, unmistakably close.

"Marry her. Once my agent returns from his last mission, her father will be out of the picture and you'll inherit twice the noble lineage if she's yours," came the woman's now distinctly familiar voice.

"Easier said than done," Beren scoffed.

"What? Did my letter from 'her father' not convince her yet?" the unknown woman asked. "Please, if you can't manage to seduce a pretty girl with my help then what good are you?"

As Caprice lingered in shock, thinking about what the woman just said, she could tell Beren was bristling outside.

"I would marry her gladly, even without knowing

I shall get her father's estate to add to my collection. But a bitter wife who loathes me—"

"I bore of this, boy. I have a whole nation to claim and rule," came the woman's haughty response, and suddenly…

Suddenly Caprice recognized who the woman was.

Lady Iztira.

The Chancellor of the Exchequer was plotting to murder her father and seize her whole noble house, as well as the Union itself.

45

THE MATRON

*A*s Aleena and her crew all worked at hacking down the village wall, the battle grew closer, and closer still.

Unfortunately, their progress was not going quickly. The spades were ill suited to the task of chopping down a tightly intertwined log-wall, and the group she had was working with a frenzy, but not well.

All of a sudden, the sounds of combat seemed to come to a halt. No longer were there gunshots and clashing weapons, just stomping feet and the impact of metal on wood.

A cry went up in the air, and Aleena had only to look to the side to see a Kron — more savage and angered than she'd ever seen Ramtok or Saghar appear — standing around the corner of the barracks, pointing at her and her group.

*   *   *

It didn't long after that for Aleena and her group to be taken and brought before the Kron leader.

The shifters were tied up by the hands, but Saghar and Ramtok made sure she was given passage between them unbound. If unarmed.

There, in the midst of the village, strewn with corpses, stood a ring of warriors. And at the center, a towering woman that dwarfed even her own two men. She had a mighty glower upon her greenish face, eyes boring intensely into Aleena as she stood, hands upon hips. Looking impatient.

"Matron Ugra," Aleena said, recognizing her instantaneously.

"That's right. And I am tired of waiting, elf," she said, her voice gravelly and unpleasant to the ears.

"We have been working as quickly as we can," Aleena said.

"Events transpired against us," Ramtok said, butting in, which earned him a glare from the powerful Matron.

The towering woman closed the distance between

them and backhanded the mighty Ramtok across the face with a loud, sickening impact.

"My clan's waiting is at an end," Ugra declared definitively. "You shall lead us to this hidden city of yours without delay. My people shall wander no further."

Aleena could do little more than nod.

"Yes, Matron Ugra," Aleena said.

Though as of yet, she'd not had the chance to even speak with Thia about the Kron's proposal.

At least, not since Thia's first rejection.

46

THE NOBLES

aprice had managed to return to the manor before the Viscount could discover her. Though her nerves were a wreck.

She had gotten news of her father's intended assassination, and a planned coup, but she remained captive.

As her mind was in turmoil thinking of how to escape or at least get word to her father, Beren came to her. He caught her at her door in the midst of her pacing back and forth, and he put on a rather smarmy, wry smile.

For her part, she could barely force her own faux-pleasant warmth, clasping her fidgeting fingers at her waist.

"Good morning, my dear," he said, leaning one

arm against the frame of the door, hedging her in as he stood there in his crisp black suit with crimson cravat.

"Good morning to you, Viscount," she said, her voice smooth but she was no longer able to will it into being as seductive of a purr as she usually did.

"Tell me, pet," he said, letting his gaze slide down to stare upon her cleavage, his fingers raising up. And for a second she thought he was going to lewdly grasp her breasts, but instead he touched the emerald upon her choker.

"Yes, my Lord?" She asked, trying to play it cool as she was so close to a man that was in on the conspiracy to kill her beloved father and oust her family.

"Would you consent to marry me and be my darling pet of a wife, if I agreed to save your father's life?" he asked. His head was tilted to the side, but his gaze lifted to hers, and a smirk graced his lips as their eyes met.

47

THE REBELS

osa towed the body of Faze along with her newfound friends, the two formerly despondent deserters seeming to warm to her as the trio walked.

But then, that might all be due to the fact she offered them their only shot at long term survival. After all…

"You two seemed about as desperate as I was just a short while ago," Rosa said.

"Oh yeah? You look like you know what you're doing," Caslian responded, obviously reading more into Rosa's attire and appearance than was there.

"We really can't thank you enough, Rosa," Levek chimed in, despite the long day of hauling Faze, after a long night of fleeing the front. "Beyond getting away and settling down somewhere, we really had no idea how to go about the in-between parts."

"Hey, that's life. Or at least, that's what I'm learning life's like beyond the city walls," Rosa corrected, feeling a little too humble after all that occurred to boast so brazenly.

"Life beyond the front is going to be an adjustment for me," Levek confessed.

"But so much better," Caslian was quick to offer up, seeming on the guard for negative thoughts.

"Right. I just… I've not left the front in so long I can barely remember life without the boom of mortar," he said.

Rosa could see in his haunted gaze that Caslian was being diligent for good reason. It didn't seem to take much to plunge the shell-shocked man into a morose state.

"Well, you know what I say? Live a little. Hell, it might be very little if the folks back at the city are real upset at me for bringing you two along," she joked.

"Are you ser—" Caslian was interrupted as they heard the sound of approaching footsteps along the road.

"Hello?" Came a man's voice, sounding unsure. "Who goes there?"

It was too late to avoid being detected; their chatting had left them exposed. So Rosa and Levek lowered the makeshift gurney and crouched.

"If you're bandits, we don't have anything for you to take!" came a woman's voice, quavering with fear.

Caslian and Levek looked to each other, before Cas moved quietly forward to peer out onto the road.

Rosa followed after, and together they peered out, finding two tall strangers on the side of the road. One man, with messy hair, shielding his wife and holding a crude cudgel, nothing more.

"It's okay," Caslian said, rising up, hands out to show she was harmless, despite the gun in her pocket.

"Don't go out there!" Rosa hissed at her, and Levek made a grab, but it was too late.

"We're not bandits," Caslian said, climbing up onto the road from the ditch between the woods and them.

"You're… you're military?" the man asked, looking Caslian over with confusion, just as Levek came out to join her.

The man brandished his cudgel between the two, but at their distance it was not threatening. Merely a toothless gesture of protection.

"No… no," the man muttered in disbelief, sounding crushed. Clearly believing he was caught and about to be apprehended. His wife sobbed loudly, pressing into his shoulder blade.

But then Rosa emerged alongside the others in her tattered and dirty leathers.

"Calm down fella. We're not military. At least, they're not any longer," Rosa said.

"Yeah, we're just passing through. You can go along your way. We won't bother you," Caslian said reassuringly.

"Wait… you're not… you mean," the troubled man looked between them. "They're deserters, honey," he said to his wife, wrapping one arm around her to comfort her.

"That's right," Rosa said, though Levek shot a glance her way, uncomfortable with giving too much info away.

"Oh thank heavens… we've been on the run for so long. Searching for a place to settle down in, we thought we'd finally gotten far enough away from the city when… when you came out," he said, cradling his wife in his arms and stroking her messy hair to reassure her.

"Where are you headed?" Levek asked, the older man's brow furrowing in distress by Rosa's judgment.

"We don't know," the wife said through her tears.

"Anywhere. We just… we need to go where they

can't find us. So we can be together, to live as husband and wife," the man said, brows furrowed, sounding so desperate.

"Why couldn't you do that in the city?" Caslian asked.

The man very carefully, very slowly, guided her wife out from behind him to his side, and helping wipe her tears away with his thumbs he kissed her on the lips.

"It's okay, honey," he said, and she slowly calmed, looking into his eyes for reassuring.

The man very carefully pulled back the woman's blonde hair, and showed them her lightly pointed ears, marking her as a half-elf.

Realization dawned on the trio immediately. Not a one of them was blind to the situation, even as Rosa felt the long inbred notion of disgust towards such a thing. Even in her, it vanished soon after and she felt only pity for the couple.

"What's your names?" Levek asked.

"Lura," the woman said.

"And Roland. Roland and Lura Malik," he said, holding his wife in his arms, squeezing her hand which held a brassy looking, unimpressive wedding ring.

Rosa sighed and ran her fingers back through her own hair.

Levek and Caslian looked to her, and it was clear to see the sympathy in their eyes for the couple.

"Fuck it," Rosa said. "Come with us, you two. We're headed to sanctuary, you might as well come along."

Rosa was already climbing back down to get Faze's unconscious form.

"How much more shit can I get in with an extra couple, huh?" Rosa muttered to herself as the two couples smiled and greeted one another, relief washing over them.

They were all headed to sanctuary.

ALSO BY J.E. & M. KEEP

Series:

Possessed by the Vampire:

Claimed

Hunted

Caught

The Warlord:

The Warlord's Concubine

The Warlord's Queen

Her Master

Her Master's Madness

Her Master's Corruption

Novels:

War-Torn

Her Descent

When Dreamers Wake

Chanting the Ancient Lay

Corrupted Hearts

Magic Academy

Unleashed

Vile

Outcast 1 & 2

Novellas:

In Her Dreams

Brutal Passions

The Enforcer: 1

The Enforcer: 2

The Fembot

Bound as the World Burns

Shorts:

The Seductive Nymph

The Curious Nymph

Wherever in the White House: Saved from the Lizard Lady

The Angel and the Demon

Packing' It In

Packing' It In: Not All At Once

The Virility Elixir

The Elven Babe: Stuffed

The Elven Babe: Dragon

The Elven Babe: Demonic

Shifters in Heat

Dancing for the Vampire

The Queen's Secret Lover

The Fertile Elf

Beast and Beauty

Bundles:

Darknest: A Dark Fantasy Anthology

Erotic Dragons Boxset

The Elven Babe: Trilogy

Wicked Monsters Boxset

ABOUT THE AUTHORS

Joshua and Michelle Keep are best-selling authors of romance, fantasy and horror, located in Newfoundland Canada. Fifteen years of joint-authorship together has earned them an enthusiastic readership and a reputation for unique, well-written stories.

Exploring the heights of romantic love and the depths of darkness, they focus on characters developing, growing and falling for one another amidst an engaging plot. Working to make sure a Happily-Ever-After exceeds your expectations.

Full time authors now, in years gone by they were a historian and corporate-ladder-climbing supervisor, respectively.

* * *

Connect with us:
admin@jmkeep.com

http://jmkeep.com
http://jmkeep.com/newsletter
http://pathforgers.com
http://twitter.com/jmkeep
http://twitter.com/jekeep